To Emma & Liam

llkombe.com

Book Design by Tan-chiehlu.com
ISBN
978-0-9958086-1-4

Take me to the Deepest Blue

L. L. Kombe

"The sea, once it casts its spell, holds one in its net of wonder forever".

~ *Jacque Yves Cousteau*

PROLOGUE

He was falling into a deep, undisturbed sleep and he could feel it closing it on him—the darkness, or the abyss—whatever that was awaiting him on the other side. Surrendering his willpower to stay awake, he let his eyes slowly shut, and waited to slip out of consciousness.

When he opened his eyes again, she was the last thing he expected to see.

But there she was all the same.

CHAPTER ONE

It hurt more than she had expected. The stings she felt where her tail used to be now pierced more deeply into her. The pain shot through her lower body, and the sensation now felt as though it had split in two. *Legs.* Nervously, her hands gripped the unfamiliar limbs that materialized as her scales faded away. But the pain didn't end. Mercilessly, it crawled deep under her skin and into her veins, forcing her to lurch back and forth like fish struggling on dry land. This unbearable agony was reminiscent of the time she accidentally scraped her arm on a sea urchin, but ten thousand times worse. Slowly but surely she could feel herself running out of air. With her two hands wrapped around her neck, she could feel her gills disappearing. *This is it.* She had to get to the surface if she wanted to complete her transition. As she emerged from the water, her arms flailed around her. There were loud splashes and her heart pounded hard as though it were plotting an escape from this foreign, human body. She recalled the words of the Advisor from their ocean grid. *Don't attract attention to yourself. They will find you. Just lie in silence and wait for them.*

Were they really coming?

As far as she could see, Narya perceived nothing but utter darkness. Her eyes were not accustomed to this world's colors. It was never completely dark underwater. Even the darkest caverns sparkled with reflections from fishes' fins, and on most nights, they had the moonlight as their trusty beacon. This, by far, was a different kind of night from the ones she was used to. She closed her eyes and listened to the waves hitting the rocks that encircled her. This sound she knew. On cloudy afternoons, she had ventured out of the waters with her more adventurous friends, and they would use their elbows to crawl onto the warm, sun-scorched sand to retrieve books from the secret chest the Changed Ones had left for them. They didn't always have the best selection, but every once in a while, aside from various magazines, she found an exceptionally good book among the more ordinary ones. She would make her way to a nearby sandbank and dip her tail into the water while she read, her elbows sinking into the warm sand as she flipped the pages with her sand-stained fingers. On those days, she felt most human and looked forward to the day when she could actually live the life of one—temporarily.

That day was today.

But now, with her weakened limbs and her acutely parched throat, she felt less than ready to tackle all the challenges that came with transition. The pain had brought forth an uncertainty that scared her to bits. She had never felt this exposed. What if she were discovered? Throughout the ages, they had been able to remain relatively unknown save for myths and tales passed down by the few humans who had had a glimpse of their kind. Fortunately for them, these were soon dismissed as fabricated stories never to be taken seriously except by children. But should an actual discovery take place, the Elders predicted that this would put all their lives in imminent danger. As far as they knew, humans loved experimental research and the discovery of new species. It certainly wouldn't be in their best interest to reveal themselves to this curious breed.

As Narya took slower and deeper breaths, her eyes fluttered and she began to search for the Changed Ones. They were assigned to help the Explorers to transition and help them settle into their temporary lives. She felt the water slowly drying from her body and a palpable tinge of fear tugging violently at her stomach. With no one in sight, she grew more nervous, like a lone cuttlefish that stumbled upon a moray eel in a darkened cave. Her throat felt unbearably dry. She sensed the calming waves calling to her, bidding her to return to her rightful home. She could jump right back in, she looked back to the ocean. Of course, she would have to face the embarrassment of not lasting above water for even a single night. The shortest record was set by her cousin, who managed to stay human for only three days before giving up and turning back into a mermaid. She vowed to never return above land. But even now, Narya could detect a small hint of regret in her cousin's eyes and the excitement that flashed ever so subtly when she recounted her short expedition to a world she briefly passed through.

She shook her head, chasing these doubts away and remembering why she committed herself to this daunting journey. Ever since Keames left for land and didn't come back when he promised he would, she had decided to see this world for herself. What was so enchanting about it that he would deliberately forget about all that he loved underwater? Almost everyone she'd came across who had lived on land as an Explorer inevitably returned to the waters. They never divulged much; their experience would remain their secret—not one to share with anyone else. This reticence only made her more curious and impelled her mind to chase after a plausible explanation. Keames had returned once since his first transition. His eyes gleamed as he told of the few details he was willing to share about his life above water. She had always been curious about humans, a breed that was so close to their own, but so indecipherably different. And yet, she'd never want to exchange her life underwater for one without the freedom to glide with dolphins, or feel the water enwrap her body like a second skin, or to simply live out the purpose of creation. She was, first and foremost, a mermaid, and she didn't intend for this to change after this expedition.

Nine transitions were what most merpeople had. Some were known to have less, but it often depended on age. She had read that cats possessed nine lives and now wondered if merpeople had anything in common with felines. Her first transition had just been used. And she *did* want to give this a try, as she was curious about humans and their exotic lifestyles. Secretly, she wanted to know what it was that had kept Keames so captivated and unwilling to return home.

She could be just as content spending the rest of her life under water with everything she needed. Being the daughter of their ocean grid's Elder gave her more space to swim freely without many restrictions. She got along with everyone and had a special connection with sharks, which most merpeople avoided. This entitled her to roam through deeper caverns whenever she wished and this kind of freedom made her fearless. But now fear was all that she felt. And it was consuming her by the second.

A rustling of footsteps startled her and made her turn around in search for the source of the sound. *Were they here?* She combed her fingers, damp with seawater, through her long, flaxen hair. It reached all the way to her waist, and she wondered how odd she must look as she wrapped it around her body. Being entirely naked made her even more apprehensive, and she tried to shield what she could with her hair.

"Are you all right?" The deep, masculine voice startled her. She wasn't expecting to see a man. She had thought the Changed Ones in charge of female Explorers were all past mermaids. Their eyes met, and she saw a young man, not much older than she was, staring back at her with an incredulous expression. His hair was short and curly, and she was tempted to reach out her hand to touch it to see if it was as soft as it looked. He had handsome, boyish features, but there was a soulless look about him that made him appear sad and older than his years. His light brown eyes blinked apprehensively, and he appeared equally surprised.

Were they all this inexperienced?

"I—I'm Narya." She expected him to know who she was. But she couldn't see the recognition in his eyes. Perhaps he had mixed up the pick-up point for another merman due to come ashore tonight. She looked about her nervously. *Where were the others?*

"Right . . . I'm going to get some help, okay? Just wait right here." He gestured with his hands as if to calm her.

She wondered if she was being abandoned as he walked away hastily before suddenly halting his steps. Had he remembered something? His fingers fumbled to unbutton his grey and white checkered shirt and he quickly threw it toward her.

"You can use this for now. I'll be right back." He turned and disappeared into the darkness.

Great, she thought. He was obviously scared of her. Maybe they all grow unaccustomed to seeing merpeople after living as Changed Ones for so long. She gladly took the shirt and draped it around her body. That felt a little bit better. It wasn't cold or anything, but the act itself made her feel more sheltered. As she had learned from books and magazines found in the secret chest, this was how humans slept—under a cloth, or blanket. A small grin appeared on her face. This was her very first human item.

From a distance, she saw two figures rushing toward her. *They're here.* Still kneeling on the sand, she straightened her back and kept the shirt tightly wrapped around her.

"What on earth are you talking about, Nick. I don't understand—oh . . ."

A young woman stood beside the man that had given Narya his shirt. She wore large, fashionable glasses—the kind with thick black frames often seen on models in magazines. Her features were not as delicate, but she was nice to look at. She sported cropped brown hair that reached her jawline with subtle blond highlights. Her eyes looked cold, but they retained a trace of kindness. She stared at Narya with an unreadable expression. *Do I look that unpresentable? Aren't they supposed to introduce themselves first?*

"I'm Narya." She assumed the man didn't explain who she was and wondered if they could even understand her. Surely it was impossible for them not to. Merpeople knew almost all the languages spoken on lands that surrounded them—at least around the coastal places. They had been taught the written form by past Explorers more than enthusiastic to share this exotic skill. She had used the dominant language of this particular island and didn't expect to be met with such puzzled looks.

"Right. And I'm Louise." The woman forced out a smile, but her eyes were hard, focused on her with an intensity that she didn't know what to make of. "What are you doing here alone? And . . ." her eyes trailed from Narya's hair to the shirt covering parts of her naked body. "And why on earth are you naked?"

Narya felt slightly irritated by her question. "I—I don't have any clothes," she said. They were supposed to come with a change of clothes. This was in the briefing before she swam to the pick-up point. No one told her that the Changed Ones would have so many questions. Why was she being interrogated as though her presence here wasn't welcome?

"You . . . you don't have any clothes for me?"

Louise stared at her with a blank expression before she burst into laughter.

"Oh man, you must have had a lot to drink. Either that, or you were high or something. All right, let's get you into some clothes, and we'll see where we can bring you." She walked toward Narya and knelt down beside her. She studied her closely, her intense blue eyes concentrating as if trying to dissect her thoughts. "Hey Nick, you want to go get my bag back at the lab? I think I have my workout clothes in there."

"You think she's okay?" Nick asked. He stood beside them reluctant to leave and avoided looking directly at her nakedness.

"Well, I'm no nurse, but I don't see any wound or anything. Except . . ." Louise stared at Narya's legs.

Her first transition had left them blotchy and extremely red in some places. These were the stings she had felt earlier. The transition was now complete, but she had been told that the redness would stay for a few days, and she would be too weak to walk properly. They were supposed to bring crutches, or at least extend their arm to support her until they could make it to a wheelchair.

"Why are your legs so red? And . . . are these jellyfish bites?" Louise pressed her thumb into the redness.

Narya thought it was strange to have someone touch her somewhere that didn't exist minutes before. After a close inspection, Louise seemed convinced they were indeed from jellyfish, and she nodded to herself. "I think we have some aloe vera back at the lab, too." She turned and saw that Nick was still standing in the same spot, his hand folded on his chest as he stared at Narya's bare legs.

"Nick, I'll need those clothes for her, unless you want to walk through campus with a naked girl in your arms." Louise shot a glance toward him that sent him running in response to her request.

She nudged Narya with her elbow and grinned mischievously. "So what did you drink before you woke up like this, huh?"

When Nick came back with Louise's bag, they gave her a bright yellow T-shirt with "The Ocean is My Home" printed on the front, and a pair of track pants that were too large for her. She had no shoes, but she didn't mind walking barefoot on the sand. It was soft and reminded her of the ocean floor in her favorite cavern.

"Can you walk?" Nick eyed her suspiciously as she tried to steady herself on two legs. When she felt she was losing her balance, Nick caught her arm and put it around his neck. He didn't say anything, but she assumed he would help her walk the rest of the way. She tilted her head sideways to study his profile. He didn't appear to be much of a talker and seemed like the quiet, gloomy type, with an indecipherable past. She let her gaze linger far too long, and he met her eyes with an arched brow and a quizzical look that made her heart jump. She turned away abruptly and cleared her throat. Maybe humans have different social codes when it comes to interacting with others. Underwater, merpeople spoke to each other by touch or glance, as their thoughts were transmitted this way. Spoken language was used only when they happen to float above water, or as practice for those due to leave as Explorers. She assumed that humans could not read her thoughts. The Changed Ones, after they make up their minds and forfeit their status as merpeople, supposedly lose the ability to speak in the same way. She opened her mouth and wanted to say something to Nick, but she was unsure what to ask him, or what might be appropriate to ask a Changed One on the first day.

"So, where do you live?" Louise turned to her suddenly before she had a chance to start with a question of her own.

"Where do I live?" Narya was puzzled that she would ask. She wasn't prepared to live alone and had expected them to take her in. They were assigned to her as caretakers. She would be housed, taught, and trained on how to behave like a human before she could make an informed decision about whether she even wanted to stay.

"Yeah, are you too stoned to know your own address or something?" There was sarcasm in her voice, not the malicious kind, but Narya didn't quite understand her. *Stoned? What did she mean?*

"Sure, maybe." She shrugged and looked expectantly at Nick. He seemed to be less aggressive than Louise when it came to questions. Maybe he would care to explain some of these human slogans she wasn't familiar with yet.

"Where am I staying?" She turned to him for help. Nick furrowed his brows and appeared to be just as confused as she was.

"Hey Lou, maybe she can just rest at your place for today, and we can figure things out tomorrow."

"My place? No way. I told you I had that TA get-together

tonight. Why don't *you* take her? You have all that extra space."
Louise threw his shirt in his face. Nick expertly caught it mid-air and
slung it over his shoulder.

"You want me to take in a strange girl, who appears to be
high, a day before I have to hand in my thesis?" There was resistance
in his voice, and he tried not to look directly at her.

Narya felt slighted by their exchange, and found it rude
that they were trying to get rid of the responsibility they were given.
She wanted to remind them of their duties but was reluctant to do
so on the very first day. A confrontation with the Changed Ones
assigned to look after her didn't seem like a wise decision. Besides,
she was exhausted from the transition, and her body was sore all
over from the pain. She needed to save her energy to recover and not
exacerbate her already weakened condition.

"Well, I'm sure she's harmless." Louise walked to her side,
took her other arm, and wrapped it around her neck. The simple
gesture made Narya feel warmer inside, and she was grateful for
Louise, however indifferent she appeared to be.

She had very little strength to stand, and walking was a
struggle she was not ready to face. She couldn't understand most of
what they meant by 'stoned,' or 'strange girl,' but she figured they
were now ready to help her in her transition. She threw her head
back and let her eyes wander aimlessly over the starry sky. It was
the same sky she stared at whenever she went up to the surface, but
tonight, the stars seemed more distant.

When they reached a large building, Narya squinted to
make out the words in the dark. *Gerace Research Centre, Bahamas.* She
remembered from the briefing that one of the Changed Ones was

a student here. So she must be with the right people. The doubt she felt about her two caretakers vanished, and the thought of finally taking on the role of an Explorer made her feel exhilarated and a bit lightheaded.

"Alright, I'm off," Louise said. "Jean is probably wondering where I am." She ducked and untangled herself from Narya's arm. "She's all yours, Nick."

A small snicker escaped her as she waved goodbye, leaving Narya with Nick, who looked as flustered as the girl they had rescued from the beach.

"You'll be fine!" She shouted as she walked away, seemingly eager to be free of them.

"Okay . . . well, I guess you're stuck with me for now."

There was neither enthusiasm nor annoyance detectable in his voice. But Narya still smiled at him apologetically. She had meant to go with Louise, but this would have to do for now. No one said transitions were easy. Still leaning on his arm, she felt Nick slow down, and her gaze followed his finger as he pointed toward a three-story building ahead. He stared skeptically at her wobbly legs.

"Three flights of stairs," he nodded perfunctorily. "I hope you can make it."

Before Narya could explain she was too tired to try walking, and that stairs would indisputably be an impossible task, she felt herself slipping away. Her eyes were closing and she knew the will to keep them open was no longer hers. She stood on solid ground, but it might as well have been crumbling beneath her. Now she could feel waves gushing through, crashing against her body, and she willingly melted into the water that called out to her.

"Hey! Hey!"

She could hear him, but he sounded so far away, his voice echoing in the deep, deep ocean floor.

When she woke, she found herself lying on a bed tucked in a thin, blue blanket, alone in a room with mismatched furniture. She was no interior designer, but she had flipped through enough magazines on the sandbank to know this was nowhere near fancy. Large world maps and posters of different shark species were plastered all over the walls. On the desk across from the bed, she could see books piled high atop each other and several papers scattered carelessly on the floor.

Her skin was not yet used to being completely dry, and she desperately felt the need to splash water over her body. Or maybe soak in a bath—one of the tips given at the briefing. During the transition phase, it was important to keep herself hydrated; it would ease the panic, she recalled someone saying. She felt as though her throat was parched, and she needed something to keep it overflowed with water or she might faint. She hadn't tried to drink or eat anything yet. These were all part of the first experiences as a human. Nick was nowhere to be seen, and she wondered if Louise would take over now and guide her through her first morning as a human.

Her head laid on white, crisp pillows that made her want to linger for a while. Grudgingly, she forced herself to get up. Sitting up with her back against the pillows, she uncovered the blanket to reveal her legs. Grinning like a child who's found her favorite toy, she stared proudly at her new limbs. They were long, slim, and straight. The skin on the rest of her body was naturally tanned but her legs were pasty white, and it made them appear as though they didn't belong to her. She tried bending one leg and wiggling her toes, hardly able to believe she actually had legs. Her tail had been so beautiful, meticulously maintained, with the most intriguing mix of turquois, violet and golden scales. With an ardor that even Keames found to be impressive, she constantly cleaned her scales against beds of sea grass whenever they came across one. Funny how she didn't miss her tail at all—at least not for now. Still on the bed, she observed her legs with childlike wonder. She hadn't really tried standing on her own after so much help from Louise and Nick yesterday. But she felt ready to tackle her first steps as a human. She staggered clumsily out of the bed and gently put one foot on the ground. Feeling the hard, cold tile on the sole of her left foot, she giggled uncontrollably at this new, weird sensation.

"Hi." Nick stood beside the open door and wore a quizzical look. She wondered how long he has been there. He held a mug in each hand, and extended one to her.

"Coffee?"

"Okay." Narya took small, unsteady steps, holding onto the edge of Nick's bookshelves as she slowly made her way toward him. "Sorry, I'm not used to this." She smiled apologetically.

"Sure." He sounded unconvinced as he watched her attempting to grab the coffee mug.

"Be careful, it's super hot." He turned the mug so that the handle was within her reach.

"Man, whatever you had last night messed you up good." He shook his head.

There was still no smile from this brooding young man. She wondered what might have happened to him to render him this unapproachable.

"I didn't have anything. Except seawater, I suppose. I choked on a lot of it last night coming up." She carefully took a small sip from the cup. It tasted bitter and she made a face.

"You were . . . in the water?" Confusion lingered in his eyes as he tried to make sense of what she said. "Anyway, drink up. Coffee helps with most hangovers."

"Hangovers? Is that what they call it now?" She didn't know this was a code name for the transition. As she attempted to take another sip, she raised her eyes. In the morning light, she saw his face clearly, unlike the blurred figure she first took him for. He had dark, tanned skin, with large brown eyes that looked like they had seen through too many of life's harsh realities. He was taller than she remembered him; she noted his broad shoulders and the bulging shape of his arms—built like a merman. *He must be a swimmer, then.*

Nick let out a small laugh and scratched his head. His eyes flickered as he watched her grab the coffee mug as though it were a bizarre contraption she'd never seen before.

"Look, I've got something planned for today, and I can't be late . . ." He glanced at his watch, and his smile instantly faded.

"Uh, listen, Louise will be here in a bit—and she'll get you home." He took a large gulp of coffee and rushed to the desk to pick up some of his books.

"Thank you for everything. I—I didn't expect someone like you . . . but thank you."

"Right." He held her gaze with a more confounded look, but he had no time for questions. "I guess I'll see you around." With that, he hurriedly exited the room and she heard the door slam.

What an unexpected beginning to her first day as a human. She supposed nothing would seem normal now. Tired of standing, she crawled back to the bed and curled up under the blanket. Rest was her best remedy for now, she closed her eyes as she prepared for the next dream that was to come.

"No, I am not waking her, *you* do it!"

Narya heard a woman's voice as she awoke from her dream. It was a good dream, too. Swimming along with the current, she was racing with Grey, one of the sharks she had befriended years ago when she realized she possessed the gift to feasibly communicate with them. Sharks and mermaids didn't usually mix. Dolphins, yes. Whales, it depended on their size; humpbacks were gentle giants, but they could cause serious accidents if they did not swim out of their way in time. As for sharks, they usually steered clear of them for obvious reasons. It was easy for sharks to confuse merpeople with other fishes that they preyed on. But once Narya made friends with one, it was hard not to embrace the entire group.

In her dream, she and Grey sped through the corals, zigzagging in and out of caverns. They couldn't slow down, like they were held captive for too long and finally set free—and it was such a thrill to swim like that. *Swim.* She opened her eyes and slid her hand down her waist and felt the foreign limbs that hung unto her lower body. Now that she was temporarily human, swimming was no longer an option. Once she dipped into the seawater, the transition back into a mermaid was inevitable. A single tear rolled down her cheek, and she let it linger there. The dampness alone soothed her.

She turned her head toward the sound and saw two indistinct figures standing by the door. She blinked then saw Louise and Nick, the only two people she had on her side for now. They were her sole support in this new life—until they deemed her human enough to travel and brought her to wherever Keames was.

"Is she awake?" Nick took a brisk step forward. He had another cup of coffee in his hands. Coffee must be a favorite drink.

"I'm awake." She didn't know how long she had slept, but from the window, she could see the sun setting. *Oh no.* She groaned loudly. "I missed the entire day?"

Louise nodded sympathetically. "Yep. That's what a bad hangover will do to you." She came over to Narya and sat on the bed. "So, are you ready to go?"

"Sure . . ." Her hair was completely dry now and still had no idea how to manage her long, loose waves of curls. They were constantly in her face, and she struggled to comb through them with her fingers. Maybe Louise could give her beauty tips. Her hair looked fashionable enough. This should be a fun first day.

"Hey . . . can you cut my hair?" She grinned like a child, anticipating the prospect of getting a makeover, something that seemed to be common among young girls according to the magazines she read.

"You want me to . . . cut your hair?"

The sound of Louise's laughter almost made Narya jump from the bed. It was one of those deep, throaty laughs that came from the core of one's stomach. She was still laughing, as though Narya had uttered the most ridiculous thing.

"Well . . ." She peered at Louise from under her hair. "I mean—I thought that's one of the things that we could do." She wasn't so sure now whether this was a good idea. Maybe they had a strict schedule for her. She didn't pay much attention at the briefing when they went over a typical first-week schedule for the Explorers.

"No, no, no. I don't cut hair. I think I could, sure, but you'd probably regret you ever asked. Come on." Louise stood up and pulled Narya by the arm. "Let's get you home."

"But . . . I thought this was . . . home."

"No, this is *Nick's* home." Louise enunciated the words slowly as if Narya were hard of hearing.

"You still don't know where your home is?" Nick asked, leaning on the threshold of the doorway. He still eyed her suspiciously but appeared genuinely concerned about her confused state of mind. "Lou, maybe we should call the police."

"What? No—no, why would you call the police?"

Narya tried to stand, but she stumbled into the bookshelf,

hitting her knee hard against the wood. "Ow!" She sat on the floor rubbing her left knee. As clueless as she was about most human things, she knew how the system on land worked. With her ambiguous identity, being interrogated by the police would surely spin things out of control.

Nick moved to rush toward her then stopped himself as though he remembered he shouldn't exhibit any real kindness or concern. He kept his distance, but his tone was softer.

"I mean, we don't have to, but it seems like you don't know where you are."

"But I *don't* know where I am." Tears welled up in her eyes, and she tried to steady her shaking voice. "You two brought me here." Her gaze shifted to Nick then to Louise, who looked just as perplexed. "I mean, weren't you waiting for me on the shore last night?"

The same look of confusion spread across both their faces. Narya's chest tightened. They *hadn't* been waiting for her. She just showed up—a naked girl on the beach with nowhere to go, and they took her in out of kindness. Did she confuse the pick-up point?

"Look," Nick gave Louise a look before continuing. "You can stay here for tonight, if you want to, but we need to get you home somehow." His voice was low and comforting, reminding her of a still ocean.

She nodded distractedly. This was more than bad. She had no one. She was utterly and hopelessly on her own.

"Yeah, maybe it'll come to you." Louise sounded hopeful. She crossed her arms and looked at Nick. "I have to go. I got quizzes to mark. Can you . . ." She lowered her voice but Narya could still hear her. ". . . *deal* with this?"

"Yeah, yeah." Nick was uneasy about having a strange girl in his house, but he felt responsible for her. After all, he was the one who found her.

CHAPTER TWO

"You know, I'd offer you the option of eating in, but unfortunately I'm really not a good cook, and there are plenty of great places to eat around campus."

They had been sitting on the couch for over an hour now. Narya silently stared at her legs as Nick pretended to flip through his books, occasionally eyeing her in case she started crying again. It was now dinnertime, and he wasn't sure if she was hungry since she hasn't spoken since Louise left. He, on the other hand, was starving and still had lots of work to go through tonight. He could never focus with an empty stomach.

"Do you want to go? It's really just around the corner." Nick got up, grabbed his keys from his pocket, and dangled them in front of her in the hope of waking his guest from her daydream. Narya was deep into her thoughts. She and the Changed Ones who were supposed to meet last night had missed each other on the beach. No one had prepared her for what to do should the pick-up go wrong. And she had no idea how to locate Keames. Was he even in the same area? She knew she was on the San Salvador island in the Bahamas, and this is where he had first surfaced. But it has been a year and a half since she last saw him, and a lot could happen in that time.

"Narya, right?"

She glanced up. This was the first time she heard her name

said out loud since she got here.

"Yes." She felt pitiful that the tears were coming again, and she buried her face in her hands, hoping to hide them.

"Hey—hey, don't . . . okay." He left out a soft sigh. He wasn't exactly annoyed with her, but he wasn't happy that his stomach was churning loudly now from excessive hunger.

"Yes. I'm just . . . very confused right now. But I'll be fine. We can go." She wiped away her tears and was about to slide off the couch when she realized she had no tail. It was time to try walking again.

"Do you need some help?"

Nick knew she would have trouble standing and reached out to help her, but she stopped him midway with a raised palm.

With one leg on the ground, she gently placed her other foot down. She felt stronger than she had yesterday. She released her hands from their clutch on the couch's armrest and let the weight of her body settle. A proud smile spread across her face. Her eyes flickered with excitement as she looked up to meet his questioning gaze.

"Did you see that?" She could hardly contain her joy, and as she laughed, her smile crinkled her nose. It was one of those moments Nick missed most about his old life. Genuine happiness. It must have looked something like this.

"Um . . . yeah. I guess you're . . . standing." It was hard not to smile along with her, this girl with her weird and unfathomable ways.

"Can you walk?" He stood about a meter away from her and held out his hands. It was like teaching a child how to walk, and the mental image of his younger self, guiding a toddler, surfaced. He shook his head and willfully chased it away. *Katie.* Though he was able to keep her face away, the sadness that came with the memories of her still lingered.

"That's good. Try to come to me." He slowly backed away so that Narya would move toward him. This was beyond weird, but by the look on her face, he saw this was a major breakthrough for her.

"I don't know. Let's see." Narya hesitantly took a small step forward. Her hands were barely touching his, but they were close enough that he could catch her if she fell. He nodded encouragingly.

"Good, good. Keep going."

With each step she took, he backed up more, making her squeal and laugh at the same time. She was walking on two feet. This sudden improvement emboldened her, and she sprinted ahead—a move she instantly regretted. She lost her balance and fell right into Nick's open arms.

"Are you sure I'm not too heavy?"

She was on Nick's back, her arms wrapped around his neck. Her legs dangled freely and she grinned as the sole of her feet felt the sea breeze glide over them. A first for her, and her feet. Embarrassed by having to be carried, she wanted to close her eyes and pretend this wasn't happening, but there was simply too much to see.

"For the tenth time, it's fine," Nick said, laughing heartily. Her smile was infectious and her behavior a little ridiculous. It was hard not to fall prey to this kind of combination. She weighed close to nothing, and he found himself entertained by her childlike reaction to everything around her. It all seemed new and exciting. She ooh-ed and ahh-ed from the moment they exited the door.

Nightlife in San Salvador was, in fact, enthralling in itself. Beach bars were crowded, overstuffed with people, and different music blasted from restaurants cramped side by side. There wasn't a corner that wasn't filled with loud laughter or some form of wild rowdiness.

"All right, we're here. Can you walk?" After almost twenty minutes with Narya on his back, he was slightly out of breath, and he slowly squatted down so she could steady her legs on the ground before moving.

"I think so." She steadied herself awkwardly and accepted Nick's help when he held out his hand. Once she was able to stand on her own, her eyes watched the colorful light bulbs that hung above the bar sign, and she listened to the buzzing sound of people around her excitedly chatting. Inhaling deeply, she smelled the ocean and could almost taste the salt in the air. All that she was used to was now beginning to fade. She took in everything with a whole new sensory system. While she could detect different scents underwater, nothing could compare to what she was experiencing now. And taste . . . she hadn't even gotten to that part yet. She had seen pictures of intricate food plates on magazines and wondered how they would taste on the tip of her tongue. The noise of a restless night—people talking, laughing, shouting—they were a sharp contrast to the quietness and serenity she was used to underwater. Tonight was going to be a first of so many things, and she had an urge to jump up and down but doubted her inexperienced legs would sustain her.

"Wow! This is amazing." Her smile lighted her face, and a dimple creased her left cheek.

"Sure. I guess it's a nice pub . . ."

Nick wasn't sure what to make of her amazement at the local eatery and pub.

Where could she be from? Her English sounded American enough, and she didn't look indigenous, so he assumed that she was a temporary visitor to this island, much like himself. She was of average height, with a slim built and a head full of thick, long, and wavy flaxen curls. Her features were delicate—light grey eyes with an interesting golden hue, and full lips that now grinned widely like a child's. As he watched her, he realized she was very beautiful and wondered how he didn't see this before. It's been a while since he'd noticed anyone, really. But there was something about her that seemed downright familiar. He couldn't pinpoint when or where he had seen her. Or maybe she looked like someone he had met before. The Bahamas was filled with people who came and went as they pleased. No one really had any concrete plans, at least no one he'd come across. Somehow this sort of instability soothed him and he found comfort in his identity as a passing visitor with no plans for the foreseeable future.

"Can we go in?"

Her eyes shone with anticipation and her legs shifted from where they stood, as if she were going to jump. Nick caught her by the arm and knew she would need his help if she was going to enter the pub in one piece. He felt like a personal bodyguard for a mental patient. Well, an attractive mental patient, he'll give her that.

"All right." He took her arm in and looped it around his. "Let's go."

Since Narya knew nothing about most of the items on the menu, Nick took the liberty of ordering for her. Two Daily Specials, which was basically a mix of grilled seafood, along with a shrimp and tuna paté. One of his favorite dishes at his regularly frequented pubs.

"So that'll be all?" Lauren, the waitress who usually worked the weekend shift, smiled cheerfully, her eyes darting to Narya.

Nick rarely brought anyone here, except Louise and Pete, his supervisor at his program. Maybe she thought that he was on a date. He hasn't been on one since he and Louise called it quits years ago. Nick cleared his throat as he waved no and purposefully averted her gaze.

Narya grinned at the whole scene. Another couple across from them sat intimately close, their foreheads touching while the guy caressed her hand and whispered something obviously meant to make her throw her head back and laugh out loud. At another table, a few young men were gathered happily and already tipsy as they roared with laughter at whatever they read on the menu. It was a regular Friday night, but the girl that sat across from Nick was anything but ordinary.

"Are you . . . not from here?" He tried not to sound too doubtful, but he had to find out, if only to satisfy his own curiosity. Louise would have to do the rest tomorrow. He had a busy schedule from dusk until dawn.

"No, I'm from here." With her chin resting on her hands, Narya answered casually, her eyes smiling as she watched the drunken young men let loose with more loud banter.

"Right here? You're from San Salvador?" He didn't believe her, but she didn't seem like the lying type either. He wondered if she was still hungover—or worse, an addict like Louise speculated her to be.

"Um, sure. I mean, near here." Her guilty look revealed her attempt to make something up. She clutched her hands on her knees and stiffened as she anxiously anticipated his next questions.

"Right." He nodded doubtingly. "Well, do you remember where you live now?"

"Where I live?"

He could see she was starting to get nervous and immediately regretted his questions. He had made her uneasy again and tears were ready to burst from the reddened rim of her doe-like eyes.

"I mean, it's okay if you don't want to tell me. I just want to make sure you get home okay tomorrow." He quickly lowered his head and pretended to read the drinks menu.

"I see." Her voice was small and he cursed himself silently for paving the way for what was now doomed to be an awkward dinner.

For a few good minutes, they sat in silence, Narya fiddling with her hair, frowning as she tried to untangle them, and Nick drumming his fingers on the table, looking aimlessly around the pub. He wished that Louise were here. She was good with these kind of situations. When they were together, she was always the one to break the ice whenever they met new people. He was never good at making small talk. And for a long time now, he hasn't really met anyone new. He was so damn comfortable in his own bubble, doing his research, spending his time with the ocean. Trapped. And painfully familiarizing himself with his guilt for what had happened.

"Can I try that?"

He glanced up and saw her pointing straight at him. He wasn't sure what she was looking at. He turned his head for a quick glimpse behind him but she obviously meant something on him. His face. And then he saw her reach for his glasses. He usually wore contacts, but he liked to remove them in the evenings when he was working on his papers.

"These? You want to try my glasses?"

She nodded enthusiastically, and she held out her hands.

The evening was only getting weirder, but Nick shrugged it off. He wanted to make peace with her to get through dinner without her tears making him uncomfortable. He gladly took off his glasses and handed them to her.

"Like this?" She carefully unfolded his glasses as if handling something extremely fragile, and steadied them on her ears.

The large black frames looked ridiculous on her tiny face, but he supposed they looked funny on him too. He'd had these outdated glasses since high school, and he never found fault with them, so he'd only updated the lens prescription. He laughed softly when she kept blinking and couldn't keep her eyes opened.

"I don't think you actually need them," he said as reached over to retrieve his glasses. His hands accidentally brushed against her cheeks and he jumped at the cold touch.

"Hey, are you feeling cold?" The temperature must be more than 25°C here, and there was no way anyone would be cold in this weather.

"No. I think—well, I'm always cold." She took a sip of water.

"Hey, this is good water! Unsalted!" Her voice was high with excitement as she took a few more gulps. When she saw him watching her, she cleared her throat.

"It's just my body temperature." She smiled sheepishly and finished the water in one large gulp.

Nick crossed his arms, trying to make sense of the odd girl who sat across from him. Nothing about her made sense, and he felt a need to find out more about her—like she were a clue to a riddle.

Narya knew that she had to mask her identity better. Louise and Nick were humans, and not her support group of Changed Ones. And while Nick seemed discreet enough, being the quiet guy that he was, she couldn't very well tell him that mermaids, like fish, were always cold. Perhaps by the time she made her decision to stay changed, her body temperature would eventually rise to normal. And what would her choice be, she wondered. She hadn't given that much thought. She still had to find Keames and decide what 'they'

were. Once that's figured out, it'll be easier to make her choice then. Her father liked Keames well enough. But once he left the waters and failed to come back, she knew he wanted her to stay behind, find another suitable merman, and continue with her life underwater where she belonged.

Ever since the new system was introduced by the Elders, everyone was allowed, even encouraged, to get a taste of being human. Before then, a few would venture out on their own, and risked exposure as they had no support on land that they knew of. It was never fully explained to them how the Transition Committee was formed, but it was understood that there were merpeople who stay changed that lingered on land, and they had agreed to be part of the transition process; to allow their curious, fellow merpeople to live out a human life temporarily. It was thought that this kind of monitored freedom would prevent them from being accidentally discovered. With rules and protocols, the curious merpeople would be able to explore the land with help and extra sets of eyes to keep them safe. And when her turn came along, she couldn't turn it down. She craved adventure and wanted to see for herself what she was missing.

And why some of them never came back.

"Here you go!" Lauren came back with two dishes of the Daily Special and placed them on the table. Before she left, she winked at Nick, as if wishing him luck on his date.

"Bon appétit." He gestured for Narya to start.

"Oh, right." She stared at her plate blankly, and hesitantly picked up the fork. She had practiced with other mermaids during the preparation stages for the transition, but never with a human staring at her. She fidgeted in her seat and laughed nervously.

Nick watched her fumble awkwardly with the fork, as though unsure of how to use one properly.

"You can use your hands," he suggested after a length of silence. He could tell that she was embarrassed, though he wasn't sure why—and he subtly offered her a way out. He put down his fork and knife and started picking at his food with his fingers.

"See?" He shoved a few french fries into his mouth. When her face relaxed into a smile, he grinned back at her.

She scooped up some of the paté and licked it off her fingers.

"So, what is this?"

"Shrimp, fish, and some crabmeat."

She started to cough, trying hard not to spit the food out. She looked horrified and repelled by what she was chewing. He offered her a glass of water, but she waved him away, half-choking on her food.

"It's okay. It's fine. I can eat . . . *fish*," she said, still coughing. Her face was reddening by the second, and she tried not to shudder at the thought of what was in her mouth. This was one of the obstacles she would have to overcome. She had to appear normal. It was a game of pretense and she could do it. She heard the waves rolling in and thought of running toward the beach and rinsing her mouth with salt water, but that would look weird and inappropriate. She shook her head and took another deep breath before taking another bite. It's not that bad, really.

She lasted a few more seconds before she staggered toward the shore and threw up all over the beach.

"She *what?*"

Narya could hear Louise's high-pitched voice from inside

the room. She had had a good sleep, but it had been filled with dreams of being back in the water. Without fish patés. She felt mortified when Nick had run after her and patted her back as she vomited every bit of fish she ingested. They must be talking about the incident now. She hid her face under the pillows, unable to get up and face Nick after what had happened.

"Not so loud, she'll hear you."

"So what? Anyway, you have to bring her back now. I just got a call that I have to sub for another TA that got a bad case of flu. Flu—in the middle of April! There goes my entire week!" Louise sounded furious and spoke through clenched teeth.

"But today's the tagging. I can't miss it." Nick's voice was firm and Narya knew that his face must look serious. Like the concerned look he had when he thought she was sick with the fish paté.

"So? You can bring her. *Or* she could stay here."

"She can't stay here on her own."

"Why? She's not a child."

"No, you don't understand—you weren't there yesterday. She couldn't even hold a fork—she's . . ." His voice trailed off when he saw Narya appear in the hallway with a blanket wrapped around her.

"Hi." She smiled weakly, still feeling sick from the day before. She didn't want to stay here, but being alone was not an option. She'd rather be with him, if he'd take her. And Louise, who wasn't so fond of her to begin with, was already in a foul mood today.

"Hey, I heard you threw up yesterday." You better?" She asked with little concern in her voice. Nick shot her a dirty look. She stared at Narya with lingering suspicion.

"I'm okay, really." Narya would much rather be with Nick, even if it meant she had to eat more fish patés.

"So, can I come with you?" She directed her question at Nick. Her eyes pleaded him to say yes.

He scratched his head and contemplated the situation then threw his hands up in surrender.

"All right, why the hell not. Come on, have something for breakfast—not fish—and we'll go."

He went into the kitchen and made her a cup of coffee— the dark liquid thing. She made a face when she took a sip, but the bitterness awoke her senses. Whatever magical ingredient was in this drink, it made her feel ready to tackle her second day.

"I hope you're okay with boats?"

Only when did they approach the dock, did Narya realize where they were going. It didn't occur to her to ask Nick to expand on the details since he had mentioned it was work. In her head, she pictured his work environment to be a closed room with books piled high on a desk, and a laptop, as she'd seen him typing furiously on one. Right now, what she saw before her was a small fishing boat like the ones she used to spot from afar, rocking gently above the tides.

"Yes, yes. I'm okay." She just had to make sure to not fall in. After all, being on a boat might be interesting. She'd always imagined what it would be like inside such a constricted area right above the waters. She treaded carefully along the dock and had an urge to hold Nick's hands in case she tripped and tumbled in. She couldn't transform in front of him. That was golden rule number one.

Nick waved at someone inside the boat, and he signaled for her to hurry. By the way he was rushing, she could tell that this was an important day for him. She has been observing him for the past two days, and she had never seen him irritated, angry, or anything other than calm. It must be nice to be so composed, so sure of oneself. She had never felt more unsure of her capability to get through a day without more missteps.

"Well, you're early!" An older man, in his forties, shouted sarcastically at Nick.

He threw him a pair of goggles and laughed heartily. He was tanned, like everyone else on the island, and had a head full of greying blond hair. His eyes were shielded by his sunglasses, but Narya was keenly aware that he was observing her.

"Who's the skittish girl?"

"A friend." Nick nodded perfunctorily at Narya before hurling the goggles back. "Pete, I told you that I can't go in there."

"Why, you afraid of sharks or something?" He laughed again, this time louder, as if it were the best joke he'd made all day. "Come on, Nick! You can't stay on the boat forever. You have to see them for yourself again. Underwater!"

"I will. Just—not yet." Nick said firmly. His eyes hardened as he stared longingly into the vast expanse of blue before him. The boat was both a shield and an obstacle between him and the sea. Yet it was his choice to be here. To breathe in the smell of the comforting saltwater that surrounded him, and lulled to sleep by the sound of the rolling waves.

"All right, fine. I'll let you off the hook this time. But one day—*one day*," Pete said emphatically, pointing at Nick with a chewed pencil. "You're going to get in there and you're going to fall in love with it all over again. Trust me, boy." He slid the pencil behind his ear, removed his sunglasses, and turned abruptly to Narya with an impish grin as he dangled the goggles in front her.

"What about you? Care to take a dive?"

They were now far from the shore. The island was a dot,

and Narya was beginning to feel a churning in her stomach. She tried to steady her hands as she held on to the metal railing at the side of the boat. Home was only a splash away, but she was risking everything she had by being out here. Pete, who she later found out was Nick's professor at the Marine Institute, was going to tag a shark today. She's never seen it done, but she'd come across plenty of sharks who had the strange device stuck on their fins. They appeared to be unbearably painful, although both Nick and Pete repeatedly assured her that the tagging process was a brief, minor discomfort for sharks. She winced at the thought of witnessing the process, but she had to bear it for now.

"Nick! Dump that bucket now!" Pete shouted from the rear of the boat with a drink in his hand.

Nick grunted as he carried a large bucket filled with dead fish and poured it overboard. Narya held on to the rim of the boat as she tried not to gag at the bloody sight.

"Get that bait ready!" Pete's excitement grew as he braced himself for the shark to appear. This never got old for him, no matter how many times he had done it before.

"Are you okay?" Nick turned and found Narya beside him, her body curled into a ball as she peered at the ocean from a crouching position.

"Oh, damn. Can you even swim?" He pulled out a worn-out lifejacket from under the bench and handed it to her.

"No—I *can't* swim." She hesitated before she took the lifejacket. She was going to say something else before a heavy thud made her lose her balance, and she almost fell overboard into the floating, chopped-up fish parts.

"Whoa! Whoa, I got you!" Nick pulled her back and she held on to him tightly.

He pointed to the middle seat. "Don't stand so close to the

edge of the boat. Sit here."

She wanted to ask what the thumping sound was, but she thought better of it and sat down obediently.

"A shark!" Nick smiled broadly, his face to the sun, welcoming its blazing brightness. With his hands expertly handling the pole, he slid a fish bait onto the hook and got into position as he waited for the shark. It was as though he belonged right here on the vast blue. Out here, he transformed into someone entirely different—he came alive. He stood close to the rim of the boat and didn't appear scared of the water at all. She wondered what he meant when he told Pete that he couldn't go in.

"Have you ever seen one? Up close?" He sounded like Pete now, overexcited about something she had encountered every day as a mermaid.

She found his rare smile contagious and grinned back.

"Nope. Not yet."

Pete threw a large net into the water. "Nick! Do you see it? On your right!"

Nick maneuvered the pole toward where the net was. It was then that Narya spotted the shark, her first time seeing one from above water. A sheer black, beautiful fin emerged, and she thought it looked familiar. She quickly scanned the area, and although she couldn't be sure where they were, by the distance from the shore, she guessed this was Grey's territory. But it wasn't Grey or she would have recognized it immediately, but it was definitely one from their ocean grid.

"Do you know this shark?" She regretted her question as soon as she had uttered it, assuming it to be a stupid question. Humans didn't interact with sharks like she did.

"Yeah, well, sort off. I saw this one a few times before, and Pete's swam with it a while back." Nick was busy pulling the bait back, and the shark was chasing after it at an alarming speed.

Narya was glad he didn't think her question was out of the ordinary. She was more comfortable now since this was familiar territory. She stood up and took small, careful steps toward Nick.

Suddenly, the shark paused in its chase. Her heart stilled. *No, not possible*. Did it just recognize her? From where she stood, she could read the shark's body language—it was now tracking her scent.

"Hey, what the—"

Before Nick could finish, the shark leapt out of the water, its jaws wide open as it aimed for the boat. For her.

It was a mako shark, magnificent in every way, and Narya's eyes grew large as she watched the notorious fish flip itself in the air. She has never seen this before. The shark was making itself known to her. But why? In her mind, she ran through all the possible reasons a shark might be making contact with her. If it managed to flip the boat, she would be exposed, and that would be the end of her transition—possibly for everyone else as well. She glanced nervously around her and felt maddeningly trapped. But wait—she *was* trapped. The shark must think she was trapped by humans on the boat. It could still recognize her mermaid self by her scent. She recalled stories of whales and sharks attacking fishing boats with the goal of freeing trapped fish, and it dawned on her that she was putting Nick and Pete in imminent danger.

"Are you sure you can't turn back now?" She moved away from the edge and wondered if the shark could easily break the small fishing boat in two.

"No, no, it's okay. They do this all the time—" Nick reassured her and started to make his way toward her when another loud thud threw him off balance. He fell down hard and landed on his arm.

"What the hell?" Pete ran toward them with his drink still in his hand. Nothing came between the man and his drink. Another thud. He was now on his hands and knees, his drink spilled across the deck.

"I think it's angry," Narya muttered. Should she dive in and lead the shark away? That might be the only way to calm it. She held on to the rim of the boat and stumbled toward the edge.

Another thud.

"Hey! Come back here!" Nick shouted as he watched her extend her hand beyond the boat's edge.

She closed her eyes, knowing the shark was coming for her before she touched it. *It's okay. It's only me.* As soon as her hand felt that familiar smooth skin, the disquietude that numbed her mind only moments before thawed away, revitalizing her with a nostalgic sense of belonging. Her fingers softly caressed the tip of the shark's snout, and it stayed still, instantly hypnotized by her touch. When she opened her eyes, she saw the shark's wet skin glistening under the sun, its eyes solemnly staring back at her. *I'm okay. I'm okay.* She smiled faintly as she steadily lowered her hand, and the shark obediently went down as if by command.

"What in God's name . . ." Pete stood with both hands on his head, certain that something disastrous might happen.

Nick stood in awe as he witnessed her ability to communicate with one of the most feared beasts of the ocean. Not many girls he knew would be brave enough to even be on a fishing boat in shark-infested waters, let alone touch one. He stared at her in disbelief. When the shark disappeared from view, it occurred to him that neither he nor Pete had spoken. They simply stood in silence, just as hypnotized by Narya as the shark. It wasn't until she turned around that Nick realized he had held his breath the entire time.

"So, how did it go?"

When they got back to the shore, Louise was waiting for them at the dock. The sun was setting, its glorious beam shining directly at her, and she had to shield her eyes with her hand when she approached the boat.

"Well, I would say it went quite well!" Pete got off the boat, and as he stepped onto the dock, he turned back. "You said your name was—what, Natalie?"

"Narya." Nick and Narya answered in unison.

"Right, Na-ree-ya." He nudged Louise with his elbow as he walked past her. "That's a good catch for Nick, huh?" He tried to keep his voice low, but they all heard him.

Louise winced at his remark.

"Narya, why don't you come back next week? I think you'll come in quite handy for our next expedition!" It didn't sound like a question but more of an expectation to be met. Pete didn't turn back to see if she had acquiesced to the request as he walked away from the dock.

"What the heck is he talking about?" Louise asked Nick.

He wondered what she'd think if she had seen Narya with the shark. It wasn't unheard of. Some divers he knew in the field had touched a shark's snout, putting it into a kind of trance. But in this case it was different. That shark was on full attack mode, and she had calmed it—like a magic trick too perfect to be true—and commanded it to back away. However hard it was to believe, the shark actually obeyed her.

He tried not to let his thoughts trail off into supernatural beliefs; it this was all beginning to sound absurd, if only in his head.

"You know, he's always tipsy in the morning." He pretended to shrug it off. Louise didn't need to know. She already thought that Narya was some kind of freak. And they had to find a way to bring her home today; the last thing Louise needed on her list was one

39

more questionable trait about Narya.

Narya had remained quiet since the boat ride back, and even now, as Nick helped her off the boat, she appeared to be somewhere else. He wondered what other secrets she could surprise them with. Too bad she wasn't sticking around longer for him to find out.

CHAPTER THREE

They sat around Nick's kitchen bar with a plate of Cheetos on the counter—the most popular snack for him and Louise for as long as he could remember. But after one look at Narya's face as she popped one into her mouth, he concluded it wasn't her favorite.

"Do you know who was supposed to pick you up?" Louise asked.

Nick thought she sounded too aggressive, but he understood that time was of the essence to her. She had papers to correct, and it was her turn to check the lab tonight. She had mentioned again earlier that they could turn her in to the police, and he had to persuade to drop the idea. He barely knew the girl but felt it his duty to make her feel safe here. He knew it irritated Louise that he was suddenly protective, but he was convinced they could help her on their own.

"No. I mean—I just know they were supposed to be there."

"Well, where were they taking you?" Fiddling with the Cheetos in the palm of her hand, Louise was becoming more impatient by the minute. Narya's vague answers certainly weren't helping her case.

"I'm not sure. Just somewhere for me to . . . recover." Narya bit her lips. She wasn't sure how much she should divulge. Louise obviously saw her as suspicious. And Nick—she stole a quick glance at him. He had been kind to her, but she recalled the words of the Advisor at the training: "Trust no one." She had heard that even some of the Changed Ones were not to be fully trusted and could be malicious toward one another. It was so unlike her community where there was little to argue over. There has been conflict between neighboring grids over the seaweed harvest, and other trivial things that bothered some more than others, but nothing escalated to a point where anyone was hurt or in imminent danger.

Louise narrowed her eyes, as though deciding whether to kick her out or not. Or worse, report her to the police. She had no identification on her—this was supposed to have been arranged by the Changed Ones. She lowered her gaze and clutched her knees. What else could she do or say to prove she was no threat, that she needed only a place to stay without raising too many questions?

Nick broke the silence.

"Hey, it's okay. I mean, if you can't take her for now, my place is big enough for two."

Narya could tell he was treading carefully with Louise, leaving her the last word. She felt reassured relieved to see Louise's tense face relax into a mildly exasperated expression.

"Alright, fine," Louise said. She threw her hands up and waved them around dramatically. There was detectable irritation in her voice, and she forced out a smile with pursed lips.

"You can stay wherever you feel comfortable. And Nick, you're the one with the extra cash to spend, so you can take care of her expenses."

Narya and Nick simultaneously released a sigh of relief as Louise rose from her interrogator's seat at the kitchen counter.

"Hey, I'm starving," she said, pointing toward Nick's empty fridge. "You guys want to go grab a bite?"

"Right. No seafood for this one." Lauren nodded and laughed as she took down their orders. She gave Narya a sympathetic smile. It was obvious her seafood paté incident had caused quite a memorable scene, and she shrank into her seat.

"I'll just take French fries." Narya watched Nick trying to suppress a grin. "And, maybe, uh . . . water?"

She glanced at the drinks menu and felt dizzy at the sight of all the choices. She recalled reading about some of these drinks in the magazines. Too many of them and she might have trouble walking, talking, and making level-headed decisions. Already in an unfavorable situation, she really had to keep her wits about her.

"Aw, come on. It's been a long day for all of us. Why don't you have a Bloody Mary? Or maybe something lighter?"

Louise stole the menu from Narya's hand and glided her fingers over the drink items. She wetted her lips as she searched for a more suitable drink for their new companion.

"What is . . . a Bloody Mary?" The name itself made Narya want to gag. The bloody image of the chopped up fish on Pete's boat was still fresh in her mind. Even the stench of the bucket was still palpable. She pulled one of her sleeves to her nose and sniffed disapprovingly.

"I don't think that's a good idea . . ." Nick said.

Louise dismissed his advice brusquely and waved her hand in his face.

"Oh, what are you, her legal guardian? Let the girl have some fun! Let's do a piña colada for you. You seem like the fruity drink type. Lauren!" She slammed the menu down on the table and signaled for the waitress.

Louise and her determined ways were becoming familiar as

she got to know her.

"Well, she can crash at your place tonight, then." Nick shook his head disapprovingly at Louise's choice of drink for Narya.

"She'll be fine! We'll just monitor how much she drinks. Right?" Louise winked playfully at Narya. She seemed less skeptical and more cheerful after only a few beers.

They had already made two bar stops in celebration of Louise having finished marking the term papers of a class in which she was the teaching assistant. She was a fast talker, with a low, firm voice and didn't care much about anyone else's opinion. Nick always deferred to her. They had a kind of bond that reminded Narya of hers and Keames. Where was he now? This was a large island. He could be anywhere. As she listened impassively to Nick and Louise arguing about the feeding behavior of the mako shark, she let her mind wander elsewhere. She rested her head on her hands and looked around aimlessly.

She caught a glimpse of the television at the bar. *Keames.* He was smiling at her. No, he was smiling at the camera. His blonde hair was longer now and swooped to the side. His eyes were as blue as she remembered as he gazed at her. He said something, but the sound was muted. She leapt up, her eyes glued to the screen in front of her.

"What?" Louise said. Her eyes followed Narya's gaze and landed on the screen above them.

"Yes, he *is* yummy," she said knowingly and grinned at Narya. "You like him, too, huh?"

Nick glared at the television with a feigned indifference.

"I . . . I know him." Her voice trembled.

Louise smirked and rolled her eyes. "OK, sweetheart, *everyone* knows who he is, alright?"

"I mean, he's . . . he's my *friend*." Narya settled on this word, since 'merman partner' was off the list.

"Ken Lauer is your *friend?*"

"Well, not just a friend. He's my . . ." She was having trouble speaking. Of course Keames would have a new name as a Changed One, but she never expected him to be on television for the whole world to see. Shouldn't the Elders have rules about that? Being someone so high profile would surely put them all at risk if he were discovered.

"What, boyfriend?" Louise scoffed with unmasked disdain. The alcohol has made her more blunt than usual.

Nick arched his eyebrow in anticipation of Narya's response.

"Yes," she said quietly. Keames was no longer there. The screen changed to a commercial featuring a singing crab. Something about fresh seafood pizza. Her ears were ringing and Narya had to grab the back of her chair to avoid losing her balance.

"Wait—wait! Are you telling us that *Ken Lauer* is your *boyfriend?*" Louise half-smiled, her eyes mocking such an unlikely scenario. Here was yet another bewildering fact about this odd girl.

"Well, I . . . I haven't seen him in a while . . .".

Nick was intrigued now. "You actually know him?" He waited for her to confirm the unlikely fact.

She wondered when he started appearing on television and whether it had changed him.

"Is he famous now?"

Louise paused, debating whether to take her on seriously or not.

"Well, I mean, yeah. He's not exactly Leonardo DiCaprio, but he's up there. Especially popular with girls who are suckers for romantic chick flicks."

"Like yourself," Nick said teasingly.

"Yes, like myself. I'm am not ashamed to admit that I enjoy watching Ken Lauer with or without a shirt on." She giggled as she discarded her straw and took big gulp of her Bloody Mary.

"So you *really* know this guy . . ." Nick's eyes were kind, and they sharply reminded her of Keames—not Ken Lauer—when they were both underwater, undisturbed by commercials.

"Yes." She had to find a way to get to him. This chance encounter might have made her life easier. A movie star shouldn't be that hard to trace. She looked up expectantly.

"Do you know how I can find him?"

The rest of the night was a blur. Nick tried to open his eyes, but his lids felt heavy, and he had very little willpower left. As he sat up in his bed, he felt a sharp headache and groaned softly. Someone shifted beside him. He turned and saw Narya's long, flaxen hair spilling over onto his pillow. She lay on her side, her back facing him. They were both fully dressed. Obviously, nothing happened between them, and he let his shoulders relax. He watched her sleep and wondered how she ended up in his bed. Where was Louise? After a quick survey of the room, he was relieved to find no sign of her. How did they even get back to the house last night?

The last thing he remembered was Louise concocting a plan to trace Ken Lauer. It involved her hiring and paying for a private investigator. That was when he knew she was no longer sober. After her fourth Bloody Mary, she had no idea what she was talking about. And he had been on his fifth beer, with some tequila shots in between, all at Louise's relentless insistence. When she had laughed hysterically at something Lauren said when she brought their next round of drinks, he grabbed the two drinks she had ordered and gulped them down before she had a chance to get more drunk. That was when his memory faded. He craned his neck to see if Narya was still sleeping. With her eyes closed, she looked beautiful and bewitchingly exotic—like someone from another world. He wanted to linger just to observe her for a while, but a noise from the kitchen distracted him. A quick glimpse back at Narya reassured him that the sound hadn't woke her. He rose gingerly and left the warm bed, tiptoeing into the kitchen. Louise was busy putting ground coffee into the filter.

"How'd you sleep?" She looked as miserable as he felt, and as she turned on the coffee machine, she yawned loudly and stretched out her arms.

"I don't remember a thing, Lou." He took mugs out of the cupboard—the ones they had bought while in Italy a few years before—and placed them on the counter. 'Ciao' was written on one and 'Bella' on the other. He smiled as he thought of their times together. Not really that along ago but an eternity since he had felt as happy and carefree.

"Really?" She suppressed a laugh, covering her mouth with her hand. "Me neither." Her long bangs fell and covered the upper rim of her dark glasses, and it was these moments when Nick used to find her irresistible.

He wanted to swipe her bangs from her eyes and hold her close enough to smell her hair. Her jasmine-infused shampoo was her signature scent, and he wondered if she had changed it. But his desire soon was replaced by a sense of guilt, and he clenched his hand into a fist as he walked toward the fridge.

"How did Narya do?"

"She didn't even touch the piña colada I ordered for her, so I'm sure she remembers everything."

"Hmm." The coffee was ready, and he poured a generous amount into his 'Ciao' mug.

"Do you think she was serious about Ken Lauer? How weird is that?" Louise asked, well into her first mugful. "I mean, she's *already* weird. But what are the odds that a girl with nowhere to go actually knows someone famous like Ken Lauer?" Her voice rose, and Nick signaled for her to be quiet.

"I don't know," he said. "Didn't she say that she hasn't seen him in a while or something?" As impossible a scenario as this, he believed her. There was something about her; a childlike innocence that made her an unlikely liar.

"Hey, I read somewhere recently that he was filming his new movie near Vancouver." Louise sounded like she had a plan. He gave her a warning look to stop her in her clever trail of thoughts.

"No, Lou. I am *not* going back there." His voice was determined, and he shook his head. But she had done her research on Ken Lauer. Unfortunately, at least for her, Vancouver was the last place on earth he wanted to go, and it would take more than a dumb excuse like stalking Ken Lauer to get him on a flight there.

"Oh, come on! You haven't been back there since—well, you know . . . That place is going to get run down if you don't take care of it once in a while. Or at least clean it up and put it up for sale or something." She spoke cautiously, not wanting to open a can of worms.

He didn't answer. Staring into his coffee, he pressed his lips together and exhaled. He hated even talking about it—the harrowing past he'd been fighting to put behind him. He detested being anywhere that reminded him of that time.

"I'm sure Narya would love the chance to go and track down her boyfriend."

"Hi." Narya's voice in the hallway startled them both. She stood unpretentiously, morning hair and all, in Nick's T-shirt. "What are you talking about?"

"I—I have no money, but once I do, I promise I'll pay you back!"

Her eyes pleaded with him, and the sympathy nestling inside him was dangerously making its way up, and he knew she was close to convincing him. How do girls do this? He cleared his throat and tried to leave the kitchen, but he felt himself cornered. Both women possessed the ability to make him feel quite defenseless.

"It's not about the money." It was too early in the morning for a major discussion like this one. And coffee—ever since he got Narya hooked on caffeine, he was down to one cup per morning. With Louise in his kitchen, he was limited to a pitiful half-cup that did nothing to clear his head, much less a serious hangover. He sensed that he was wavering, and it unnerved him to know that Louise had probably caught on to his hesitancy. Of all people, she knew how to take advantage of his weaknesses.

"Yeah, he has plenty of that, trust me." Louise said.

"You don't like Vancouver?" Narya's eyes were light grey, and in the morning sun, they took on a different shade, making them appear almost golden. She regarded him with such hope that he had to look away.

"No, not exactly. I . . ." He didn't want to have to explain. Louise was the one who came up with this idea, and now Narya was stuck on it, obsessed by the prospect of finding Ken Lauer.

"I just—I have to go. This is the only way for me to get to the people who were supposed to take care of me."

"Okay, who are these people again?" Louise had redirected her attention. Skepticism filled her sharp gaze as it fell on Narya.

"Just . . . people that know me."

"Uh-huh, and you have no idea who they are or where they live?" Louise's unfriendly tone made Narya shift uncomfortably in her seat.

"Well, I don't really know anyone here . . ."

He tried to ignore her desperation—the expression that made her look all but too vulnerable. Tears filled her eyes, and he felt a crack in the fortress he built around his guarded conscience.

"Okay—okay, fine. We can all go." He raised both hands, signaling his defeat. If anything, he said this to deter Louise's attention away from Narya. Damn, he gave up way too easily. Uneasiness crept into his mind, warning him about his sudden need to protect Narya. He tried not to think about it and took another sip of coffee.

"Really?" Narya folded her hands together as if she were praying, and she squealed before jumping up and down and giving Nick a hug. He steadied his cup so that he wouldn't spill hot coffee all over her. Feeling her arms around him gave him chills since she was constantly cold. But he was used to the cooling sensation now—if anything, it soothed him.

"Yeah, yeah. It's fine. You don't have to pay me back or anything. We'll just try to get you home." He tried to smile, but he could feel the burden of that place weighing on him. It wasn't going to be an easy journey back.

"Oh, we have to tell Pete! I'm sure he can give us a few days off. No tagging next week, right?" Louise hastened toward the door, her bag in her hand. "See you later! Hey, Nick, you're buying my ticket, too, right?" Before he even had a chance to answer, she bolted out the door.

She had played him well. As if her animosity toward Narya was all a clever ruse to make him agree to the trip.

"You're going *where*?"

"Vancouver." Nick debated all morning when it might be

best to bring up the trip to Pete. He knew they were heading into a busy shark-tagging season, but this was the only way for Narya to find her companions, or whatever Ken Lauer was to her, and Louise insisted she was long overdue for a vacation.

He sat with Pete—at Pete's insistence when he found out Nick was suffering from a hangover—at a local beach coffee bar, though both of them had two shots of whisky in their coffee, also Pete's idea.

"We're planning to leave next Saturday." He knew Pete wouldn't exactly be against it, but he was still his academic superior and couldn't afford to get on his bad side in his last term before graduation. "Unless you want me to stay."

Pete waved nonchalantly. He was an easygoing guy and was known for it; and he was one of the most brilliant marine biologists with the most credentials. Nick did his research before flying all the way to the Bahamas to be part of Pete's research team. Although this was not his only reason to be on the island.

"I'll let you go on one condition." He let Nick ponder what that might be while he took a sip of his spiked latte. The milk foam stuck to his lips as he smiled.

"I have another tagging scheduled for the day after tomorrow. Originally, I had Max coming in, but I'd like you to do it instead. And bring that shark whisperer with you."

"Narya?" Nick hadn't given that day much thought until now.

"Yeah, Nar-yee-a."

Nick cringed at Pete's mispronunciation of her name.

"Bring her along and I'll grant you your vacation." Pete put down the coffee mug and nodded cockishly at his student. This was his bargain and he was going to get it. Confidence oozed from him like the alcohol stench on his breath.

"I can't promise anything, but I'll try." Nick drummed his fingers on the table. He didn't know why but he felt uncomfortable asking her. "She doesn't know how to swim, and I don't know if she'll want to go again . . ."

"Sure, I understand." Pete chuckled softly, and signaled for the waiter to bring the bill. And he turned back to Nick, still smiling. "But that's my condition."

His professor's voice was firm and he recognized his tone to be serious—which was rarely the case.

The ocean was inexplicably calm. Narya could only imagine what the others were up to down below. On days like this, she would swim alongside Grey to places usually forbidden by the Advisors. Darkened Waters, as they called these off-limits areas. These were where the deep sea creatures roam. Fish that have yet been named or discovered by humans, with curious physical traits and unpredictable behaviors. No one really knew them very well, and only seldom do any merpeople encounter them. This was one of Narya's favorite things to do besides reading onshore. The Darkened Waters fascinated her just as much as the land above. Today, as she sat on the sand, her eyes gazing out to the borderless ocean, her heart ached to swim freely and daringly like she did before. If she couldn't find something that convinced her to stay, then she would leave here, give up the rest of her transitions and remain content with her life underwater. What was it that made some unwilling to return to a world that was already so magical and intoxicatingly beautiful?

The water looked irresistibly cool and, hypnotized by it, she stood up and took a few steps forward. When the waves gently rolled in and drops of seawater landed on her legs, she felt it: that tingling sensation, the pain—ever so mild—but still palpable. She looked down and saw the faint, glittery reflection of fish scales appearing where the water had splashed. Most merpeople during their transition would shy away from the coastal area and move into the city. She looked out to the ocean and assessed the risks. This was so close to home and she felt the proximity as comforting as it was alarming to have seen the scales resurfacing.

Cautiously, she dipped her toes into the water and felt the pain intensifying. From where she stood, she stared at her feet beginning to take the shape of her colorful fish tail.

"Narya!"

She didn't know whether to look toward the waters, or back to shore. She followed the sound of the voice and turned back. A figure was running toward her. Nick. She stepped out of the water hastily and tried to cover her feet with the warm sand to dry it out. The pain was fading and only a few specks of fish skin could be detected on the sole of her feet.

As he got closer, she waved animatedly at him.

"Hey, I got some news," Nick said, trying to catch his breath. "And a job for you."

Tilting her head sideways, she waited for him to continue and reveal what that might be.

"How would you like to work for Pete? As his assistant for the tagging?"

CHAPTER FOUR

Louise eyed her with downright suspicion. She didn't trust this girl, however innocent and pure she seemed. And what's more, she sure had Nick under a spell. She hadn't seen him pay anyone this much attention since—well, her. But that was a while ago, and she knew their relationship had been off the table for too long for her to have any jealousy rights. Still, she looked out for him, as he did for her. She watched Narya like a hawk, waiting for her to reveal who she really was underneath that cunning façade.

Narya was busy helping Nick untie the rope for the anchor. Her hands fumbled with almost everything she touched—like she'd never done the simplest human tasks.

Since Louise had gotten to know her better, she scratched off the possibility of Narya being a drug addict. Only the other day she'd begged Nick to let her try a cigarette, and she almost cough to death. She shook her head and flinched at the sight of her. As irritated she was by Narya's presence, she knew she didn't have an agenda. Nor did she seem like a criminal, or someone with a dubious history. But she was so full of mystery. Nothing about her made sense. And she had clumsy hands. *Can't even untie a damn knot.*

Louise stepped forward to offer her a hand. "Here, let me do this. Why don't you go over there and help Pete with the fishing rod?"

Narya nodded and smiled gratefully. She hurried toward Pete and the sudden movement made the boat swerve. Louise shot her a reproachful look.

"Slowly!"

"You're having a good morning." Nick stood beside her, his hands busy with the rope. He nudged her with his elbow.

"Yeah, yeah. This wasn't part of my plan. You know, to have her onboard." She rolled her eyes. "Didn't you say she can't swim?"

"Well, I don't know. Ask her." His boyish grin made Louise want to smack him on the head and kiss him at the same time.

"It's not really any of my business. And frankly, I couldn't care less." She paused. "When did you two become such good friends?"

"Are you jealous?" Nick grunted as he pulled the anchor into the boat and sat down, already exhausted.

He still loved it—the boat, the deep blue sea, the unknown adventures that awaited them in the open waters.

"Of her?" Louise waved her hand dismissively.

On most days, she didn't feel threatened by any other woman who showed interest in Nick. It had been almost three years since they decided to take it slow. Somehow that had transitioned into an indefinite break. She used to blame the accident, and she also blamed Katie. But now that time had passed and healed most of their scars, she was less resentful, and most of the time just blamed the damn ocean. It was hard to keep a grudge against something she loved so much. It was their dream to be here, studying under Pete in such proximity to one of the most pristine waters in the world. And the sharks—it was their common interest in these magnificent creatures that had first brought them together. At a bookstore in downtown Vancouver, when they both had reached for the same book on *Carcharodon Carcharias*, otherwise known as the Great White shark. At first, Louise was reluctant to let go, but when she saw that face and those light brown eyes, it was not hard to pretend to be more courteous than she normally would have been.

She still loved him, but it was less possessive, much less dramatic, and she felt that familiar feeling only during select moments like these. For the past few days, her feelings had grown stronger, and she knew they had been triggered by Narya's presence. It bothered her to see Nick so intrigued by someone new. The girl was odd, but there was something about her simple, quiet beauty that was mesmerizing. Her face was pleasant, almost childlike, and those doe-like eyes only added to her innocent appearance. And Louse had to admit a head full of long, wavy hair was eye-catching, irritatingly so. Nick always had a thing for girls with long hair, despite that throughout the years they were together, she had insisted on keeping hers short out of defiance.

"Hey! Louise!"

She hated hearing her full name called out. Especially by Pete, with his raspy, old-man voice. As much as she admired him, she disliked everything about his personality. Despite the fact he was brilliant at what he did, he was unabashedly obnoxious (and proud of it), dismissive of other people's ideas (especially hers, as apparent from his comment on all the papers she had submitted), and openly perverted. She noticed the way he blatantly stared at her when she was in her wetsuit. It made her want to punch him. And she could. She had a black belt in four different kinds of martial arts. She could kick his ass hard. On most days, she shrugged it off, but on days like this, when her mood was already dampened, her rage escalated faster than usual, and it was getting hard for her to contain it.

"Yeah?" She snapped and felt Nick's gaze on her back. Pete never asked his students to address him formally, and he didn't care for formalities. But her voice had an edge to it, and she knew that she had to try harder or she was going to lose it.

"Yes, Pete?" She turned back and made a face at Nick. He gave her a disapproving look.

Right. She needed to be on her best behavior if she wanted to go on that vacation.

"Hand me my notes, would ya? They're somewhere in my bag." He pointed at his khaki bag, stained with sand and spilled coffee. She made another face as she grabbed it. His things were always messy, filthy, and most of his notes were illegible due to his bad handwriting. How did a guy like this ever manage to have a such a stellar academic career?

"Here you go, Pete." As she handed it to him, the boat swerved and she tripped on his bag. Before she landed on her face, Narya stepped in and caught her in her arms. She steadied herself with Narya's help, noticing she had strong arms, almost like a swimmer's.

"Are you alright?" Her eyes were earnest, almost annoyingly so, and Louise gave her a wry, half-smile.

"I'm fine. Thanks."

Pete was shouting from the tail of the boat as he pulled two beers out of the cooler and handed one to Nick.

"Alright, kids. It's a fine day for shark tagging!"

"What, we don't get one?" Louise never missed an opportunity to point out Pete's views on the lesser sex, another thing she disliked about him.

He scoffed and threw another beer her way.

"The other one looks underage. Ha ha!" He elbowed Nick jokingly and let out a hearty belly laugh.

"Might as well skip this one, Narya," Louise muttered. "This guy only ever buys cheap beer, and they're never cold." She read the label on the beer with a disappointed look.

"I think we're close." Nick opened his beer and took large gulps. He was excited and always in his element out here. Though he hasn't gotten over that incident yet, he could still be near the ocean, if not immersed in it.

"Roger that! Let's drop the bait!" Pete signaled for Louise to get the bucket.

She hated this part of the job—the stench of dead fish. She groaned and went to fetch the bucket.

"I hear you can't swim," Louise said as she poured the shark bait overboard. But from what she's observed so far, Narya didn't appear nervous being on the boat. In fact, she looked as if she belonged. The sea breeze made her long hair dance, and she sat comfortably near the rim of the boat, relaxed and at peace.

"Oh, yes." There was guilt in her eyes, and her hands clutched tightly around the metal handle of the boat.

Louise eyed her suspiciously again. She had very little patience for liars, and even less if they're bad at their own game of charades.

"Look! There it is! That's our shark!" Pete pointed toward the sea.

From the short distance, they could see a large black fin approaching the boat. The shark swam calmly toward them as it was successfully lured by their bait. Louise took in its gigantic size, its gleaming skin visible underwater. She stood, fascinated, with her arms crossed in front of her.

"Beautiful as hell, aren't they?" She muttered under her breath, addressing no one in particular.

Pete walked toward Narya with a smile. "All right, sugar. It's your turn to shine."

When Narya saw the shark's fin emerging from the water, she recognized it immediately. There was a faded scar on its pectoral fin. Her heart sank. It was Grey, and a sense of doom overwhelmed her. She started to back away from the edge of the boat. Perhaps she should jump into the water and put a stop to an adventure that was rapidly getting riskier.

"Hey, are you all right?" Nick stood with Louise and Pete to get a better glimpse of the shark and saw the sudden shift in Narya's mood.

"Yes. I'm okay. Just a bit . . . *seasick*." She never thought she would have the opportunity to use this word.

Pete was shouting and laughing at the same time. Oblivious to her reluctance, he signaled her to get closer. "Narya! Get back out here!"

She wanted to turn back, but how? She was on a boat in the middle of the ocean and near her grid since Grey was right here. She was home, and these people were trespassing. They wanted her to take part in tagging a shark. Grey. She thought of her own predicament and all that she wanted to find out for herself during her time of transition. She also needed to get to Keames, and Nick was literally her ticket out. Reluctantly, she took a few careful steps toward Pete.

"Now, listen," he said. "I've been trying to get to this one for the past few months. It's an aggressive one, this shark. So I need you to help me get to it." He pointed at her with a don't-mess-with-me look. "I need you to do that thing you did with the other shark."

She knew exactly what he meant. He wanted her to be bait. To lure Grey close enough so that he can tag him. But that would be betrayal at its very core. From the side of the boat, she saw Grey fast approaching. He would recognize her in no time, and then she'd be forced to commit the act of treachery that would certainly not bode well with anyone underwater.

"Hey! I'm not getting any younger over here!" There was impatience rising in Pete's voice, and that was her cue to act.

"Okay." She blinked as she watched Grey's silhouette under the clear blue water. As she leaned forward, she stretched out her left arm and raised it slowly until her hand was above her head. Grey sprinted out of the waters and his snout touched the palm of her hand. They stayed like that for almost a minute. She wondered what would come next. From the corner of her eye, she saw Pete taking something from his bag—a large gun of some sort. She dropped her hand instantly. *Go. Go now.*

Pete was about to aim the tranquilizer shot when he saw what Narya had done.

"What the—"

Grey dove back into the sea, splashing seawater onboard as he sped off.

Narya felt the droplets of water burning her lower body, and before she could find a towel to wipe her legs and feet, she caught a glimpse of Pete staring at her with an unreadable expression.

Nick knew by Pete's stiff body language that he was pissed. They were all in the lab, Louise and Nick eyeing each other, unsure of what to say. Pete paced across the room, chewing on his lucky pencil. Narya was absent and therefore exempt from the rage that would inevitably come. He had asked her, as politely as he could have, to bring him a cup of coffee from the farthest bar on the beach strip before he slammed the door and started mumbling to himself.

"You know she did that on purpose, don't you?" He faced Nick, his eyes wild, laughing to himself.

Louise cleared her throat and gave Nick a warning look.

The soft laugh usually preceded the meltdown. They were both accustomed to Pete's tantrums, and at least now they knew how to predict them.

Nick tread carefully. "What do you mean?" He wasn't sure if his vacation was still a go. In any case, he'd be relieved if Pete forbade them to go. But it would certainly break Narya, and he wanted to remain optimistic for her sake.

"You saw her! She was talking . . . to that goddamn shark!" He was visibly shaken and flabbergasted by the incident.

Louise rolled her eyes. "You're not serious, Pete. Besides, it's not the first time someone managed to hypnotize a shark by touching its snout." As much as Pete was stuck to this idea, she wasn't convinced that Narya was a shark whisperer.

"No, no . . ." He was onto something now. He chewed his pencil more fervently, spitting out pieces of wood as he moved around. Frustrated, he forcefully kicked the aluminum trash can. The crashing sound echoed through the room.

"Even that first time," Pete said. "The sharks—they paused right before they approached the boat, didn't they?" He inched close to Nick and, seeing his stunned expression mirroring his own, it dawned on him that he wasn't the only one feeling doubtful about Narya.

Nick wanted to keep these thoughts to himself rather than admit them aloud, but he did go over the events in his head. The sharks had sensed Narya's presence on the boat and paused to . . . what? Smell her? He tried to dismiss this ridiculous theory.

"I . . . can't say. Maybe it's the boat," he said, trying to appear oblivious. But Pete was approaching him with that don't-fuck-with-me look that appeared every once in a blue moon.

"Nick, don't play dumb with me. You were there both times. Didn't you notice the sharks and their strange behaviors? There's something about that girl . . ." He wanted to say something else but decided against it. He held Nick's gaze before he his face relaxed into a sly smile.

"Alright, fine. Fine! Don't let me keep you. Go! I'll see you all back next week!" He needed time to think and waved them away nonchalantly. "Wait!" He reached into his pocket and dug out a crumpled fifty-dollar bill. "Here. You can give this to her. Tell her . . . I'm going to hire her part-time when you all get back."

He sat down grudgingly, scribbling notes while he continued mumbling to himself. Nick and Louise left quietly, not wanting to risk their teacher throwing another tantrum and holding them hostage to more of his incomprehensible ramblings.

Nick exhaled his relief as he closed the door quietly behind them.

"That lunatic!" Louise said, walking past Nick, who stood by the door, busy with his own troubling thoughts.

"I need your last name." Louise's fingers sped across the keyboard as she searched for cheap flights into Vancouver.

Nick was busy in the kitchen, fixing a simple dinner. When she volunteered to book their tickets, he had been ushered into the kitchen, challenged to improvise and create something edible with frozen vegetables and a pack of shrimp in his fridge.

"My last name?" It didn't occur to Narya until now that she required one. This was why transitions with the Changed Ones proved to be so useful. And here she was, preparing to travel without a last name. She wanted to run into the washroom and hide from Louise and her incessant questions.

"Yeah, do you have one?"

"Um . . . yes." Her eyes darted nervously around the room.

One of the papers left scattered on Nick's kitchen counter was visible. *Biological Information System for Marine Life and role for biodiversity research by H. Yamamoto.*

"Yamamoto." She thought the name sounded a bit foreign, but it might work.

"Really?" Louise looked at her dubiously. "You don't look Japanese. Are you mixed?" Her skin was too tanned to be considered Japanese, but her features were slightly exotic, hinting at a trace of Asian with her almond eyes that arched slightly at the end.

"Yes." Narya stared back steadily into Louise's questioning gaze.

"All right." Louise typed the name as she spelled it out. "Y-a-m-a-m-o-t-o?"

Narya nodded and rearranged Nick's papers so the one authored by Yamamoto was no longer visible.

"Passport number?"

"What?" She hadn't been briefed on any sort of identification number by the Elders.

"Wait, you don't have one? Or did it expire?" Either she was raised in a cave, or she was plain stupid. Louise was getting annoyed.

"I guess—I need to get it . . . again." She tried not to sound too dubious.

"Yeah, yeah. I guess we'll have to stop by the Embassy tomorrow. U.S., I'm assuming? I hope you have other I.D.s on you."

Narya was unsure of what to say in response.

"Dinnertime, ladies!" Nick walked in with a big bowl of improvised seafood pasta. Narya craned her neck with anticipation. She hadn't realized how hungry she was until she smelled the food. She froze as she spotted the shrimp collection on top.

"Oh, don't worry. This one's for you." Nick handed her a separate dish with pasta noodles and tomato sauce, devoid of seafood. He gave her a quick wink. "No shrimp."

"Okay. Here we are—third floor." Nick walked out promptly when the elevator door opened.

Narya reluctantly followed behind. She had not the faintest idea of what would happen.

When Louise asked her that morning to bring all the necessary documents, she had nodded and answered mm-hmm to everything until Louise was satisfied and left for her morning dive. Nick volunteered to take her to the embassy, knowing that she'd have no idea where it was.

She stood before an office clerk while Nick sat in the reception area, flipping magazines. This was going to be disastrous. The night before, after he and Louise were cleaning up in the kitchen, she had used Nick's laptop to look up passport information. The booklet seemed harder to obtain than finding a conch pearl in the middle of the ocean.

A young, bright-eyed girl with a high ponytail and a loose chiffon shirt greeted her cheerfully at the counter. "Hi, how can I help you?"

"Yes. I . . . need a passport." She kept her voice low, hoping this would be as uncomplicated as ordering a drink.

"Right. Are you re-applying, or did you lose your passport?" The question sounded routine as though she was asked it a dozen times a day.

Narya was baffled, and she started to stammer. "Um . . . I don't . . . I'm not sure . . ."

The girl stared at her more guardedly, her eyes moving to the faint scars on her neck where gills used to be. She had thought they might attract unwanted attention, but neither Nick nor Louise had said anything. Nonetheless, she regretted now not having covered them.

"Well, let me see if I can help you. Do you have any other identification on you? " The girl's hand accidentally grazed hers, and when she felt the coolness, she recoiled and her eyes lit up in recognition.

"What is your name?"

"Narya . . . Yamamoto."

"Narya," the girl muttered.

She excused herself and hurried off to a back room. The door was shut, and Narya was left at the counter waiting, already dreading the outcome of her coming in here. A few minutes later, the clerk returned, her face more solemn, and she asked Narya to follow her.

Nick looked up from his magazine and watched with a puzzled expression as Narya was led into a hallway in the off-limits area.

She was brought into a spacious office with tall windows that looked out to the sea. A woman in her mid-forties glanced up from her paperwork. Seated behind her large desk, she held a stamp in her hand, which paused in mid-air as Narya was escorted in.

"Ah, hello," the woman said.

"Hello." She was unsure what to make of this meeting. Had she been caught without a passport? Was she going to be detained?

"Narya, I am so sorry. I had no idea that—" the clerk began in an agitated voice, but the woman silenced her with an imperious sweeping motion.

"Alicia, you can go now." The woman commanded an invisible authority, and her mannerisms seemed familiar.

The door shut quietly as Alicia exited the room.

"I'm sorry," Narya said. "I just need a passport—" She too

was met with a dismissive wave.

"No need." The woman removed her glasses and rubbed her temple. "Alicia—the girl you just met—was supposed to meet you at the dock. She was caught up in . . . well, a rather important *date*, and couldn't make it on time. For that she is truly sorry, and has been reprimanded accordingly." The woman squeezed out a faint smile before continuing.

"Narya, we've been looking for you ever since." She stood up and came out from around her desk with a friendlier expression and her hand extended.

"My name is Jane. And I was a former Elder in our ocean grid. I'm now here." She gestured around her office with a cold smile. "You probably shouldn't use your real name up here. Do you have an alias?"

"Alias?" She was trying to make sense of it all. Was she actually conversing with another mermaid in an office in the U.S. Embassy?

"Yes, another name for you to use while you're here. Or . . ." She eyed her contemplatively. "Perhaps you can keep it. I suppose you've already made friends around here?"

"Yes." She wondered if she should say anything about Louise and Nick and their research subjects.

Jane nodded contemplatively. "Right. Well, in that case, I suppose there's no sense in changing it now."

"You . . . you are a Changed One?" Narya needed to confirm this. She had finally met one of her kind in the least expected place. She quickly glanced around her and saw framed certificates in acknowledgment of doctorates and various distinguished titles then turned her gaze back to Jane, a former mermaid. She still had broad, swimmers' shoulders and an elegant posture supposedly distinctive to merpeople. According to rumors she had heard, several mermaids had become professional ballerinas. But the woman who stood before her was someone who held an important position in the U.S. government. *How convenient.* Mermaids working at the embassy in a coastal region.

Jane smiled at Narya, her pale, grey eyes crinkling as she did so. She went back to her desk and opened a drawer. "As delayed as it may be, Alicia can take over for now for your transition. And you should probably meet with her once a day as you get settled in."

"Yes," Narya replied. She felt oddly intimidated by the former mermaid, and her shoulders stiffened—like she'd been caught doing something wrong.

"And where exactly are you going?"

"Vancouver. I . . . want to meet someone. A friend from the grid." Her answers were short and abrupt. Though it was unlikely, she didn't want Jane to read her mind and discover who her new friends were.

"I see. Well, just make sure not to go to the beach while you're there." She put her hands into her jacket pockets and carried on speaking. The brief friendliness that was just there a moment ago had vanished.

"That should be all. Alicia can assist you with your picture and help procure the other documents needed to process your passport. She'll also give you your weekly allowance—for your expenditures while you're on land. That is, if you don't change your mind before this week's up." She said tersely, eyeing the young mermaid with a contemplative look.

"Right . . . Thank you." Narya started to walk away, and Jane cleared her throat.

"One more thing. I'd be wary of your human friends. Don't get too close to them. And don't divulge anything." This time, her gaze was cold. There would be no room for discussion, as Narya could tell that this was not a request, but a direct order.

"I understand," Narya muttered before making her exit. Outside the door, she gasped for air as though she'd been holding her breath throughout the entire interview.

Alicia was standing outside with a sheepish smile. "She can be a bit intimidating, huh?"

"Yes." As much as she thought she'd be angry with her, Narya couldn't bring herself to scold the girl who stood before her with one of the guiltiest expressions she'd ever seen.

"I am *so* sorry," Alicia said, biting her fingernails.

Narya could see part of the same faded scars on her neck, cleverly masked by a silk scarf.

"It's okay. I'll just need my passport. I'm . . . traveling with some friends."

"Oh, did you find a group of Changed Ones to show you around?" Alicia asked, looking puzzled.

"Yeah. Yeah, I did." She smiled reassuringly. *A little white lie wouldn't hurt anyone.* "They're great."

"Oh, that's good news!" Alicia smiled broadly at her. "Okay, I should get the documents prepared for your passport. We'll get your picture taken here, and you can come back in two days to pick it up."

"Thanks! Sounds great!" Narya wanted to ask her a multitude of questions about her life as a Changed One, but she didn't want to spoil her trip by having anyone meddling into her preparations now. *She'll be here when I get back.*

"I should go see Jane and get her to sign a few things then. Speed things up for you." She clutched her pile of files and started walking away.

"Oh, and how was the date?" Narya asked.

"Turned out to be quite uneventful, actually." Alicia turned around and lowered her voice conspiratorially as though she were about to disclose classified information. "Human guys, as you'll find out, are usually not that interesting." She hurried away before Narya could answer.

Lingering on what she had heard, Narya returned to the waiting area where Nick sat waiting for her.

"Hey, so what happened?"

His concerned gaze momentarily locked with hers, and she emphatically decided that Alicia's statement couldn't possibly apply to all men on land.

Louise stuffed her duffle bag into the overhead bin as they settled down in their respective seats on the plane.

"I don't usually say this, but you need to do some serious shopping."

While packing that morning, Louise was astonished that Narya had nothing to pack for the trip. She had to run back to her apartment and grab extra clothes, even buying a few pairs of underwear for Narya at a local drugstore. She had been horrified to learn that Narya didn't feel the need for underwear.

For the past few days, she had worn Nick's T-shirts paired with Louise's jogging pants. They were too large for her, but Narya didn't care for her appearance that much. She was simply passing by with no one to impress really, except maybe Keames. As her thoughts drifted to him, she felt butterflies in her stomach. Louise had searched the internet and found out what film he was working on, and where the film set would be for the next few weeks. She also discovered it was no longer based in Vancouver but in Squamish.

As she sat between Nick and Louise on the plane, she felt trapped. She'd never been on one before, and the thought of flying terrified her and made her question whether Keames was worth all this trouble. She declined the window seat that Nick so generously offered her, claiming she'd love the sight of the mountains when they neared the Canadian Rockies. Inexperienced with mountainous landscapes and with little enthusiasm for anything else other than jumping back into the ocean, she tried not to think what was about to take place. The distance between the air and the ground. Clouds . . . mid-air. She thought she was brave and daring enough to leave the water. But this was another level of challenge she had not anticipated.

When the plane engine revved, she almost jumped from her seat. Her teeth chattered as she glanced around her, surprised to see that no one else was affected by this horrifying sound.

Louise sneered. "I don't suppose you've ever been on one of these before. Alright, kids. I'm getting my beauty sleep. Enjoy the ride, Narya." She yawned loudly and yanked down her eye mask.

"First time flying?" Nick asked, flipping through the airplane magazine. He was nervous too, but for a different reason.

"Yes. First time." Her hands fumbled with the seat belt. It was too loose for her, and she tried not to think about what would happen should the plane swivel upside down. She had just watched *Alaska* with Nick the other night, a frightening introduction to flying to be sure.

"Here, let me help." He put down the magazine and reached over to adjust her seatbelt. She instantly recognized the scent of his after shave—a musky yet refreshing fragrance.

She didn't realize how much she's gotten used to living at his place—at such a proximity to a human. A guy. A few times they had bumped into each other in the middle of the night in front of the bathroom door. He'd nodded sleepily and let her use it first. She enjoyed being around him but had begun to sense a kind of awkwardness between them. He was the first one who found her at the beach, and he'd been playing the part of her guardian; she'd gotten used to depending on him. But she wasn't sure what he felt toward her. Did he see her as a burden? On most days, she felt convinced he wanted her there. At other times, she found him to be distant and indifferent and it befuddled her to no ends.

"Is your family in Vancouver?" She asked, wanting to focus on something other than flying. She swallowed hard as she felt the plane move. They would take off soon, and in her head she counted down from one-hundred.

"Well, no . . . I don't have any family left."

"I'm sorry." She realized that she chose the wrong question to ask, but she was beyond nervous now and couldn't focus on anything else but her own panic. She took the safety-instruction pamphlet from the seat pocket in front of her and fanned herself.

The question didn't faze him, and he shrugged it off. "That's OK. You want a snack?" He unzipped his bag and took out a piece of chocolate bar. He dangled it in front of her like it was something she might crave.

She shook her head and closed her eyes. They weren't even flying yet, and she was already nauseated.

"Hey, hey. Are you okay?"

"Yeah. No. Well, I don't know." The plane accelerated, and she tried not to imagine the wheels on the ground and what would happen when they lifted off. Her body began to tremble and she couldn't make it stop. With her eyes tightly shut, she could hear Nick shuffling in his seat and unzipping his bag again.

"Alright, here. Try this." She felt him place something over her ears. It was soft and spongy as it gently cupped her ears. A soothing melody resonated throughout the plane. She opened her eyes. No one else seemed to have heard it. Nick smiled reassuringly at her. He pointed to her ears, and she touched the headphones covering them.

"That's for you. It'll calm you down." He scrolled his phone screen, looking for something. "Let's see . . . I don't think you'd be a fan of heavy metal, right?" He laughed to himself as he kept scrolling. "Um, maybe something more . . . acoustic. Jason Mraz?"

She had heard music before: at bars, from Nick's laptop, and occasionally from the radio that blasted from the boat when she went out with Nick and Pete. But never like this. She closed her eyes and listened to the guitar strumming, and the soft, angelic voice that sang words she'd never heard before. The music put her mind at ease and it was like she was home again—swimming against the current, her arms teasing the water as she moved forward.

She didn't realize that she had been smiling until Nick tapped gently on her shoulder.

"Look." He pointed out the window. A sea of white clouds surrounded them.

They were flying.

The city hadn't really changed all that much, but the air seemed stuffier. Perhaps he was used to the clean air on the island, free from unending street traffic congestion that only worsened by the year. There were a few more high rises in his neighborhood. As the taxi driver turned the familiar corner, dread began to fill his mind as his house came into view. He wasn't really prepared for this, his homecoming. His home seemed larger, emptier, devoid of anyone waiting for him. From the outside, nothing seemed to have changed. Granted, he was still paying the gardener, and he had arranged for a new paint job a few months ago since he was planning to eventually sell the place. He'd had several offers in the last month but couldn't bring himself to accept any of them, even those way above his asking price. His real-estate agent thought he was nuts and had stopped bugging him with interested offers. Maybe he wasn't ready to let go yet. Memories. Katie. Seeing it so close now, the threshold only steps away, the sight of his old home made him want to run. But Louise had already skipped her way up to the porch and, still holding bags in her hands, she signaled impatiently for Nick to open the door.

Here goes—a trip down memory lane.

"This is much bigger than your other place!" Narya exclaimed. She took in the high ceilings, the large, gold-framed paintings of abstract artwork that hung on the white walls—a stark contrast to the shark posters in his two-bedroom apartment.

"Yeap. Nick here leads quite a charmed life," Louise remarked sarcastically as she opened the closet in the luxurious foyer and hung up her jacket.

"I call guestroom number three! That's the one with the large Jacuzzi, right?" Her eyes shone with excitement as she made her way up the stairs with her bag.

"No, that's guestroom number two. On the far left." Nick lifted Narya's bag and slung it effortlessly across his shoulder. It was so light, practically with nothing inside.

"Lou, be careful with the vase in that room! I'm still planning to sell this place!" Nick shouted after her as he walked toward the staircase.

Narya lagged behind, her eyes surveying the lavishly decorated house. As she passed the tall bookshelves near the threshold, a family picture caught her attention. Pausing to gaze at it, she recognized a slightly younger version of Nick standing behind his parents who sat on their living room sofa. He had his mother's kind eyes. The young girl beside him bore a striking resemblance to his father, and her warm smile reminded her of the sun. Her left arm rested on Nick's shoulder, and the picture displayed their closeness. There was something else about the girl—something so familiar— that made Narya take a step closer to inspect the picture. A necklace with a small pendant in the shape of a seashell around her neck. She wondered why she was unable to peel her eyes away. She'd seen this necklace before. Squinting as she took in the details, she tried to remember whether it had a pearl nestled in its core.

"Is that your sister?" Her fingers glided along the glass surface of the framed picture. It was dusty, presumably forgotten for a while.

"Yeah, that's Katie." A shadow cast across Nick's face, and he hurried to where she stood and turned the picture face down. "Come on, let's go upstairs. I'll show you to your room."

She was done exploring her room. It was grand, just like the rest of the house, but it was also devoid of memories. No trace of anyone having ever stayed here. She found the lack of personalization boring and decided to venture out.

Louise's low voice behind her made her jump. "Are you lost?" Her arms were crossed, and she eyed her as if she were an intruder. But she was smiling. At times, it was difficult to tell whether she was seriously angry or jokingly sarcastic.

"No. I'm just looking for Nick."

Louise's moods were tricky to decipher. They constantly shifted like ocean tides. Unpredictable, wild, and inarguably beautiful at the same time. She gazed curiously into Louise's face and wondered whether she was still skeptical of her.

"I see." She frowned as Narya stepped closer and threatened her comfort zone. "Why the hell are you looking at me like that?"

"Oh, nothing." Narya smiled self-consciously. "Can I come in?"

"Sure, why not." Louise swung the door opened and waved her inside.

She stepped across the threshold and walked toward the bed where Louise had her suitcase opened. She was busy rummaging through her things and occasionally opening a drawer nearby to inspect the objects inside. It was hard not to notice her familiarity with the place.

"This is a big house," Narya said. She fiddled with Louise's luggage tag, a cartoon shark, smiling as it flashed all of its glorious teeth.

"Mmm-hmm." Louise sat on the bed crossed-legged, digging for something deep inside her backpack.

"Have you been here before?"

She snorted and rolled her eyes. "Why, did Nick finally tell you?"

"Tell me what?" Narya sat up, curious to know what she had to say.

"Oh, well, that we dated for a few years." Louise took a deep breath and rolled off the bed to open a drawer and pull out a pair of socks. "Oh, great, I was looking for these." She threw the socks into her luggage. "Anyway, it's complicated. I don't want to bore you with the details." She wanted to end this conversation, as if she might already have divulged too much.

Narya couldn't quite picture Nick and Louise together. Not that they didn't suit each other. But she found the more time she spent with Nick, the more possessive she felt toward him. "Was it serious?"

"Well, kind of." Louise pursed her lips and rested her glasses above her forehead.

Narya had never noticed how her blue eyes sparkled, or how Nick might have been attracted to her. But she was beginning to see it now. Louise was intimidating in many ways, to be sure. But there was also a magnetic charm about her, something that made one crave her approval.

"I mean, I gave up a research position in Seychelles for him, so that's gotta say something, right?"

"Really? Why did you do that?" She didn't know much about Africa, but from the way Louise said it, it seemed to be somewhere she still wanted to be. Why would she give up the appealing prospect of being somewhere so idyllic to her?

Louise frowned and made a scoffing sound.

"Haven't you ever liked anyone so much that you'd give up stuff for them?"

Narya let the silence answer for her.

"Well, anyway, I don't really want to talk about this anymore."

"Okay." Her ability to read people's mood was improving. She now knew when to stop probing, especially with Louise, who preferred to keep a distance from everyone, except for Nick.

"So, where's Katie?" Narya asked, her eyes drifting to the busy city scene outside the window. Lines of cars formed below them, and the smoke sputtering from tailpipes was visible everywhere. She began to understand why Nick preferred the Bahamas.

Louise kept her back to her, and although Narya couldn't see her face, she knew she was annoyed, especially after her incessant questions.

"She died two years ago in a diving accident. "Narya knew that her questions should end here, but she wanted to know, and her curiosity got the better of her. "Where?"

"In the Bahamas," Louise said, folding and unfolding her clothes.

Her eyes glazed over and they held a genuine, profound sadness that made Narya want to wrap her arms around her, if only to console her for a little while. This was a side to Louise that she had not seen before.

There had been something strikingly familiar in Katie's picture that Narya couldn't put her finger on. Now, the pieces were coming together at an alarming speed, as though they were attracted to each other like magnets. The same seashell necklace. She's seen it once before. Underwater.

"Hey, you girls ready to go grab a bite and stretch your legs?" Nick stood by the door. He was smiling, but his eyes were tense.

Narya wondered how long he had stood outside Louise's room, and how much of their conversation he'd heard. That diving incident that tore him and Katie apart. He must have endured many sleepless nights—and her heart broke for him, because now she knew.

She had been there when it happened.

CHAPTER FIVE

Narya couldn't peel her eyes away from the car window. She'd seen mountains before, mostly in pictures or movies she and Nick had watched when they stayed up late, while indulging in midnight snacks. During a hike with Nick a few days earlier on Cat Island, she saw one for herself—Mount Alvernia—but it was nothing compared to the astounding sight that shook her to the core. Glorious snow-capped mountains standing behind rows and rows of lush green forests. A crystal-blue lake at the bottom mirrored the picturesque landscape. If someone had told her that she'd be granted this view before boarding the plane, it might have helped. But how do you describe such a place with mere words?

She stayed silent through most of the drive, her thoughts busy with Katie and the incident that she played a part in. Now, her worries evaporated into thin air as she stared out the car window, willingly held captive by the beauty of a side of nature she'd never witnessed before.

"Here we are—Joffre Lakes," Nick said, grinning as he watched her still entranced by their surroundings. "You like it?"

Louise rolled her eyes and exited the car. "Like it? God, look at her. Good luck bringing *her* back to the Bahamas."

Nick followed swiftly behind. He opened the trunk and

started unpacking their camping gear.

If this was going to be their home for the next few days, Narya wasn't sure if she would waste any time sleeping. Her eyes studied the lake, wondering whether there would be any familiar species below, but this was a new territory and it even smelled different. She inhaled deeply and smiled at the foreignness of it all.

"I wonder what movie this is. Probably a rom-com of some sort, huh?" Louise asked, nudging her.

"What?" She was still in the midst of taking it all in—the mountains, the inviting color of the lake, the towering pine trees that surrounded them like an otherworldly fortress.

"Your *boyfriend*, the movie star? Never mind . . ." Louise chuckled wryly and bent down to open her tent.

Narya hadn't thought about Keames since they had arrived. Now that Louise reminded her, she couldn't help but wonder if this trip was in vain. Could this actually be? Keames, an actor? She tried to picture Keames posing in front of a camera, flashing his smile and basking in the public's adoration. He had always been a modest merman, despite all the achievements he could boast of. One of the fastest swimmers on his grid, he'd won all the races in the past five years. Being the eldest son of a well-respected Advisor's family certainly made him one of the most eligible mermen, but he never was one to brag or crave public attention. The Keames she knew was a modest, kind, and at times, shy merman. Had he really changed all that much since he left for land?

By the time they finished setting up camp, the sun was dipping into the orange-lit lake. A rare quietness filled the air, and all three of them lay in their sleeping bags, gazing upward, simultaneously enthralled by the starlit sky.

A few minutes passed in silence, and a loud snore came from Louise's sleeping bag. Narya turned, startled by this foreign sound. Seeing the shock on her face, Nick burst into laughter and she joined in. She shifted to her side, her eyes lingering on Nick's dimples. Whenever he smiled, she couldn't help but feel that she accomplished something great. The more time she spent with him, she came to realize how rare it was to make him laugh. His usual expression was indifference. He was hard to read, but she felt that the shell he hid behind wasn't voluntarily constructed. It had been cast on him like an encumbrance he couldn't shake off. And now that she's unveiled Katie's identity, she'd come to understand why.

She would put off asking him about Katie for now. She didn't want anything to ruin this moment. Nick appeared relaxed and genuinely enjoying just being here. There must have been a time when his smile wasn't a rare occurrence.

"This is nice," she said through a half-yawn as she stretched her arms.

"Yes, it is." He put his head behind his arms and closed his eyes, his lips still curved upward.

"I'm nervous." She had to confess to someone. The thought of meeting Keames tomorrow seemed like a daunting task that would seal her fate. To stay or to leave. Nick's smile faded, and he opened his eyes and stared at her as if he could read her mind. She knew that humans and merpeople could not communicate this way, but sometimes she thought Nick could read her thoughts as easily as anyone underwater.

"Of course you are. And that's okay."

The warmth of his voice made her want to put her arms out and curl up beside him. But she was acutely aware of the distance she needed to keep from Nick since she had uncovered his past.

"Thank you." She looked up at the sky again. This was the

same constellation she had stared at night after night when she swam to the surface for a clearer glimpse of the moon. She felt like they had been in disguise all this time, and that she was finally seeing them clearly for the first time.

A loud, rustling sound of something being dragged along the ground shook Narya from her sleep. She rubbed her eyes and blinked before she made out the shape of a kayak.

"Sorry I woke you." Nick 's face came into view. "I'm going out for a quick row." He took a few steps before turning around. "You want to join?"

She nodded eagerly at his invitation and quickly unzipped her sleeping bag, pulling out the clunky pair of boots that Louise gladly had donated to her.

"Here, put this on." Nick grabbed a lifejacket from the kayak and handed it to her.

"Oh, I don't need that."

Nick looked puzzled. "I thought you were scared of the water. Are you sure you can swim? It's quite deep out there." He casted a worried glance at the lake behind them.

"Oh." It didn't occur to her that lake water might be an issue. She eyed the kayak and wondered how good of a rower Nick was. If she fell into the lake, would the change take place?

Gingerly, she took a few steps toward the edge of the water. When she neared the rocks, she held her breath in, dipped her hand inside and gently splashed some water on her legs. *Nothing.* Not even a tingle.

"I'll be fine." She nodded confidently, walked back, and grabbed the end of the kayak.

His puzzled expression faded into a smile and he let out a

soft chuckle.

"I don't know what you just did, but you can't test the depth of that lake by putting your hand into it." He picked up one of the oars in the kayak and handed it to her. "Just . . . try not to fall in, alright?"

He held the kayak steady while Narya settled awkwardly into her seat. This was her first time in such a confined space above water, and the excitement made her uncontrollably giddy. Another first-time experience. She likely would not be able to share this with the others—the idea of a mermaid during transition treading so close to the sea was scandalous enough. She smiled as she imagined Jane's solemn face, warning her to stay away from the waters. If only she could see her now. The fact that this must remain a secret made it even more thrilling.

"All right, you ready?" Nick pushed the kayak out into the open waters and then swiftly hopped in behind her. He expertly maneuvered his oar, taking them out at an exciting pace. The morning mist slowly dissipated, and the sun was beginning to make its grand entrance. The lake glittered with reflected sunlight and snow-capped mountains. The breathtaking scenery was beyond any words she could think of out of all the languages she knew. She absorbed it all speechlessly, falling more in love with the place by the second.

This was the first time she had used an oar. How could Nick manage his so effortlessly? She could only assume they moved along smoothly because of him. The water was clear and pristine, as though it were calling her; she responded by dipping her hand into the lake. A cooling sensation soothed her skin, sending a gratifying responsiveness through her veins, rejuvenating her whole body. The water was her temptress and she was willingly lured into her trap. She closed her eyes and was transported back into the water realm, imagining dipping her whole body into the lake, savoring the illusion of that achingly familiar feeling.

"Taking a break already?" Narya couldn't see his face, but she knew from his mocking tone that he was smiling. He smiled more and more these days, and it pleased her to see him like this—like he was thawing out of bad spell. Or a bad incident. Her thoughts drifted back to Katie and to the Bahamas.

"I'm not really scared of the water, you know," she whispered. She didn't lie often, and it was embarrassing to admit that she was uncovering her own lie.

"I figured. Why did you lie about it?"

"I guess . . . I'm trying to forget about something in my past." She couldn't tell him the whole truth, and she struggled to find the right words. "For now. I'm steering clear of the water. But eventually, I'll go back again."

"Right." This seemed to have struck a familiar note with him. He sounded relieved, like he had just admitted his own fear of the water.

"Can we go further out?" Narya asked. She was consumed by the surrounding beauty, and so boldly fueled by excitement that she wasn't ready to go back. For the first time, she began to doubt whether this world didn't possessed unfathomable powers and that she was not falling prey to its seduction.

Nick didn't respond. They were gliding faster now, and the movement of his oar was swifter and stronger than before. He led them into deeper waters, and she found herself liking him more by the stroke.

It had been more than half an hour since they left shore, and Narya could feel the sun warming their backs, gently reminding them that it was time to leave this idyllic place. Pulled back into reality, she could only imagine Louise wondering where they were. Or did she already know Nick's old habits? She began to feel a tinge of envy thinking of their closeness. Were they still attracted to each other? And why should it matter to her now? They rowed in silence, both preoccupied with their own thoughts. Tired, she took her oar out of the water and placed it on her lap. The water dripped onto her legs, each drop rendering her more vulnerable to the temptation of diving in.

A loud splash near them awoke Narya from her trance, and as she looked for the source of the sound, all she saw was a fish's tail dipping back into the water. Now she knew she couldn't hold back any longer.

"I'll be right back." She didn't have time to explain her unstoppable urge to be one with the water, or how staying above water had been such a heart-wrenching struggle. She had to take this chance before they flew back to the Bahamas where she would be surrounded by the ocean and its temporarily forbidden borders. At least here she was free to swim—even just for little while.

"Wait—what?"

Before Nick could stop her, she dived in fully clothed. She felt the weight of her wet clothes, but it was a small burden to bear. Aware that there was a human watching her, she slowed her pace lest she scare him with her usual mermaid speed. Soon she was giggling uncontrollably, and she raised her head above the water, peeking childishly at Nick.

"Are you crazy? It's like five degrees in there!"

He sounded mad. The usual calm in his voice was gone, and she detected a palpable concern in his eyes she hadn't seen before. It felt nice to be cared for like this. She wished he knew that mermaids were not bothered by the cold.

"It's not that bad," she said. "I'm always cold, so it doesn't really make a difference."

He eyed her with suspicion and a faint smile.

"You are the weirdest person I've ever met."

"Thank you." She couldn't care less what he thought of her at this moment. Her arms flapped against the water, and she laughed so hard she could hardly keep her head above water. It wasn't salty like the kind she was used to, and the breathtaking landscape that encircled them deepened her trance-like mood.

"I think you should get out of there before you get sick." He attempted to pull her up. As his hand touched the water, his arm shot up and he looked at her in shock. "The water is freezing! You have to come out right now!" He stretched both his arms out and motioned for her to let him help.

She beamed at him as she swam ahead obediently then impishly tugged at his arm. When he fell in, the sound of his scream was muffled by the splash he made in the water.

"I'll bet it was cold!" Louise stood by the shore with her arms crossed.

She looked neither angry nor amused by the fact they had returned soaked from head to toe. She appeared indifferent, perhaps even a little jealous by the way she was hugging her arms. But he couldn't be sure; it has been too long since he had read her like that.

"Yes, well—I didn't go in voluntarily. She did." He let out a loud sneeze. Looking over his shoulder, he saw that Narya still had her feet in the water, hesitant to leave her new haven. He still was in disbelief that she had been so unaffected by the freezing lake water.

"I'm going to change out of these clothes." He glanced at Louise, who followed Narya with her eyes.

He hadn't seen her like this since they were together. She was probably one of the most confident person he knew, but she was easily ticked off if she found any other girl showing the slightest interest in him. Today, he had seen the same glare in her eyes. But he didn't feel that Narya showed any sign of interest. If anything, she was more intrigued by the lake than his company. But it did raise a small doubt in his mind. Was *he* attracted to her? He watched her standing by the shore, still in her damp clothes, waving to Louise, who looked less than enthusiastic, to join her. He strained to get a clearer glimpse of Narya—the wave of long curls that cupped her face and her blurred silhouette suddenly triggered something in his memory. He felt a shift deep within himself. Like his darkest secret was being unlocked. The familiarity about her had paved the way for unwanted nostalgia, the memory of someone he loved.

After changing into dry clothes, Nick sat quietly in the tent and willingly let in the memories that both pained and soothed him.

Katie had loved the water—obsessed was more like it. When he first introduced his younger sister to the world of diving while on a vacation in Maui, she thought she hit jackpot. This was her newfound passion and her first love. At the ripe old age of twenty-one, she had only started to discover the world, to travel, and to align her passion with her career. One day, she announced to him over a plate of macaroni and cheese, their regular Friday-night dinner, that she was going to be a diving instructor in the Bahamas. Without consulting with him first, she had already accepted this job offer and had bought herself a one-way ticket to begin her idyllic island life. He couldn't possibly let her go alone. The only placed she'd ever traveled to by herself was San Francisco, and that was a closely chaperoned trip. Their great aunt hosted her throughout her stay and demanded strict curfew hours. This was something entirely different and foreign. Playing the big brother card, he insisted that he would escort her there and stay until she had settled in.

When they arrived on the island, they had rushed into the water like fish that craved release into the open sea. There was no time to lose; they had to scratch an itch for being separated from the water for so long on the flight over. They both loved to be immersed in the deep blue, encircled by colorful species of fish, coral reefs, and the complete silence that made it all the more inviting. On their third morning, when the adrenaline started to wear off and the jetlag began to kick in, he was torn between sleeping in or tearing himself away from bed by five o'clock in the morning to go for an adventurous dive. They would be exploring the 100-foot Theo's Wreck off Grand Bahama island—a desperate request from Katie. He still remembered turning the second alarm off on his phone at 5:13 a.m. He had thought the number was oddly ominous; it reminded him of Friday the 13th. Being logic minded, he chose to ignore a silly superstition and grudgingly dragged himself out of bed.

By the time he got to the beach, Katie was already geared up, and he sensed her impatience before he even approached her. He could still see her, jumping up and down and shouting at him, her voice comically high as she begged him to hurry because the tide wasn't going to wait for them. How true that was. The tides, the waves, and the ocean waited for no one, nor did they have the ability to mourn any loss they were responsible for.

Deeply infatuated by the sea, they seldom saw harm pushing their limits, so in they went. They had chartered a private boat from a man named Bob, who bore a striking resemblance to Bob Marley with his long dreads and a hazy look in his eyes. Getting on that boat was a decision Nick would regret for the rest of his life—every minute he breathed and mourned for Katie.

When they arrived at the diving spot, and the captain of the boat shut off the engine, Katie turned to him and waved. That was the last time he ever saw her alive above water.

"Hey! Are you sleeping in there?" Louise's voice freed him from his memories. Some days he preferred to linger and dwell on thoughts of Katie. Today, though, he was thankful for Louise's nosiness.

"Yeah, I'm coming out."

As he unzipped his tent, Narya popped her head through the opening and gazed at him with her large, innocent eyes.

"I'm sorry I pulled you in like that yesterday. I didn't realize it was that cold."

Her voice was barely audible, but her eyes flickered and he realized that she didn't regret it at all. In fact, she must have enjoyed seeing him falling into the water. He laughed lightly. For some reason, he found himself more and more incapable of keeping a straight face when he was with her. Seeing her lessened the strain he had carried by himself for so long. He stared at her now with a curiosity that made his heart flutter. She was removing the pieces that had cluttered his core for so long and replacing them with fresh air. He found it easier to breathe just by being around her. This odd girl he had found on the shores of the Bahamas in the middle of the night was slowly but surely healing and piecing back together his shattered soul.

CHAPTER SIX

"Do you see him yet?" Louise craned her neck, trying to get a better view of the film set.

They stood a few meters away from the dressing van, their paths blocked by a 'Do Not Cross' yellow tape. Glancing over her shoulders, she found Narya less excited. Either that or she was nervous to see him, because she'd been extremely quiet and withdrawn since they got into the car. Something was bothering her—maybe the fact that her lie was about to be uncovered? Louise never believed that she and Ken Lauer were an item.

"This is your moment to shine . . . Where the heck is that boyfriend of yours?"

There were other fans standing amongst them, mostly teenage girls with large placards saying "I love you, Ken!" or "Take me home, Ken!" Louise remembered that phase, though she never really went through it. She was more the studious type, fascinated by sharks since her childhood, and finding marine life far more interesting and attractive than boys her age. Until she met Nick, but that was years after high school. She searched for him in the sea of squealing girls and saw him standing near a fire hydrant by the sidewalk. He looked bored and a little frustrated. He was pinching his left elbow, a habit he never had gotten rid of since he was a teenager. When they first started dating, she especially liked to probe him about his childhood. Being the analytical researcher that she was, she wanted every piece of information she could find on her current boyfriend so that she might better understand what made him the man he was. But Nick was as secretive as an undercover CIA agent. He stayed tight-lipped about his family history, and the only subject he would elaborate on with more than a few words were impersonal details she didn't care about. He didn't disclose much, and when she found out through Google that his parents had died in a home-invasion robbery when he was sixteen years old, she stopped probing. He and his sister had been away at summer camp when it happened. As an orphaned teenager, he had to grow up overnight into a man, strong enough to take care of himself and Katie, his twelve-year old sister.

He was quiet but certainly didn't mind a crowd; he was too confident to be intimidated by anyone she knew. And she knew a lot of cocky guys of little substance. Bringing Nick out was like showing off a rare trophy. Being good-looking didn't hurt either. They got a lot of stares when they went out together, and she enjoyed the extra attention. What girl didn't?

Nick was a lot more contemplative than other guys she knew. His experiences in life influenced and shaped him. He preferred solitude, and he naturally gravitated toward diving, lured by the silence and peace it offered when he was underwater. He had admitted to her on several occasions that he preferred the company of fish over humans. She initially laughed at his candidness, but in time, she could relate to this odd preference. It wasn't that Nick was cold-blooded or shy. He was a top student in his program, and a damn good athlete, excelling at almost every sports she could think of. But he cringed when shoved into the spotlight, possibly a side-effect of journalists swarming around his home, his school, and his after-class swimming lessons. She'd like to think that whenever he dove into the deep blue, he was safely confined in a world tucked away from the chaos above land, enjoying the new role he had taken on: a small, insignificant addition to the exquisite processions in the ocean, going wherever the waves took him. She may be romanticizing his underwater hobby, but she believed that the ocean was his true love—after her, of course.

"I see him."

Louise heard the whispered words and followed Narya's gaze through the crowd. A handsome blond man with the body of a Greek god sat on a park bench with a beautiful, otherworldly creature beside him. Louise recognized Hailey Storm, his costar, with her elf-like features and a head full of meticulously arranged dark curls that perfectly framed her stunning face. Ken leaned close against her, his nose rubbing her neck as he whispered something no doubt ridiculously scripted.

"What are they doing?"

Narya must be unaware of the surrounding film crew and the cameraman; she was probably not familiar with the movie scene. Poor girl. She's oblivious to almost everything with exception to marine biology. During a heated debate on the tiger shark's predatory instincts, she had contradicted Nick and her at every turn, as though she were the academic expert.

Louise thought back on their discussion and felt the sting to her ego, and she decided to let this go on for a bit longer, as she found herself actually enjoying seeing Narya fuming away. It was harmless, since technically, it was all just an act.

A hush fell over the crowd, and she was not immune to the swooning effect that Ken had on every girl. The Greek god was now passionately kissing the elfin creature in broad daylight, and she heard envious sighs in the crowd. The kiss grew more intense, and she suspected that she—along with all the other girls—were wishing they were sitting with Ken Lauer on that lucky bench.

She was shaken from her thoughts by a loud thud. A crew member's chair had landed by the bench where Ken and Hailey were sitting. She looked through the crowd. Who would have done such a crazy thing? A disgruntled fan? That chair looked pretty heavy, so it must have been someone stronger than a teenage girl. She turned back toward Narya, eager to make a sarcastic comment, and her heart skipped a beat with the realization of who the offender might be.

Narya's face was red with rage and her eyes blazed as she glared at Ken Lauer. The oddly innocent, frail-looking girl they had found on the shores of Bahamas had thrown that chair in the actor's direction. *Damn!* She hoped that he knew what he gotten himself into, dating a total wacko to begin with. Before she could pull Narya aside to calm her, two largely built bodyguards headed their way. "Oh, shit." She looked to where Nick had been standing a few minutes before, but there was no sign of him. The stocky bodyguards looked intimidating in their black suits and identical sunglasses. They looked like they could have stood in for *Men in Black* characters. One approached Narya from behind, and the other was speaking through his headset. Their stiff body language signified that they were not going to let Narya off the hook so easily. As much as she might like seeing Narya carried off and charged with God-knows-what, she felt compelled to help her—for Nick's sake.

"Hey, hey, hey, it's just a misunderstanding . . ." Louise stepped between the two men and smiled brightly at the younger bodyguard, but neither paid any attention to her. One forcefully grabbed Narya by the arm and began to pull her away.

"Hey! Hang on one second!" Nick pushed through the crowd to get to them. He stretched his arms wide to block the bodyguards' path. "What's going on here?"

"This girl deliberately threw a chair at the actors, that's what's going on here." The older bodyguard, with hair greying at the sides, chewed his gum loudly as he spoke.

"Look, I'm sure it's just a misunderstanding . . . she probably didn't mean it—"

Louise saw that Nick was getting flustered as the vein on his forehead became more visible.

She tried to hold it in, but she started to laugh hysterically when she realized how comical it all was. As far as they knew, Narya could be a crazy fan who claimed she was dating Ken Lauer. This was all too much.

"Oh, for the love of God . . ." She turned away in order not to annoy Nick, who was doing his best to prevent Narya from getting arrested. She covered her mouth to stifle her laugh when a familiar figure appeared. Her jaw dropped for the second time today—this was too dramatic to be true.

"*Oh, shit.* I mean . . . hi."

Ken Lauer stood in front of her, looking as shocked as she felt, staring at the flaxen-haired girl uncomfortably wedged between his two bodyguards. She looked tiny and waiflike—an unlikely suspect for an assault crime. She hoped he would be gracious enough to forgive a crazy fan, and it was worth the effort to try and talk him into letting her go.

"Listen, my friend here obviously made a mistake. I don't think she really—"

Before she could finish, he had stopped the bodyguards with an authoritative hand motion.

Louise craned her neck to get a better view of the drama that was spinning out of control. It was like watching a movie within a movie. She couldn't see his face clearly with all the fans thronging around and raised hands pressing the camera button on their phones. *This is going to be the tweet of the year!* Everyone seemed to be holding their breath, waiting to see what he would do next. Was he as kind and gentle as he seemed on-screen? Maybe he was just curious and wanted to see for himself the obsessed fan who had attacked him with a chair. He waved then smiled apologetically.

"It's okay. I know her. This is all a very big misunderstanding."

As an A-rated actor, he sure had trouble masking his discomfort. At first, the bodyguards were unwilling to let Narya go, but at his insistence and assurance that she was not a threat, they loosened their grip on her and signaled Nick to take over in case she tried anything else.

A large gathering began to form around them as girls gawked at Narya, wondering who in the world she could be. Assaulting Ken Lauer with a chair and getting away with it? Fingers busily typed on phones. This was going to be all over social media.

Nick held Narya's arm and tried to pull her away from the limelight before she shook free and walked toward Ken. She appeared outwardly calm, but her eyes relayed an angry message.

"Let's meet somewhere to talk later, yeah?" Ever so confident onscreen, the Ken Lauer that Louise witnessed now looked like he'd been found guilty of an unforgivable crime. His eyes darted from left to right, painstakingly aware of the growing numbers of spectators, all witnesses to a conflict he had not anticipated when he woke up this morning.

"Where?"

Louise watched admirably as the awkward girl she knew brilliantly transformed into a woman in charge. There was a look in her eyes she'd never seen before. Assertiveness? Rage? If she hadn't known better, the dynamic between these two was that of a bickering couple—boy cheats on girl, girl confronts boy. But Narya—with her oversized T-shirt and a pair of worn-out Nike shorts, standing opposite the meticulously dressed Ken Lauer—made them look like an unlikely couple.

"Are you seeing what I'm seeing?" Louise whispered to Nick. He seemed as confused as she was, unsure of what to make of this encounter.

"Pemberton Valley Lodge. Around five? Maybe . . ." Ken sounded more apologetic by the word. His gaze moved from Narya's furious face and landed on Nick and then Louise, and his face took on a different expression. "Your *friends* can take you."

"Okay." Narya didn't look at him as she walked away, leaving both of them speechless as they followed her out of the crowd.

"Ho-ly . . . SHIT."

As they got back into the car, Louise couldn't help but give Narya two thumbs up.

"I can't believe how well you handled that." She was still laughing as they made their silent walk back to the car, and she tried her best to keep a straight face after Nick gave her a warning look.

"So, is this like a big reunion for you guys? Because it seems to me he had no idea you were coming."

Louise felt a pinch on her arm, but she had to probe.

"I don't want to talk about it."

It was the first time she had seen Narya sulk. Today was a first for many things. She turned back to Nick. He wasn't as amused as she was, but she didn't mind. What a thrilling way to start the day.

"No."

Louise looked at her and dismissed her with a wave of

her hand. They would accompany Narya to the Pemberton Valley Lodge for her big date with Ken. And at Louise's insistence, Narya would look exceptionally good for the occasion. But when she sifted through Narya's bag, the only other outfit that Narya was the gym clothes that she had given her on the day they found her at the beach.

"Okay. I rarely say things like this—but, girl, you need to go shopping."

Narya initially enjoyed the idea, as this was one of the many activities she looked forward to before she came ashore. But after more than a dozen unsuccessful outfit trysts, she felt like a puppet with no mind of her own. She liked bold, vibrant colors, but Louise had her own stubborn take on fashion and what would work for Narya. All the dresses she had picked out from the many racks they went through were heartlessly discarded by Louise, who had taken over as her personal stylist.

While they were busy in the dressing room, Nick aimlessly wandered around the store. Narya peered through the small opening of the curtains and saw him yawn as he browsed the aisle stacked with women's clothes. She found herself smiling at the sight of him. It was the first time she had seen him so palpably uncomfortable in his surroundings. It was a refreshing side of Nick that she liked seeing. Maybe she could sneak out before Louise came back. Nick certainly needed a break from all the shopping that didn't concern him. But before she could plot her escape, Louise stuffed another dark-colored item in her shopping basket on the floor.

"I'm waiting!"

She was not the type to take no for an answer. What Louise wanted, she got.

On most days, Narya found this to be an admirable trait, but not today. She sat on the metal chair inside the change room, staring at her own dull reflection in the mirror. Louise had made her try on a short, black dress with an open back that neither pleased her nor made her feel attractive. She wanted to throw her arms into the air and give up, but a hand pushed through the curtain, holding a shimmery purple dress that glittered with a purpose.

"Here, try this." She peered down and recognized the tips of Nick's shoes.

The color reminded her of her mermaid tail, and nostalgia swelled inside her and compelled her to take it. She wasn't sure about the lightweight material, or the unusually shaped patterns made out of sparkling beads that covered the dress. But most of Louise's selection had turned out disappointing, and she saw no harm in trying Nick's suggestion.

She slipped into the dress and was instantly awed by the soft, silky material that caressed her skin. When she looked down to study its magical fabric, she swayed a little, and the glimmer it produced made her giggle. It made her feel like she had her tail back. As she turned to get a glimpse of herself in the mirror, she let out a small gasp.

The ankle-length dress hugged her figure so well that it accentuated every curve she had. She brushed her hair to one side, and her long, wavy, flaxen locks fell perfectly across her bare shoulder, complementing her look with an ethereal glow. She spun around, stunned by the way the scintillating color of the dress shifted as she moved. Excited by this new find, she swayed from side to side and watched the purple fade into silver and magically morph back into its original color. Like a school of purple tang fish clashing with a group of silver sweetlips in an unlikely collision. It reminded her of home.

"I like it." She said it loud enough so that Louise could hear her on the other side. She could hear Nick laughing close by and she smiled. They were finding more common ground by the hour.

Louise pulled the curtain open and gaped at the smiling Narya, who proudly held her chin high to face her critic.

"Wait, what? This purple disco dress?"

"Yes. I like this one." She made sure she enunciated every word. It was her dress and she was putting her foot down. She glanced over at Nick and she thought she saw a smile meant for her, which made all the difference for her. She stuffed all the other dull dresses that Louise had emphatically made her try on into the basket and handed it to her. This was the dress, and no other one would do.

As they walked back to the mall's parking lot, Narya struggled with the unfamiliar height of her heels. If people thought sea urchins' stings were painful, they should try fitting into a pair of brand-new, three-inch-high shoes. As beautiful as they were—expensive, nude suede shoes—she was confident this would be a one-time experience for her. Since they had stepped beyond the mall's sliding doors, Louise already had caught her several times when she lost balance trying to dodge the unforgiving potholes on the pavement.

When they at last reached the car, Nick opened the door, and she slid into the backseat as carefully as she could to preserve her new dress. She's never felt this kind of material against her skin before. She'd seen and heard of silk, but this was the first time she had slipped into a dress that enwrapped her body with such a delightful sensation. Her first dress. She caught a glimpse of herself in the rear-view mirror and realized she was actually looking forward to her meeting with Keames. She had managed to cool off when Louise explained he'd been acting, and repeatedly reassured her that the intimacy shared was staged. They were simply two professional actors doing their job. But no matter how many times she tried to justify the kiss she saw, it still bothered her that he was able to do that so freely, and probably on many other occasions, with different women, due to the nature of his work. Perhaps tonight, he would be able to reassure her in person and erase the doubts crowding her mind.

"Look at you, all excited!" Louise's voice still had a trace of sarcasm, but it was friendlier, and she appeared equally enthusiastic about the makeover project. "Oh wait, we totally forgot something here …" She sifted through her purse, purposefully digging for something. "I own two shades of lipsticks, so I hope this one will do." She groaned when her phone rang.

"Naturally, you'd be calling me now, Professor . . ."

The irritation in her voice left no doubt she was talking about Pete who had been calling her incessantly throughout the trip.

"I need to get this. Will you, uh—do this?" Louise shoved her lipstick into Nick's hand and made a quick circular motion around her mouth with her finger before she exited the car, leaving him and Narya alone, staring blankly at each other.

"I don't think I'd be good at this."

After an awkward silence, he handed Narya the lipstick and watched her take it hesitantly. She stared at it, oblivious as to what should be done with the object. She'd seen magazine ads of girls wearing lipsticks but had never come across a page showing a girl actually applying them. She opened the small tube gingerly and peeked inside. The stick was hidden and, without a second thought, she dug her finger into the tube.

"No! No, wait!" Nick unbuckled his seatbelt and snatched the lipstick out of her hands, but she had already smudged her face with a big chunk of it with her index finger. She looked up at him, unsure of what she did wrong.

"Wow, okay, you really are clueless. Look, this is how you

open it." He slowly twisted the bottom of the tube and a very uneven pale pink stick revealed itself.

"Sorry. I don't know how this works." A sheepish smile spread across her face, knowing she had ruined Louise's lipstick.

"Yeah, well, I don't think this is an expensive one . . . and it's okay—this is salvageable." He took out a pocketknife and expertly sliced off the smudged corner of the lipstick. "See?"

He leaned closer, embarrassed by what he was about to do.

"I can't believe I'm doing this."

Narya mirrored his action and stretched her neck out. She assumed that he was going to help her, and she smiled, waiting for him to apply the lipstick for her.

"No, you have to—part your lips. Okay, first, you have to stop smiling," he said sternly, at the same time suppressing a reciprocal smile. "Like this." He parted his lips slightly and he motioned for her to do the same.

"Oh, okay." She felt ready and focused her gaze on him as he moved in closer with the lipstick in his hands.

He kept his eyes on her lips while she watched him. She'd never noticed the small scar above his left eyebrow, nor the mole that was cleverly disguised in the center of his chin amongst the stubble that he sported. She examined his features and his tanned, muscular arms and smelled the musky cologne at the side of his neck. Hypnotized by their closeness, she reached out and gently glided her fingers across his cheek. Their eyes locked and Narya stopped breathing. She felt like her secret was out but had no idea what it was. He stared back at her as if he could read her mermaid mind. His light brown eyes were scrutinizing every inch of her soul. The peculiar transparency she now felt had morphed into a deep desire to be kissed by this man who held her gaze so fixedly—as though something tragic might happen if he looked away.

"All right!" Louise swung the door open, making both of them jump back and causing Nick to drop the lipstick.

"Apparently Pete seems to think I'm your personal babysitter, Narya. He was asking all these weird questions about how you're adjusting to the climate here. What a nutjob." She climbed into the car, becoming aware of the silence only after she had buckled her seatbelt.

"What? What's going on?" She turned and saw Narya with only her upper lip painted.

Nick stared ahead and cleared his throat before putting his hands back on the wheel.

"Nothing, nothing. Shall we go?" He started the car and the engine roared, dispelling the uncomfortable silence.

They sat by the cozy fireplace in the lobby, waiting for Ken Lauer to show up. There weren't many people around, mostly retired couples, some quietly reading their books and others in a jollier mood, sipping their drinks by the boisterous bar.

Nick aimlessly flipped through a Vogue magazine and felt inexplicably irritated by all the brand-name ads featuring all these ridiculously famous people. He turned the page and a large portrait of the perfectly manicured Ken Lauer stared back at him, sporting an expensive watch, the designer item he was obviously posing for. When did this guy become the new Leonardo DiCaprio? He took a closer look at the picture and saw nothing he approved of. His skin was too smooth, his hair too blond, and there was something about his eyes that annoyed him. He glared into the camera with one of those facial expressions that had never appealed to him, reminding him of the 'Blue Steel' look from *Zoolander*. This guy was a joke.

He raised his eyes to steal a glance at the girl across from him. How did she, of all people, end up with Ken Lauer? Not that he thought she didn't deserve him. No, he was thinking more of the other way around. A pang of panic hit him hard in his chest.

"I'll be right back." He could feel Louise's eyes on him as he walked out the door. Ever observant, she sensed something was up.

Once he breathed in the cool, fresh air outside, he could feel the knots in his mind loosening. He relaxed his shoulders and took in the majestic mountains rowed up against a canvas of fading, sepia-colored sky. He used to love coming here. He'd had some pretty memorable dates with backdrops like these. His mind raced as he exhaled deeply. He hadn't allowed himself to fall for anyone since Katie's incident. He had shut out Louise and the possibility of being happy with anyone else because, frankly, he didn't think he deserved happiness. Not after what happened. It had taken him years to finally accept his parents' death. A fatal robbery, a homicide case. He knew it was foolish to think that, as a scrawny teenager, he could've prevented his parents' death, but he felt responsible for not being there, for not having at least tried to protect them. But he could protect Katie, he wholeheartedly believed he could—and he was not going to let her down.

Things had been improving by the day. They were doing fine, just the two of them. Though they were legally under their widowed aunt's custody, she was mostly away on business trips, stopping by only to leave grocery money and make sure that they didn't drop out of school. He was the true parent, Katie's guardian in every sense, and her full-time emotional support. On most nights, he would make dinner—nothing special—but Katie never failed to let him know how delicious his mac and cheese tasted, nor did she complain when he had little time to cook, settling for breakfast food at dinner.

"I could have Cheerios and your peanut butter jam

sandwiches three meals in a row." She always made sure that his culinary skills were acknowledged, no matter how simple his efforts were.

They had their own set of friends at school, but none of their friendships really came close to what they had with each other. Before their parents died, they were considered close, but after the incident, their closeness forged into an unbreakable bond, an unspoken understanding that they now only had each other to depend on. Katie came home from school in the afternoons and made sure the house was tidy and at least somewhat organized while she waited for him to finish swimming club. When he made dinner, she usually stuck around, finishing her homework at the counter, or helping him with the cooking. They didn't talk much during these times, but the presence of each other was enough to prevent the heart-wrenching reality of their parents not being there to swallow them whole.

When he met Louise, he had thought he really had it together. Her bright smile made his heart race, and every time he made her laugh, he felt like he had achieved something unattainable. Aside from being stunningly beautiful and bearing an uncanny resemblance to Natalie Portman, she had a carefree way about her, with her loud laughter and intimidating boldness in everything she did. He fell for her instantly, and she became part of his world along with Katie. Life was going well for him, and he felt almost invincible, ready to tackle anything else the world was going to throw at him. He aced all his courses in the marine biology program and even had spare time to volunteer at the local aquarium. When he discovered deep-sea diving with Louise on their spontaneous trip to Belize, he thought that life couldn't get any better. There in the deep blue sea, he had finally made peace with himself. After his parents' death, he had finally found some degree of closure and was beginning to see the bright, vivid, rose-colored sides of life. Little did he know all that was about to plummet and change forever for the second time.

He searched for Narya through the window. Her face was blurred by the etched glass, and he was struck by a déjà vu. Where has he seen her before? There were times—whenever he caught a glimpse of Narya from a certain angle—he would feel a pang of familiarity that left him dumbfounded. But so far he hasn't had any luck with finding the missing piece to the puzzle.

"Hi!" A voice startled him.

He turned around and found himself staring at Ken Lauer.

"Is she in there?" With his blond hair immaculately styled and dressed in a nice suit, he looked as though he just stepped out of a commercial.

Nick scrutinized his face carefully. He tried to smile but his eyes were constantly shifting from left to right. Was it possible? Was Ken Lauer actually nervous about meeting Narya? He found this hard to believe since the Narya that he knew was the least intimidating person he had ever come across.

"Yeah, yeah, I think she's inside." Nick wondered if he was already too late—if he'd ever be able to figure out what was so strikingly familiar about her. And now, standing face to face with Ken Lauer, he wondered whether he should run inside first and convince her that this actor wasn't the guy for her—despite the fact that he was currently ranked among the hottest men in the world by *People Magazine*.

"Great. Thanks, man." He rushed through the door, and Nick followed closely behind.

Ken locked eyes with Narya and he attempted to give her a hug. Narya lifted her arms, but then awkwardly backed away when she saw Nick and Louise watching them.

"I'm . . . sorry about earlier today."

"No, it's okay." He sounded unsure. The chair had missed him only by a few inches. He cleared his throat and stretched his hand out to Narya. "Shall we? I made reservations, and I think we're late already."

Nick saw that he was trying to avoid eye contact with him and Louise. And Narya could do little or say anything other than wave as Ken took her hand and led her away.

"Well . . . that's that," Louise said, watching Ken and Narya exit. The most unlikely couple of the year. "You want to go grab some pizza?"

Ken hadn't aged a day since she saw him last. His blond hair was smoothed to one side, and his sideburns had grown out. She was not used to seeing him dry, dressed in a fitted suit, not to mention with a glass of wine in his hand. She'd had her fair share of drinks with Louise and Nick, but she was not fond of these funny smelling liquids. She preferred fresh-fruit smoothies over alcohol any day. But seeing Ken sipping his wine with such ease made her feel small and inferior. Everything about him seemed alien and, in a way, unappealing. He chatted with their server who obviously recognized him and appeared excited and flustered about serving them. She watched his lips move and listened intently to the words he spoke. They didn't used to speak like this before, as everything was communicated through their ability to transmit thoughts to each other. How strange he sounded to her. She was more used to Louise's low, sultry voice and the occasional curse words she uttered forcefully under her breath. Or Nick's laugh when she said or did something that made her seem odd to him. Every minute that went by, she felt increasingly distanced from this man whom she thought she loved. Or had she changed since she left the waters?

"Okay, for sure, I'll be right back with your starters." Their server giggled nervously as she walked away, frazzled by Keames' stellar presence.

Interestingly, she wasn't bothered by the extra attention that he was getting. On the contrary, she felt quite indifferent to it.

"So . . . let's talk about your time here. I mean, there— where you first . . . landed. How was it?" His voice was low, almost whispering, as though afraid of anyone listening in on their conversation.

"You mean my first transition?"

"Well, yes." He cleared his throat and raised his glass to his nose. Funny that he wanted to smell his drink before he tasted it. This was his second glass since they were seated at the best table in the restaurant.

"It was fine. Nick and Louise, they . . . well, they found me."

"Right. The ones that were assigned to you." His eyes darted from left to right, trying to pick out possible spies. "Are they . . . helpful?"

She decided not to tell him the truth about her friends, not wanting to make him any more nervous than he already was.

"Sure. I mean, yes, they are. Very helpful. Well . . ."

He narrowed his eyes at her as though he knew she wasn't telling the whole truth. Before he could question her, their server returned with their food on a tray, her eyes extra flirtatious as her gaze rested on Keames.

"Thanks." His smile was brief this time, and his answer curt. She took the hint and left briskly to wait on another table.

Narya poked at her food with her fork. It didn't look like a seafood cake so she took a bite.

"What did you order exactly?"

She paused as she felt the familiar texture on her tongue. This *did* taste like fish. She put her fork down and spat out the content into her napkin.

"Sorry, do you not like this?" Ken looked concerned and poured more water into her glass.

"Not really. What *is* this?"

"Tuna salad," he said as he chewed on his seafood.

"Tuna, as in . . . the fish?" She watched in horror as he took a second bite.

"Oh, I'm sorry. I thought . . . ." Now he looked embarrassed and gently pushed her plate away. "I wasn't thinking. You haven't gotten used to the food here."

"I don't think I'd ever get used to it. Do all Changed Ones eat . . . seafood . . . ?" She bent toward him and lowered her voice. ". . . and actually like it?"

Keames looked unperturbed and smiled politely. One of those smiles she'd seen him in on the hair-products commercials. No one else was listening to their conversation. Who was he acting for?

"Well, I'm not sure. I don't really . . . meet with them very often. I have a very tight schedule." He cleared his throat and eyed the menu, looking for something else to try.

"Right." She pulled her plate back and tried picking the tuna strips off the salad, attempting to salvage the meal, as she was already starving.

"I can order something else for you."

She looked up and saw him smile. His eyes were apologetic and she could tell that he was sincerely trying to make amends.

"That'd be nice."

"I was really surprised to see you this morning," he said. He smoothed his hair with his fingers for the tenth time since they had sat down. His hair couldn't look any more perfect, but there was something about it that bothered her.

"Well, I couldn't really contact you. Louise did most of the work, and she had already seen all your movies." She thought about the kiss he had shared with his co-star. Did he enjoy it? Did he ever think of her when he was kissing other actresses?

"Listen, I'm really glad that you're here. Despite the fact that you threw a chair at me." His eyes met hers, and they burst out laughing.

"Yes, that was not really planned."

"You should stay with me for the time being."

There was no hesitation in his voice, and she felt the warmth of his hand covering hers.

"Are you sure?"

"Yes, of course. I mean, I'd have to say that you're my assistant or something, but no one would bother you."

She was slightly taken aback at the new role he had planned for her, even though she hadn't agreed to anything yet.

"Well . . . I don't know yet. I mean, I've been staying with Louise and Nick all this time, and Nick mentioned there was a job for me back on the island—"

"*Nick* has a job for you?" His voice rose, and his grip on his wineglass tightened.

"I didn't say I would take it yet. But, yes, I do have some sort of a life back in the Bahamas."

"You know, it's really not recommended for us to stay on the coast, so near to home. You never know what might happen."

"Why? Do you still have transitions left?" She wondered when would be the best time to ask him why he had never returned. Or if he ever planned to.

"No, well, I don't think so." He raised his hand to catch

the attention of a passing server. "Can we have an order of the asparagus soup?" He redirected his gaze to Narya, swallowed hard and lowered his voice. "The thing is . . . I don't think there's a limit."

"What do you mean? Everyone gets seven, at most, nine transitions . . . that's why we have to choose—" She sat up straighter in her chair and felt her body stiffen as she absorbed the shockingly new information.

Keames struggled for words. "Well . . . I mean—what I want to say is—I've tested it myself. A few months ago, my agent kept pushing me to take this movie role that required me to swim in the ocean. And I was already at my ninth transition. I thought, maybe, why not." His wiped his forehead with his napkin while his other hand tapped on the table. "But it was too big of a risk for me. I would have had a whole film crew staring at me getting into the water. Not to mention rolling cameras."

"I tried. I flew into Miami, walked down to the beach and splashed seawater on my legs." He took a big gulp of his wine. "And then the scales came back. I couldn't believe it. I jumped back into the water and changed. The transition was instantaneous. I waited another two days before trying again. And again." He inhaled deeply before he continued with his revelation. "Narya, I reached *twenty-three* transitions."

She lifted her eyes to meet his. What was equally disturbing to her, aside from this new information, was that he was able to go through all of his nine transitions without giving her a second thought. It saddened her that she wasn't in his plans for the future.

"Why did you never come back?" She tried not to sound piteous while saying this, knowing that it made her appear a little desperate. But it bothered her that she wasn't enough reason for him to return underwater.

"It's . . . it's hard to explain in just a few sentences." His face was ridden with guilt, and he took another sip of his drink as though it might render courage.

"Well, try." She said firmly as she crossed her arms—a body language she learned from Louise. "I . . . I feel different here." His fingers drummed next to his wine glass. "I mean—I feel like I matter. You know? And the things that I get to experience—it's incredible. I get to fly to a different city like every week. It's more than just a glamorous lifestyle. It's an eye-opening experience over and over again. You'll see. You can come with me. You'd be surprised how much you'd love it, too." His eyes gleamed an unfamiliar desire.

Narya wasn't sure she understood what he had just said. But it was clearly something that kept him entranced, something that even the deepest, most intriguing part of the ocean could not compete with. Would she ever find something that would trump her desire to be underwater—to make her want to give up the freedom to roam the deep blue as a mermaid?

"What are you thinking about?"

He looked genuinely concerned, and it soothed her to know that he might still care for her. But still—not enough. He chose fame, and whatever came with it, over her.

"So you're saying that each of us get more than nine transitions?"

"Well, I can't be sure—I haven't told anyone else. I don't really have many Changed Ones in my circle. Though there's a possibility that there are more than nine. And who knows, maybe a number—a limit doesn't actually exist."

A faint smile crossed her lips. No limit—no one has to be changed permanently. Her mind began to drift as she dreamed of the possibility of living two lives simultaneously. No longer having to choose whether to stay on land for good, to completely give up her freedom underwater. That meant she could spend time with her family, race with Grey, and she could see Nick and Louise whenever she wanted to—to come and go as she pleased.

"And there's something else."

He wanted to continue but the server came back with their soups, and she giggled again as she met Keames's gaze.

Narya couldn't help but roll her eyes. The girl left in a daydream-like state after he had complimented her on her dangling earrings. Narya tried her soup and, at the same time, anticipated another exciting piece of information.

"I have news from a reliable source that there are rumors about *us*."

She forgot to blow on her spoon before she took her first sip, and she had to spit it out. Keames made a face at her table manners, but she couldn't care less. She was having her first encounter of burning sensation on her tongue. With a tight grip on her cup, she easily gulped down the cool, sweet, water she craved almost every minute spent on land.

"Rumors?" She wiped her mouth hastily with the napkin after spilling water on herself.

Keames frowned disapprovingly as he watched her try to clean it off. "Well, someone saw a transition. Or at least a part of it."

"Who? Where?" This information wasn't as exciting as the last one.

"Someone from the upper grid. Somewhere in Africa, I think. An island by the Indian ocean. And you know word spreads fast. Especially among researchers—marine biologists, or whatever."

She was quiet now, her thoughts drifting to Louise and Nick, and she wondered whether they would ever expose her if they found out.

"It's not safe for you now, being so close to the water."

She dipped a finger into her water glass and watched

the ripple grow. It made sense for her to leave with Keames, but something tugged within her, and it hurt to think she wouldn't be back in the Bahamas soon. Was her heart already anchored onto something—or someone?

"Are you okay?" he asked, taking her hand in his.

She flinched slightly at his touch. Moments ago, he practically confessed he had forgotten about her—that there was something grander here for him than their lives back in the deep blue.

"Just come with me. It's the right thing to do." There was finality in his voice, and as much as she hated to admit it, she knew he was right.

She wasn't ready to be on her own. Nick and Louise were her friends, but they were nowhere close to being her guardians. Jane and Alicia could offer nothing compared to the familiarity and security that Keames could give her. She needed someone to lean on, someone she trusted to guide her through her transition journey until she was ready to make an informed decision to stay or to return to the waters. Every inch of her body resisted leaving with Keames, but she knew it was her best option for now.

The stars dotted the open sky in the most spectacular show of lights one could hope for. Nick lay inside his sleeping bag, watching the constellation, mesmerized by the beauty and serenity of it all. When he had lived here, he would make a habit of marking down the stars and planets he spotted on a clear evening sky. His eyes were now on the Big Dipper that dazzled the stellar platform.

He had stayed quiet for most of the night, and while he sensed that Louise wanted to talk about their eventful day, he claimed that he was tired and snuck into his tent as soon as they had returned to the campsite. It bothered him to know that Narya was probably not coming back tonight and it irritated him even more to think about whom she'd be spending the night with. At the same time, though, he felt relieved. This would be the end of it, then. He had nothing else to encourage him to pursue something further with her. From a distance, he watched the lake glimmer, lit up by moonlight. The canoe he and Narya had used this morning was tied up at the dock, rocking gently on the water. It had been an unexpected whirlwind of a day.

A tire brake screeched nearby the camp. He rose and stood by the entrance of his tent, looking into the darkness. Two figures approached, and he immediately recognized Narya's figure by the awkward way she walked in heels.

"Hi!" She smiled as she came closer, and Nick's first thought was that Ken had her hand in his.

"Hi," he said, staring at Ken. He wondered if the actor remembered him from earlier today.

"Hi again," Ken replied. "I'm sorry I haven't had time to properly introduce myself yet."

Nick resisted the urge to scoff at this fake humbleness. No one so famous needed an introduction. Admittedly, he was being biased, never having liked any of his movies. Not a fan of rom-coms to begin with. Nor did he like the fact that he and Narya were an item, as unlikely as it seemed.

"Right. I'm Nick."

"Uh-huh. And how long have you been . . . up . . . here?" Ken appeared to be having trouble with his words.

"Here? Not that long. But I'm pretty familiar with this area." Nick tried to remain friendly for Narya's sake, but he disliked any form of small talk. He wished that he would just get to the point. Did she bring him back here to formally introduce Ken as her boyfriend?

A few hours ago, the idea was laughable, though he tried to keep the absurdity of it to himself. Now it seemed the joke was on him.

"Really? I thought you and Louise were assigned to Narya—"

A slap on his shoulder stopped him mid-sentence. Ken and Nick shifted their attention to Narya, who appeared flustered by their conversation.

"Um . . . so Nick, where is Louise?"

"Probably sleeping." He pointed toward the tent adjacent to his and the faint snoring heard from inside.

"Right," she said, laughing nervously. "I came to get the rest of my things—and to say goodbye."

"Oh . . . right." Nick had anticipated this, the worst-case scenario. Turning away quickly, he tried not to show his disappointment. He went into the tent he had set up for Narya and retrieved her bag. She didn't have much luggage, so it weighed close to nothing. Its lightness was a sharp contrast to the heavy stone he felt weighing on his heart. This was it then.

"Thanks." As Narya reached for the bag, Ken picked it up and slung it across his bulky shoulder.

Louise popped her head out of her tent, her eyes hidden by the unkempt hair she tried to smooth over to the side. "Hey! Where are you off to? Oh, shit. I mean, *hi*."

Nick could see that she sorely regretted not checking the mirror first and noticing Ken a second too late.

Ken nodded and smiled politely at Louise; he obviously was used to girls acting absurdly around him.

"So you're leaving us?" Louise noticed Narya's bag and couldn't help but show a hint of disappointment.

Nick had been sure she wasn't a big fan of Narya and her weird ways. Perhaps he'd been wrong and was not the only one who would miss her following her hasty departure.

"I think so," Narya said without looking her in the eye.

Still halfway inside her tent, with only her head and elbows protruding, Louise said, "Well, we're taking the red-eye flight in a few hours. We still have your return ticket . . . in case you change your mind."

"Thanks—I'll think about it." Narya's eyes shone at the prospect but quickly dimmed when Ken cleared his throat, a signal for their departure.

"We should go. It was great meeting you both." He waved suavely and had started to walk away while Narya lingered behind.

"And good luck up here, you two." He winked at Louise, making her almost swoon as she smiled in reciprocation.

"We'll . . . be fine." Nick didn't fully understand what he meant, but decided to shrug it off. He didn't want to prolong any unnecessary interaction with Ken Lauer.

"Oh, right," Narya said, suddenly remembering something. She dug into her pocket and handed the lipstick back to its rightful owner.

"Thanks for this." Her gaze shifted from Louise to Nick.

He suddenly felt unsure of himself, like she was staring into the part of his soul he preferred to keep hidden.

Before she could walk away, Nick felt prompted to say something, anything at all to stall her from leaving.

"You know Pete wants to offer you a job?" he blurted out. He hoped no one picked up the panic in his tone.

Narya was intrigued. "A real job?"

The possibility made Ken stop in his track as well.

"Yeah, he wants you to be his shark-tag assistant. I mean, really, you of all people."

Louise rolled her eyes at the ridiculous idea of Narya doing something she herself was more qualified to do.

"Shark tagging—really?" Ken frowned disapprovingly at Nick and discarded the job proposal. He wasn't the adventurous type, never having dived nor did he ever plan to. "I don't think—"

"Tell Pete that I'll think about it," Narya said.

Nick nodded. "Sure." Her arm was still linked with Ken's. This had been a vain attempt after all.

"Goodbye." She was far enough so that it was only as loud as a whisper.

The strange, clueless girl they had stumbled upon was bidding them farewell, with the company of her famous boyfriend.

Nick couldn't help but laugh at the absurdity of the situation. She was like a fleeting dream—one that was deeply unsatisfying and leaving him wanting more.

"That was odd." Louise was busy stuffing her things into her duffel bag.

They dissembled their tents and were getting ready to drive to the airport. Nick always found packing a daunting task, but tonight it was especially irritating.

"What was?" He knew she would bring this up to bug him. The ever-so-observant Louise must have picked up his disappointment after Narya left.

"You know, the way she just . . . left."

"I don't think we know her enough to know what is normal for her."

He had sounded curt with Louise and wished he could take it back. *Too late, now.* She shifted her attention from her bag to him and his sour mood.

"Wait!" Her eyes brightened at the epiphany. "You're

actually sorry to see her go." There was no hostility in her voice, but she wasn't thrilled with this revelation.

"Come on, Lou. We're going to be late." He zipped up his camping bag and swung the car door wide open. *Time to head home.*

"I didn't expect that you could handle alcohol."

Keames and Narya sat side by side at the hotel bar, waiting for their drinks. When the server took their order, Narya asked for a piña colada, the only drink she knew off the top of her head, thanks to Louise's intense drinking sessions.

"I just really like the pineapple," she said with a hint of embarrassment.

Keames laughed heartily at her childish response. She felt belittled by his reaction and shrank back into her seat with the drink in her hand.

"Well, you'll have the opportunity to try many, many other drinks." A server came by and delivered their orders. "Thanks," Keames nodded perfunctorily before sliding Narya's drink over to her.

This was a fancy, exclusive bar by the way people dressed and acted. She looked to her left and saw a table of middle-aged women, bejeweled from head to toe, happily chatting away. Next to them were two young men meticulously dressed in expensive looking suits, smoking cigars. When she shifted her gaze back to Keames, she saw that he belonged here—tailor made to fit into this picture-perfect setting. Flashing her a dazzling grin, he took his shot glass and finished it on the spot.

"*That* tiny drink costs thirty-five dollars?" She didn't have any money of her own, but she'd been out with Louise and Nick enough to know what was considered expensive.

"It's more about the quality than the quantity of the drink," he said, sounding much like her father when he'd lecture her about the value of a pristine coral reef.

"I see." She took a sip of her inexpensive piña colada and watched Keames order another drink. She felt inexplicably out of place with someone she had been so close to in their formerly shared territory.

"Do you miss it?" She had been suppressing the question since being reunited with the first merman on land.

"I'm not sure," he replied casually, holding his empty glass. "Sometimes I don't think about it at all, and when I'm reminded of the waters, I try to think of something else."

His answer made Narya's heart sink. She had anticipated a drastic shift of attitude in the Changed Ones, but she had a higher regard for Keames. Before he had decided to venture out of the waters, he was dedicated to preserving the pristine ground in their grid. His passion for life underwater was infectious and had a lasting effect on everyone who came across him. Though he was likely still considered charming—especially here on land, she found herself becoming less enchanted by this new Keames by the minute.

"Where are Nick and Louise from?" he asked. "I'm assuming these are their changed names? Not very original," he chuckled to himself. "I know too many Nicks here on land."

Narya flinched at his mention of her human friends. She wanted to keep them a secret; but up until now, she had felt diminished by most of his comments and reactions and wanted to purposely thwart this unexpected curveball at him. Just for fun.

"Well, they're not actually . . . merpeople."

"What do you mean?" His eyes darkened and stared into hers, expecting an immediate answer. Anything to contradict the shocking news he thought he had just heard.

"They are . . . just people." She felt a small triumph. Keames was blinking hard, a habit of his when he was surprised. Soon the stuttering would start.

"What—are you—Narya—what—what—I can't—I just can't—what . . ." His face turned redder and he leaned closer to her.

"Do they know about us?" He was now speaking through clenched teeth.

She found his rage to be a little ridiculous but tried to keep a straight face, or she might trigger him to lose it in public. And Ken Lauer couldn't afford to do that. She let out a small smirk. When she didn't answer right away, Keames persisted, his hand tightly clutching hers.

"Narya, do they *know?*"

She was certain that Nick and Louise wouldn't do anything to harm her even if they knew, but seeing Keames so guarded unsettled her. She moved a few inches away, but that didn't stop her from smelling the alcohol on his breath.

"No, of course not." She frowned at the thought of Nick conducting research on mermaids. Would he ever be involved in such a thing? What if he had discovered what she really was underneath?

"So who is in charge of your transition? And why didn't they come with you?" It was a full-on interrogation now. He wasted no time trying to get to the bottom of everything.

She glanced furtively at him and she could tell that he quickly picked up where her guilt was coming from.

"You!" He lowered his voice again when he saw he had drawn stares from people around them. "You're on *your own?* Without any Changed Ones?"

"I'm fine." She felt defensive and compelled to let him know she was able to survive on her own. "And I'm here, aren't I? The fact that I'm able to come all the way here without being discovered, without the help of any Changed Ones—shouldn't that say something about me? Give me some credit, Keames."

His shoulders relaxed a little, and he flexed his fingers as he glanced sideways, seemingly always on a lookout for spies.

"Yes, well I suppose you are not *completely* clueless." He sighed and his eyes took her in, seeing her in a slightly different light now that he found her to be more rebellious and capable than he had initially thought.

"Okay, maybe we should go back."

"Back? Underwater?" She thought it highly unlikely but was hopeful nonetheless.

"No, I mean upstairs, back to the room. We're still not done talking about this." He grabbed his jacket off the chair and motioned for her to stand up.

Sulkily, she walked toward the exit, and he followed closely with his hand on her back. He was leading her out of the crowded bar as if she needed his protection and guidance.

"I can walk just fine by myself, Keames." She gave him a cold stare before she quickened her pace and left him behind.

The shock in his eyes was her second triumph of the night.

The elevator was a small, confined space, and another young couple entered at the same time as they did. They were on their way up to the 17th floor, where Keames was booked for the night. She watched the floor buttons lit up one by one. *Three . . . Four . . . Five.*

The doors opened and the couple walked out. The woman turned and stole a subtle glimpse of Keames and smiled. Narya wondered if he truly enjoyed his fame, or if this was only one of the things he had to deal with being a famous actor. She caught him grinning back.

When the doors closed again, he gently wrapped his arms around her waist and pulled her closer to him. She had adored his touch underwater, but this intimacy seemed foreign, almost suffocating in a way that made her body limp. She could smell the alcohol on his lips and wanted to shake herself free. Before she could stop him, she watched him lower his head, and felt his hand under her chin, pulling her in for a kiss. A human kiss. *How oddly repulsive this all is.* She had a flashback to earlier in the day, a similar scenario. The memory of Nick was like a bright gleam from a school of bait fish reflecting off each other, and it made her jerk her head back, leaving Keames stunned and speechless as he watched her back away from him.

"I . . . I have to go." She looked for the ground floor button and pressed it firmly. She thought about Nick and how free he made her feel, not trapped like this. The walls of the elevator were closing in on her.

"What—where are you going? Are you kidding me right now?" Keames was used to getting his way and rejection was not common for him, especially since his career as an actor took off on land.

The elevator bell announced their arrival on the 17th floor. They stood across from each other, both staring at the open doors and the view of the red-carpeted hallway floor.

"I'm going back to the Bahamas." She stood erect, feeling more determined than ever. If she were underwater, her tail would be fully stretched out, steadily moving to keep her in an upright posture, looking taller than the merman that stood before her. But she was on land—in an elevator, no less—and she gathered the courage to not let him intimidate her.

"To do what, Narya?" Exasperated, he looked at her as though she were a child with unreasonable demands.

She felt a spark of rage expand in her chest.

"I'm not sure yet. But I know I want to be there."

The elevators door began to close, and she could see his eyes on the narrowing gap. The doors shut and they started to moved again. She exhaled in relief.

"You know those people can't help you if you get in trouble. If you . . . slip." Keames's face was unsympathetic, and his voice had an edge to it.

"I can take care of myself. And, I trust them." She pressed her hand against her chest as though the action demonstrated full trust in her friends. Funny how much she learned about body language in such a short time. She had adapted to the human ways far better than she had anticipated. Strange how this all seemed so natural to her now. There was surely an undeniable link between them and humans; the longer she dwelled in this place, the more she believed their similarities outweighed their differences.

"They are humans, Narya. You can't let your guard down. You're too naïve to really think they're your friends!" His hands clenched into fists, and he pressed something that made the elevator stop.

She had never felt unsafe with Keames before, and this was the first time she wondered whether he could hurt her if he wanted to. He grabbed her forcibly by the arm, and she felt no pain, but his action alone made her wince.

"Every mermaid decides her own fate, even you know this."

She raised her chin and made sure he remembered who she was. As trapped and helpless as she may appear on land, compared to his Changed status, she was still a mermaid—as free as one can be.

"And you can't stop me."

His eyes widened as though he remembered who she was—

and what he used to be.

"No, I don't suppose I can." His grip loosened on her and he took a few steps back. He stood quietly with his head hung low before he raised his eyes.

"This is crazy—you know?" He pressed a button and they felt a thud before the elevator began to move again.

"I know." A small grin crossed her mouth before she caught herself.

"How will you even get back to the Bahamas?" He glanced at his gold Rolex. "You'll never make that flight in time."

"I'm not planning to fly." Her eyes were fixed on the elevator buttons. *Five . . . Four . . . Three . . .*

"Really. And how do you plan to go there?" He eyed her with a whimsical expression.

One . . .

"Swim."

"What?"

The elevator doors swung open and she leapt out as though her life depended on it. She was going back. And she was going to take the shortcut.

Nick looked out the window, and as they ascended into the sea of clouds, he caught sight of the waters sparkling in the moonlight. And in that split second, what appeared to be a whale's tail emerged from the water.

CHAPTER SEVEN

It was a strange and exhilaratingly familiar sensation to be surrounded by the waters again. She let go of the inhibitions that bounded her on land and sped freely through the current. As she swam through an underwater trench on the seabed, she passed a community of merpeople that she'd never seen before. They had fairer skins and slightly different features, and their tails were less colorful than those back home. The scales that decorated the mermaids' chests meticulously matched the colors of their tails, whereas at home, all mermaids had colorful, mismatched chest and tail scales. In this new place, they stopped and gawked at her sudden intrusion. She felt their gaze on her as she hurried on her way. There was no time to stop and explain why she was here, and she knew she was breaking the rules passing by unannounced with no formal greeting.

There was a gnawing sense of urgency she seldom had felt—like it was of the utmost importance being on land with that one specific person. She hoped that nothing would be misconstrued by this community, and she avoided meeting their curious stares. To prevent any unwanted gossip reaching her grid, she would leave the deep end of the ocean and swim closer to the surface. She hoped she hadn't lingered long enough for anyone to memorize the pattern of her tail and identify her. Lunging upward, she moved her tail as swiftly as possible and swam toward the surface, passing a lone, frilled shark, a group of spooked fangtooth fishes, and a curious vampire squid that followed her for a few miles before giving up its chase.

As she neared the surface, she joined a pod of dolphins heading in the same direction. Their pace was to her liking and she could sense that they welcomed her presence. Their movements were swift and graceful, and she was thrilled to have them as companions on her long journey back. One dolphin approached her and rubbed against her tail with its pectoral fin, and she sensed it was ready to jump out of the water for a quick breather. She reached out and held unto its fin, and they emerged from underwater, feeling invincible as they soared over the rolling waves. She lifted her head and felt enfolded by the starry night sky.

He stared at the flight of stairs and blew out his breath in exasperation. After no sleep throughout two back to back flights, he was exhausted. His mind had deliberately prevented him from taking a rest. It was filled with snippets of conversation with Katie on the day before the accident, and of things he wished he had said to her had he known they had so little time left. Narya's face would occasionally come into view and ease his sufferings. But the raw absence of her forced him to think of something else to end that feeling of dreary emptiness.

On the taxi ride from the airport, Louise speculated incessantly on Narya and Ken Lauer's mysterious relationship. It bothered him to hear their names spoken together, but he had to admit that he, too, wondered about them.

"You know what I think?" Louise said with pride, as though she had discovered something newsworthy. "I think our little friend

Narya has some exclusive information about Ken Lauer, and she's blackmailing him."

Nick dismissed her speculation with a scoff.

"Look," she said insistently, why else would he seem so nervous around her? You saw him earlier today—come on, you don't think that *she* could get a guy like that!"

"And why the hell not?" Nick snapped and immediately regretted it.

"I'm sorry. I'm just—really tired." He pulled up the hood of his sweater and sank back into his seat, letting the silence overwhelm the awkwardness.

He made his way grudgingly up the stairs with his duffle bag slung across his shoulder when he suddenly slipped on wet surface. Grabbing onto the railing, he quickly steadied himself.

"What the . . ." He looked at the ground he had slipped on and saw large puddles of water everywhere—like someone had walked up drenched in water. His eyes followed the wet trail right up to his door.

He had no idea where the glimmer came from until he saw a small figure curled up in the corner of his doorway. Still unsure, he took out his phone and turned on the flashlight, aiming it directly at the unclear figure.

Narya lifted her head and rubbed her eyes when the light shone on her. She was drenched from head to toe and still wearing the purple dress he had picked out for her at the mall. Her long, wet hair was stuck to her shoulders and back, and water dripped from her dress. Puddles on the ground reflected her dress, and she appeared to be emerging from another world, an ethereal creature out of a mythical tale.

"Hi." He stood still by the staircase, unable to say much else.

"Hi!" Narya got up and rushed toward him, water slushing

under her feet as she moved.

"You're back." He tried to grasp the fact that the girl he had been thinking of with each step he took to reach here, actually had materialized before him.

"Yes, I am," she said, unable to keep herself from smiling.

They stood at such proximity that the water from her hair dripped on the tip of his shoes. As he took a step closer, he slipped on the wet ground and grabbed unto her arm. They laughed simultaneously, momentarily held captive by the exhilarating moment of being in each other's embrace. Dawn crept in from the window in the stairwell, lighting Narya's flaxen hair and making her look even more intoxicating. He tucked a strand behind her ear, and breathed in the scent of seawater.

"Hey, so Pete just called . . ."

Nick jumped back at the sound of Louise's voice. He felt like he had been caught doing something behind her back.

Louise's eyes showed only her shock seeing Narya beside Nick. "Hey . . . when did you—how did you get back here?"

Narya smiled and shrugged her shoulders as if it were an irrelevant question.

"And why are you so wet? How the hell did you get here— swim?" Louise's voice rose, and he was glad to detect a bit of concern in her tone. Finally, someone she may care about other than herself.

Narya shrank back at Louise's questions and forwardness. The warmth she had exuded a minute before now vanished, and she retreated like a clam closing its shell.

"So what did Pete say?" Nick asked, feeling the need to step in.

"Huh? Oh . . ." Louise grimaced at the mention of their professor's name. "He wants us to do a shark tag. Like now. Can you imagine? The nerve of that guy . . . we literally just got off the plane.

I'd better get going before he kills someone." She headed toward the stairs then turned back.

"Are you both coming?"

Narya felt the waves rocking them, a bit too violently for her taste. It was never too bad underwater, and she feared she might be getting seasick. The boat, as functional as it was, felt claustrophobic. She was getting better at traveling above waters, but her stomach still churned when she saw a splash of water or incoming waves high enough to sink the boat. She stared at her naked legs, vulnerable to instant transition if she fell into the water. When she and Nick had rushed to follow Louise, she didn't have time to change into anything else. When she showed up at the dock in her evening dress, Pete gawked at her inappropriate attire.

Nick, Louise and Pete began to set up the cage that would hold someone brave enough to tag a great white.

"Narya, right?" Pete asked, a cigarette between his lips. He pronounced her name *Na-ree-ah*, smirking at her as he nonchalantly blew the smoke out. She sat in the middle of the boat, her long, windswept hair covering half her face.

"Yes," she said, her voice sounding small.

Pete's towering figure held a bucket of fish meat like a prized possession.

"Well, today is your lucky day, ha ha! What do you say you go down there in that nice contraption, eh?"

His maniacal laugh unsettled her, but she managed to squeeze out a smile. Following his finger, she saw that he was pointing to the cage being lowered into the water.

Nick, overhearing their conversation, came to her side. "I don't think that's such a good idea," he said, looking warily at the cage.

"Come on! Let the poor girl speak for herself!" Pete jokingly pushed Nick aside and shoved the fish bucket into his arms. He strode toward Narya and knelt down beside her.

"What do you say? It's a once in a lifetime experience."

She detected no hint of friendliness in his eyes as she looked past him to the open waters and contemplated diving in.

"Alright, Pete. Quit bothering her, will you? Can't you see the poor girl's about to throw up in your boat?" Louise unexpectedly cut into the small distance between Narya and Pete and pulled her up with one hand. "Come on, you hold this, and I'll get changed to get into that cage."

She handed Narya another bucket full of fish heads, leaving her unsure whether she was grateful or sickened. Her knees almost buckled when she looked down at the poor, decapitated fishes.

Pete waved his hands as though to dismiss them. "Aw, you people are no fun." He walked away sulkily and sat down near the front of the boat with his binoculars.

He seemed so determined a minute ago, Narya thought. She feared he'd come back to her, and she stuck close to Louise, her unexpected ally in this situation.

"You doing okay with that? Louise asked. "Don't spill it before we need to." Her voice was authoritative and firm. This was the Louise she knew.

"Good save, Lou." Nick patted Louise on the back as he passed by and continued prepping the cage.

"You ready?" Nick shouted to Louise, who was checking her mask and oxygen tank. Her slim figure was accented by her full-body wet suit, and Narya couldn't help but notice how beautiful she looked as she descended into the aluminum cage. She gave them a thumbs up.

Pete cackled and muttered something incomprehensible before taking another sip of his second beer that morning.

Nick beamed at Narya as if he were showing off something grand. "I bet you've never seen this before."

She wanted to agree, but she couldn't see the sense of meeting a shark behind a cage. She didn't know any shark that had deliberately attacked a free diver underwater. But she'd seen them gnawing on debris, and broken cages. She waited patiently for what was to come.

"Time to spill the casualties overboard!" Pete shouted from where he sat.

"Let's do it. You ready?" Nick held one bucket while Narya took the other in her arms, trying desperately not to gag. Together, they dumped the contents into the water and watched the meat float about before sinking. The red color encircled the boat, and Narya felt her knees buckling yet again.

"Hey, hey! Nick caught her before she landed on the ground. He sat her down gently. "Are you okay?"

"Yeah. Yeah, I think so." She still felt dizzy but at least she couldn't see the fish meat anymore. She sat up on her own, supported by her hands.

"Okay, well, just stay here. I have to—"

She felt a hard thud and the boat shook violently.

Pete struggled to stand up with two beers in his hands.

"Did you feel that?" Nick rushed to the side of the boat to check on Louise.

Another thud. This time, it was strong enough to almost throw Nick overboard, but he grabbed onto the side railing of the boat.

"Do you see anything?" Pete shouted from where he stood. A broken bottle of beer lay near his feet. "Damn it, I gotta clean this up." As he crouched down to pick up the shattered glass, another thud threw him off balance.

"Shit! What the hell is that?" He pierced his hand with one of the broken pieces and cursed first at himself, and then at the beer.

Nick struggled to stand, looking distraught at the underwater movement. "I don't know, I don't . . . I don't see—"

Narya crawled toward the side of the boat and froze as soon as she saw him.

Grey. With his distinct scar on the top corner of his fin, she instantly knew it was him. Even above water, she could sense him. But there was something different about Grey. His gentle and graceful demeanor was gone. Today, his body language appeared fierce and signaled attack mode. He was getting ready to thrust himself toward the cage.

Grey had no reason to attack anything near the surface. His preferred prey were all in the deeper end of the ocean. Neither the boat nor the cage posed visible threats to him. She saw Louise helplessly trapped in the cage, and it suddenly clicked. Grey must have sensed her near the boat just as she had sensed him from where she stood. He must have thought she was the one trapped inside the cage. He was trying to free her.

"You have to get her out of there!" Nick and Pete tried to pull the cage up.

A low, cracking sound of metal crushing raised another alarm. This was too slow for Grey's ferocious movements. He would break that cage before they'd be able to pull her up.

"Oh, shit." Nick continued to yank at the chain but there was no movement.

Pete stepped back, panting for breath. "It's stuck, isn't it? This *fucking chain*, I knew it!" Flustered and angry, he kicked the useless metal that lay on the ground.

Another thud. Someone had to move fast. Should she try and transition back to lead Grey away from the boat? She would risk exposing her identity in a boat full of marine biologists whose jobs were to discover new underwater species. She closed her eyes. *Think. Think. Think.*

"Can't she just open the cage and swim out?" It sounded dangerous, but this was the only other option. They couldn't know how angry Grey was, and once he broke that cage free and discovered Louise instead of her, she dreaded finding out what he may do out of blind fury.

"I don't know," Nick replied. His hands were clasped around the metal chain and his eyes fixed on the horizon.

He hadn't panicked like Pete, but she could see his lips trembling as he tried to stay calm and figure out a plan. Every passing second brought Louise closer to a doomed underwater fate.

"Someone needs to go down there," she said. *And it can't be me.* She looked at Nick and Pete.

Nick nodded absently and turned to Pete.

"What? Me? Are you crazy? With an angry shark? You're both out of your fucking minds!" His hand continued bleeding and he busily tied a towel around it.

"You're responsible for this shark tagging, Pete!" Nick was losing his cool, and Narya's eyes stayed on the water. Grey pounded on the cage below, and they could all feel the rhythmic thuds. It wasn't going to get any better.

"Look," Pete said, "she signed up for it herself. And—and I'm sure the shark will back off—"

"Are you kidding me, Pete? You have no better plan than hoping that the shark will *back off?*"

"Hey, hey! I'd like to see you get into the waters! When are you going to get over your fucking water phobia?"

The thuds grew louder, and Narya swore she had heard something crack. That cage would break if she didn't do something soon.

A loud splash of water silenced both men. Nick turned and his face blanched when he saw that Narya was no longer there. He and Pete rushed to the side of the boat. Her blurred figure swam toward the cage. The waves that the shark had made in the water scrambled his view.

"Holy shit!" Pete scratched his head with his bleeding hand, unaware that the towel he had used to bandage it had come off.

Nick stared into the water. It was time to get over his fear. He shuddered as he tried to visualize immersing himself into the ocean. The sound of the waves hitting the boat weren't helping. He tried to focus on all the good things within the deep blue that encompassed all that he craved to see.

Narya's transformation was almost instant. This was her second transition. If Keames was wrong, then she had, at most, seven left. She felt an immediate rejuvenation as she jumped in, the fresh seawater enwrapping her body like a second skin. She didn't have time to catch a glimpse of her tail to make sure every scale was still in place. From where she was, she could see the top of Grey's fin and the mangled cage. Louise's head was bowed, and she looked like she had been knocked unconscious. With a speed that even Keames would have found impressive, Narya swam toward the cage.

Grey stopped as soon as he felt her approach. *It's me, Grey. Come to me.*

She saw him turn and glide toward her and she felt the stone that was pressing against her chest drop instantly. Grey was now circling around her, his movement buoyant and she could tell that he was thrilled to be reunited with her underwater after so long. *It's okay. It's okay. I'm here.*

She touched his snout gently and made sure he was aware of what she was going to do before she swam out to Louise.

She gingerly opened the top of the mangled cage. Louise's stillness frightened her, and there was no reaction when she attempted to pull her out. But it was better this way—that she remain unconscious for the moment rather than witness her in her true form. She entered the cage and took Louise's face in her hands. How long had she been down here now? *What if they come looking for her?* She wrapped Louise's arm around her shoulder and swam toward the surface.

"Ok, I'm going down there." Nick said. *You fool, you waited for too long.* He cursed at himself repeatedly before he took off his shirt and got into a diving position.

Pete pointed at something in the water. "Wait! What the hell is that?"

Two figures approached the boat and as they reached the side, Louise emerged from the water. She was not moving, and he could make out Narya's face underwater before she came up. Louise's head rested on her shoulders, and he wondered how she had managed to get her out on her own.

Narya's eyes flitted nervously around. "Just take her. I'll be right back."

Nick was pulling Louise up when he caught on to what she was saying. "No . . . no! Come up *now*!" He wouldn't entertain her silly ideas now, and he gestured for her to get back onboard while Pete laid Louise's limp body on the floor of the boat.

"Narya, we need to get back to shore now!"

"Just go first!"

In a blink of an eye she was nowhere to be seen.

"Narya!" *Where the hell did she think she was going?*

"Nick I'm no expert at this . . . And I don't know if she's actually breathing!" Pete sounded breathless from the exertion of pulling Louise out of the water.

Nick felt her pulse. It was there, but too low, and he shook his head in exasperation. How did he get himself into another mess like this? He glanced back to the waters. *Where the hell did she go? And where was that shark?*

Standing by the edge of the boat, he stared into the deep blue—its dark color and tempestuous waves mirrored the storm ravaging within him. It tightened the knot in his chest, and thinking back now, it only ever loosened its grip with Narya's presence. He could hear his own heart beating, pleading for him to make a decision.

"Listen, you take Lou back now." He pulled out the emergency raft and threw it in the water. "I'm borrowing this."

He grabbed an oar and a diving mask from under the bench and threw them onto the raft. He put on the mask and fixed it firmly around his face. *This is just another dive into the ocean.* Back where he vowed never to return. Just another dive. Another deep breath.

All he had to do was jump, and so he did.

"What the fuck?—Nick!" Pete called after him, but it was too late.

He hadn't felt as free and unchained in so long. From underwater, he could hear the motor of the boat. That meant Pete was following instructions—for once. Meanwhile, he had to find Narya and bring her back to safety.

As he dove deeper, there was little he could see. The water was murky and dark. He didn't have long before he'd have to surface again for breath. He couldn't help feeling intimidated by his surroundings, despite it being familiar territory. It had been too long since he'd been down here—since Katie. As he tried to untangle himself from his encumbering thoughts, he saw her.

A vision he'd surely seen before.

I must be imagining this. It can't be real.

CHAPTER EIGHT

Right there in front of him was a creature with Narya's face, her features obscured by her long hair, flowing in all directions in the water. Her previously flaxen color took on a different shade—golden like the sunset, lit by a force unknown. Every part of her glowed—from the colorful scales that covered her chest area, to the long, spellbinding fish tail that covered where her legs should have been. *A tail.*

As a school of four-eye butterflyfish swarmed by him, flashing their bright yellow fins, the glaring brightness triggered a memory he had tried so hard to shut away for years. The image of Narya overlapped with another apparition he'd seen for countless nights in his troubling dreams. The memory of this very scene emerged from where it had been buried. That long-forgotten vision he thought had been part of his hallucination after passing out underwater during the diving incident with Katie.

The shipwreck. Katie. He blinked and was momentarily transported back to that fateful day.

They had been down there for almost four hours. He

looked at his watch again, trying not to turn back and face Katie. He couldn't let her down—not now. He was her only hope. She had to survive this. Damn it, they both had to.

He first realized they were in trouble when Katie froze while they explored one of the cabins of the ship. She had been lagging behind, but he figured she was busy taking her time fiddling with every piece of debris she came across. When he swam up close enough to see her eyes, he saw they were drooping, as though she were falling asleep. He fumbled through her equipment, checking on her oxygen level but couldn't see any obvious equipment malfunction. They had get out of here. He wasn't going to take any chances with his little sister's safety. He took her hand in his and signaled for her to move quickly. He swam speedily through the passage, past all the other cabins they already explored. He had carefully lain out a trail line in case they got stuck. This was nothing new—he'd done dives in shipwrecks before. He had taken every precaution possible. Every so often, he turned back to check on her, just to make sure she was still conscious.

Then the unimaginable happened. He felt a sudden tug and had turned to see why she had stopped. He still remembered to this day, the fear in his sister's eyes. She hadn't stopped voluntarily—she was stuck, tangled in rags of a fishing net. At first glance, it wasn't worrisome. Harmless nets were known to have slowed down divers but they were seldom treated as a serious impediment. He tried pulling at the net with his hands. It looked like it was made out of nylon, and he had even chuckled at first, shaking his head as he tried to free his sister from this harmless obstacle. After ten minutes of pulling in vain, he looked up and watched hope drain from Katie's eyes. Her eyes lost their luster, and she was slowly dozing into a deep, dangerous sleep.

He had scrambled around, desperately trying to find anything remotely sharp enough to cut her loose. He swam back to all the different cabins they had been in but had become disoriented. He lost the track of time and started to feel trapped and alarmingly distressed, imprisoned in a world he loved, one that had soothed him from all outside harm. He himself was running out of oxygen, sensing it before he even had checked his meter. By the time he got back to Katie, her head was low and her body solemnly still. He had stayed beside her, without really looking at her, holding onto the hope that she, of all people, had to survive. Eventually, the darkness came to him, too. He had felt the tightness around his throat, and he reached out to hold her hand. As lifeless as it was, it was still Katie's. He waited to be engulfed. He had been ready for it, and he waited.

He felt a small tug on his arm. At first, he figured it must be some curious fish—or worse, a shark. When he came to, a pair of curious eyes stared attentively into his. It was the face of a young woman. She didn't seem completely human. Perhaps it was because she was down here, almost five hundred meters underwater, without any diving equipment. Or the fact that everything about her seemed too unearthly beautiful to be real. Her long hair floated gracefully around her, as she circled him and Katie like a curious fish. He held out his hand to try and direct her attention to Katie, but she had already noticed her. She leaned in and he could feel her pulling him up and away from Katie. *No!* He wanted to shout and stop her, but he was too weak to even raise his arm in protest. As she led him away from the shipwreck, his anger and frustration exhausted him, and he found himself devoid of any strength to fight off this mystical creature forever separating him from his sister.

The next thing he knew he was coughing and gasping for air. When he made a fist and realized he was grasping sand, he found himself lying on the shore. The sun was rising and the skies turned a dramatic combination of purple and orange. As he watched the water glimmer from the reflection of the sun, he knew what he had lost. It didn't take long for people to gather round him—those who had shops on the beach, early surfers, and rescue divers. He wanted to go back to look for Katie, but he was too weak and couldn't speak coherently. As he lay listlessly on the stretcher, waiting to be taken away in an ambulance, he watched the dark silhouettes put on their masks and dive into the water like it was any other dives of the day. The water was still, and the sun made its glorious entrance over the cloudless, clear blue skies.

It was the perfect morning for a dive.

It didn't take long for them to bring her up. He wasn't there to see her for the last time before his decision to cremate her. He didn't need to. For hours, as he laid awake on the hospital bed, he tried to remember Katie as a child—as an annoying four year-old who tagged along whenever he went to his friends' birthday parties. Her short, blond curls dangled above her forehead, something he always found annoying and at the same time ridiculously adorable. He would flick at them for fun but also as a sign of affection. He remembered her as teenager who curiously eyed whatever he was reading on the sofa. And her bright, wide smile that would light up any room.

A few weeks ago they had celebrated her birthday with Louise. Knowing Katie, they didn't do anything fancy. They set up a small picnic in the middle of Stanley Park at dawn. The hamper was simple, but filled with Katie's favorite food: a box of salted caramel donuts, fish tacos, an overly generous amount of brie cheese and crackers, along with a few bottles of expensive wine at Louise's insistence. When she opened his present, she broke into a smile. It was a necklace; a small, delicate seashell-shaped pendant with a pearl in the middle, hanging on a thin, rose-gold chain. Something that befitted a fellow diver, he had told her.

And to that, she responded, "This is going to be my lucky charm." She put it around her neck.

"To protect me from all kinds of troubles, right?"

And he hadn't seen her part with it since. He remembered when they were in the shipwreck, and Katie had panicked as she got tangled up in the fishing net, her hand clutching that same necklace. He wondered then if she still believed that it would protect her. When they asked him if he would like to see her one last time, he declined. The lifeless, cold Katie wasn't the one he wanted to remember. He preferred to select fragments of memories—specific, vivid moments that highlighted her at her best.

It took him a while before he was able to talk about what happened. Even after Louise flew in the next day, he had chosen silence over everything. Over food, over sleep, over almost every waking minute of that first agonizing week. Some days, when he locked himself in his room, he would try to open his mouth to say something, but heard only a sound resembling a sob that escaped him.

When Louise couldn't take it anymore, she forced it out of him. And he hated her for it. He eventually said that everything had been his fault. From getting Katie into diving, for not being protective enough, for being stupid enough to agree to a shipwreck dive when they were both still jetlagged. For rushing Katie through that passage when she got stuck. For losing yet another person he loved. He didn't cry after that—no tears would come. But all the blame, the what-ifs, all the hatred for all things underwater came like an unstoppable rush of adrenaline. When Louise probed further, asking him how he had managed to get out, he was unable come up with an answer. He wasn't sure if he even knew. The apparition of that young woman seemed too ridiculous a thing to recount. When he thought back to that moment, he had convinced himself that it must have been his mind playing tricks on him. The lack of oxygen, he concluded. Now, as he stared into that same apparition, he wondered where reality drew its line. Was he dreaming? Or was she—Narya—the one that rescued him from the shipwreck that day?

Narya could feel Nick's intense gaze on her. A piercing, relentless kind of look that had so sharp an edge that she felt it cut through her. She wondered if he had remembered their first meeting.

She'd seen them before—divers. But never encountering them head-on like this. No, she, along with other curious mermaids, or mermen, would watch from a safe distance. On her more daring days, she would venture closer to get a clearer view of the humans— although she could never see what they actually looked like since they were always veiled under weird looking dark suits. They had been warned, of course, of the consequences, should they ever be discovered. So they were always prepared to escape, in case they were noticed. But that has never happened before.

That day, she was aimlessly swimming around, half-heartily looking for Grey, who usually lurked around shipwrecks. She had almost swam past it without noticing the divers inside, but something that glimmered from a distance caught her attention. As she swam closer to investigate, she saw two figures floating listlessly in one of the cabins. Typically, they would be swimming around, or at least moving, using a camera or some kind of machine to record their time underwater. But this time, it was different. Something about them made her stop. It just didn't look right. She swam as discreetly as she could to the window and peered inside. They were still not moving from where they were. Her curiosity got the better of her and she decided to brave the risks.

At first, she approached cautiously, moving her tail only when necessary. When only a few feet away from them, it surprised her that she could sense the energy they exuded. The one closer to her was taller, and she could tell it was a male by his physique, and that he was struggling to breathe. Perhaps not for much longer. It didn't take her a full second to sense that life had already left the other one. She couldn't see the face but could tell it was a young girl by the softness of her hands and the smoothness of her neck. It was her first time at such a thrilling proximity to a human. She wanted to spend more time observing them, even to just touch them for a bit longer. But when she saw the man's head drooping, she knew that she had to move fast in order to save him.

She tugged gently at his arm, afraid to wake him as she wasn't sure how he'd react. When she saw that he opened his eyes and didn't panic at the sight of her, she figured it was time to move. She took his hand in hers and linked their fingers together and began to swim away from the shipwreck. She had to look back several times to make sure he was still conscious. They passed several schools of zebra fish and a few curious turtles that swam up and tried to nibble at the diver's fins. Luckily, she didn't see any merpeople. There wasn't a rule against saving humans, but the fact that she had approached one was scandalous enough. She consciously took a different route to the surface, knowing which areas the others usually swam. When they surfaced, the land wasn't too far out, but she still contemplated whether to bring him to shore herself. The sunrise lit up every corner of the beach, and she had to move inconspicuously toward the open shores.

As she laid him gently down on the sand, his eyes were

closed and his breathing shallow. She wasn't sure whether she should try to wake him or let others discover him. While these thoughts raced through her mind, she heard voices from a distance, and the decision was made for her on the spot. She took one last look at the diver before she dove back into the ocean.

She was still there. *Narya*. He blinked to make sure he wasn't dreaming. Everything about her that had seemed overwhelmingly familiar now made sense. Had she known this all along? Did she come to him knowing she had saved him once before? Underwater, her tanned skin took on a more translucent glow, and her upper body looked as if it had been sprinkled with fallen stardust. A long, dark turquoise tail wrapped around her lower body, and it swayed with a life of its own as she floated before him. Her purple dress hung onto the bottom of her tail, an oddly beautiful accessory that appeared hauntingly out of place.

He watched her hold out her arm, and when he felt her touch, he recoiled, his dreamlike state shattered, and he knew he was running out of air. He swam upward as fast as he could and gasped for air, grabbing the emergency raft and resting his arms on the edge. Before he could go down again, Narya emerged from the water, and the sight of her made his heart race.

Her face glistened, and she couldn't quite hide her guilt.

"I . . . " She couldn't continue. She let the silence linger and hoped for him to say something first.

Save for the glittering scales that traced her upper body, she appeared to be like an ordinary girl, and it made him question what was real.

"Look, I need to go check on Lou," he said, not having anything better in mind to say to her.

"Right." She floated effortlessly in the water.

His legs were already tired from the dive. It has been a long time since his last swim. His hands tightly clutched the raft, and he tried not to think of her fish tail, but then he heard a swooshing sound as it swayed in the water. He raised his eyes to meet her gaze, and they stayed motionless—a siren of the sea, and a man, each wondering what would happen next.

Nick was the first to break away, unable to process it all at once. He could still see her from the corner of his eye as he climbed onto the raft. She was waiting for him for some kind of affirmation. He searched his mind for something appropriate to say. How does one react to sea creatures that exist only in legends and mythical tales?

Reading his hesitance, she began to back away from the raft, and he knew that she might disappear into the deep blue if he let the silence drag on for too long. He had to say something—anything—rather than losing her to the ocean.

"Are you coming?" He was taken aback by how calm he sounded.

The silence made his chest tighten, and for a second he thought she had gone. He heard a splash and saw her swim past him, pulling the raft as she went and bringing him to shore at such an alarming speed that he almost tumbled back into the water.

"Okay, so what happens now?"

They reached the shore in less than five minutes. For a journey that typically took half an hour on a boat, this was frighteningly impressive. They wound up in the reef area, with rocks that shielded them from the beach. He watched her fiddle with her hair, hesitant to leave the water.

"Do you need . . . time to change?" He felt his cheeks redden at the preposterousness of his question.

"Yes." Her voice was timid. "I think you should turn around."

He obeyed and walked away, giving her the privacy that she needed. Facing a large rock formation, he tried to focus on the different sizes and shapes of its uneven holes. From where he sat, he could hear the ocean waves rolling onto the shore, an evocative sound that he never tired of. He felt like he was one with the ocean—he couldn't imagine his life without being close to it. He supposed that he and Narya resembled each other this way. He heard another splash, and then a few small gasps before silence took over. Only the calming sound of waves being washed ashore remained. He shut his eyes, remembering the times he craved nothing more than jumping in and exploring the world that fascinated him.

A gentle tap on his shoulder roused him from his reminiscences. He opened his eyes to find Narya wearing that same lilac colored dress, her wet hair tousled in a carefree way that reminded him of the first day they met.

He wanted to say something, but words couldn't get through the convoluted web that cluttered his mind. What should he say in a situation as strange as this? Perhaps it was best to say nothing at all for now. Narya stood erect before him, consciously hugging herself. She was not only a dream come true, but a fragile one that he needed to hover over protectively. Something could set her off, and he could lose her forever. He nodded to himself and made up his mind to postpone his questions until later. There was a more pressing matter at hand.

"All right, let's go check on Lou."

"Are you sure you didn't see anything?"

"No! God, for the twentieth time, can you leave me in peace for now? I almost *died.*"

Pete swaggered around the room, his hair in disarray and he was talking through his cigarette.

A true mad scientist, Louise thought. If anyone wanted to see what a genius looked like, they'd be horribly disappointed meeting Pete, legend of a marine biologist that he was.

"But I swear I saw a glimmer of something when she brought you up. It was like . . ."

"Like what, Pete?" Her patience was waning.

She stared longingly at the hospital jello and wished he'd leave her alone so she might indulge without an audience. He had been by her bedside ever since she woke up. At first, she found it kind of endearing. Maybe he cared for her enough to be there. But after he opened his mouth and began his ludicrous speculation about Narya, she was transported back to the reality where Pete was still playing the part of a genuine asshole.

". . . like *scales.*" He stopped, contemplating what he had just said. "Fish scales." He moved to the window that overlooked the ocean.

"What do you mean?" She would devour the jello regardless and opened it swiftly, searching for a spoon on the bedside table.

"Like as if she were . . . a *fish.*" He faced her now, his eyes intense, and it sent chills down her spine.

"Okay. First—what the *fuck?* And second, you are out of your mind, Pete. Are you sure you were sober on that boat? How many beers did you have? Four? Five?" She took the lid off the jello cup and started licking it. She had forgotten how much she enjoyed chocolate. She would add this to the list of things not to take for granted while she was alive. *Not everyone gets a second chance at life.*

"Listen—just *listen* to me, Louise. Put all of your fucking logical thinking aside for now, and let's explore the impossible. Science has no limit, right? I *swear*. I saw scales on her before. On that first shark tag I took her and Nick on. This isn't just my imagination. And this could be *big*." He took his phone out of his pocket and searched as he scrolled the screen.

"Are you saying she's . . . not human?" Louise tried not to smirk. "You're saying she might be a . . . "

"—*a mermaid*." Pete finished her sentence with the word she least expected him to say. He was a marine biologist, not a five-year-old. This was beyond absurd, and she vehemently shook her head at him. Still, she couldn't stop herself from snickering. God, she loved it when he got crazy. Good entertainment, if nothing else.

"Look," he said, "I have this old colleague down in East Africa. He runs a small research facility on Pemba island, and he's made some pretty interesting discoveries." He lowered his voice despite there being no one else in the room.

"Pemba? That tiny island off Zanzibar?"

"Yeah. In Tanzania." He nodded then he showed her a picture on his phone.

At first, she couldn't tell what it was. The picture was dark and blurry, obviously taken underwater, and too hazy to make out any distinctive colors and shapes. But as she struggled for a better look, she saw what she thought could be a long tail, on top of which appeared to be a human torso. A small dot in the middle suggested a bellybutton. If Pete hadn't mentioned the word mermaid, she would never have thought this was a picture of one. She took the phone from his hand and zoomed in closer. It could be anything, really, including a large fish. She looked again and tried hard not to blink. A large fish . . . with a waist and bellybutton. *Holy shit*. She was turning crazy, too.

"Okay . . . fine." She cleared her throat and tried not to sound too agreeable, in case he got too eager to get her on board with this ridiculous mermaid theory. "So even if you and your friend aren't completely *crazy*, what do you plan to do about it? You can't just do research on Narya. She's . . ."

She was going to say friend, but she seldom considered anyone a friend after less than a month. Even acquaintances she'd known for years didn't make it to her friends' list that easily. She was cautious when it came to people, knowing that she didn't possess great people skills, but she was good at reading them. And there were only a handful of people she would consider her friends. She didn't exactly dislike Narya, but she didn't fully trust her. There was something so intangibly different about that girl. She took another glance at Pete's picture, rapidly growing less skeptical of his theory.

"Well, technically, I can't. It'd be against the law here." Pete's voice had an edge to it, and Louise could almost guess what he would say next.

"Oh, no. What are you proposing?"

"We can fly her to Pemba. You know, there are a lot of legal loopholes in African countries that we can take advantage of when we're there."

Louise could detect the excitement in the tone of his voice and rolled her eyes at his scandalous scheme.She didn't answer right away. It was difficult to know whether or not he was joking. He seemed to have thought this through. And he had that crazy, determined look in his eyes that appeared only once in a blue moon when he would come across something research worthy.

"Look. Why don't you do this . . ." He opened his bag and pulled out a bottle of murky water. "Spill some of this seawater on her leg, and see for yourself."

Convinced that he already had proven himself right, he nodded to her and left the room.

They were quiet from the time they got to shore until they reached the hospital. Nick tried to think of what he would say to her, but he couldn't manage to utter anything that wouldn't be considered intrusive. As they approached the hospital, he walked behind her, and from time to time, he would stare at her legs, wondering about the biology of it all. He couldn't help but try to make sense of this craziness. Was it a gene mutation? A possible defect? Are there more of them down there? A whole legion of them?

"I think that maybe you shouldn't tell Louise about me." Surprisingly, she was the one to break the silence first as they reached the sliding entrance doors. She stared down at her feet. He followed her gaze but could only picture her mermaid tail.

"Right." He had to agree, it was not like he had other options. Knowing Louise and her ambitions, he wasn't sure whether she wouldn't expose Narya to the world for an easy shortcut to fame. And he felt his own curiosity bursting at the seams. It was a marine biologist's dream come true. A new species of *fish*. Or at least some kind of a hybrid.

"How . . . I mean, what kind of . . . how does *this* work?" He gestured at her legs that had taken the form of a fishtail underwater only moments before. He regretted the question as soon as it had left his lips. He eyed her questioningly as he began to sweat uncontrollably, fearing that this would set her off. But she made no move to run back to the ocean, and his shoulders relaxed.

"I'm not supposed to talk about it." Her gaze was direct and sharp, as though he had stepped over an invisible boundary.

"You mean you're forbidden to talk about it? By the *others*?" He could feel her stiffen and knew he was pushing his luck. They stared at each other, and he hoped she would crack under pressure and spill everything. At the same time, he felt something tugging at his conscience.

"I really can't." Her face changed from a serious look to a kind of pleading that weakened his will and logic. He let infatuation get the better of him. And he willingly surrendered—for now, at least.

"So, are we . . . good?"

"Yep." He stared straight ahead at the busy hallway of the hospital. She surprised him on a daily basis. And this, by far, was the biggest surprise. He doubted there could be anything more bizarre to trump this.

"Let's go." He let her walk ahead of him, and they scurried through the crowd of people. As he watched her from behind, he realized how easy it was for him to pick her out of all these ordinary people. The more he observed her, the more she sank under his skin and deep into his veins. She was something essential to his very survival. He made a silent vow to himself to protect her from harm—even from himself.

At first, Louise didn't say much. It was difficult to tell if she was upset with them or if she was in a foul mood because of her injuries. She did thank her, ever so briefly, for saving her life. But a thick cloud of suspicion still lingered above them, stubbornly refusing to clear.

"I didn't know you could swim." Louise said with her arms crossed.

"It's . . . been a while," Narya said. She was palpably nervous and Nick didn't blame her.

"Mm-hmm." Louise's passive aggressiveness was unforgiving.

"Well, you're okay now." Nick tried to divert the attention from Narya. She didn't need to be under Louise's harsh interrogation limelight after what she had been through today.

"Yes. Well, thank you for that." Louise tried to sit up straight on the bed, but the action made her wince.

"Are you all right?" Nick moved to help her up.

"Yeah, I think I just need another dose of painkiller for my headache."

"I'll get the nurse," Nick said, hurrying out of the room.

It was suddenly quiet, and the sound of Louise shuffling in her bed made the silence more unbearable.

Narya wanted to help, but she also wanted to leave before Louise could shoot off any more of her daunting questions. "Do you need anything else?"

"Sure. Can you grab me that bottle of water?"

Narya nodded and casually reached for the bottle. As she handed it to her, the cap came loose, and Louise accidently tilted the bottle, spilling water all over her legs and feet.

The feeling initially was very mild, the prickliness subtle, but then she began to feel it crawling over her feet. She looked down and a few scales had already appeared. A mixture of dark purple and bright lilac glimmered from the sunlight that seeped through the curtains. She tried to dry the water off with her hands, but the scales weren't disappearing quickly enough, and she could only hope that Louise wasn't watching her.

"Sorry, I'm just going to . . . go to the washroom. Here— here's your water." Narya placed the water bottle on the bedside table.

"Sure thing." Louise didn't look up, appearing busy with something on her phone.

Narya slowed her pace as she neared a cart filled with bed

linens. Seeing no one around, she snatched a sheet and hastily dried off her legs. The colors were slowly fading now, and most of the scales were no longer visible, except for their subtle contour. She watched her human legs return to their normal state. Unsure whether or not Louise had seen anything, she could only hope that she had run away fast enough for her to miss the glimmer that shone from her legs.

She tried to remain calm when she re-entered the room. Louise was still occupied with her phone. "Hey."

"Hey, yourself. Are you okay?" Louise didn't even glance up from her phone. Narya relaxed her shoulders and sat in the chair beside her bed.

"Well, I should be asking you that question. Are you feeling better?"

"Yeah. I think so." A faint sneer on Louise's face made her slightly uncomfortable, and she shifted in her seat.

"I—um, I don't think you're supposed to drink that," Narya said, eyeing the half-empty water bottle on the table—the one that had spilled on her legs.

"Why not?"

"Well, it's seawater." Narya cursed herself as soon as she said it. She could only pray that Louise wouldn't read into this too much.

"And how'd you know it's seawater?" Louise tilted her head and casted a wry glance in her direction.

"Well—I mean, you can smell it, right?" She tried to sound as casual as possible. Now really wasn't the time to get on Louise's bad side. She didn't need any more suspicions after what happened today.

After what seemed like the longest few seconds, Louise shrugged. "Oh, yeah, I don't know how that got in here."

Nick walked in just in time with a nurse who wore her impatience bluntly on her face. They had definitely overstayed their visitor's hours.

"Someone called for some painkiller?"

CHAPTER NINE

Nick walked with Narya along the beach, as the ocean waves rolled in behind them. He was thankful for the sound as they were both exceedingly quiet other than for an occasional mentioning of Louise. They had stayed with her until the sun began to set. She seemed in high spirits and laughed heartily at the inside jokes shared with Nick years earlier.

They now neared a deserted beach area temporarily forgotten by the crowds. There were high rocks around them, forming a small overhead cliff. The waves continued to rise, and as the water reached their feet, he watched Narya cautiously stepping over the water and backing away. He couldn't believe that mere few hours ago, she was someone wholly different underwater; an obscure image immersed in water, long hair flowing around her, and the translucent glow that surrounded her like a halo.

"Do you miss it?" he heard himself ask before he cursed silently for succumbing to his unrelenting curiosity.

"Do I miss what?" She was busy averting the water, and was now treading around it. Like she was dancing with the waves.

"This." He walked a small distance away from her and edged into the water until his ankles were submerged. He missed it, even craved sometimes, like an addict trying hard to fight the damning temptation. The swim from earlier today only made his yearnings worse. He savored the feeling of the lukewarm seawater— the perfect condition for a sunset swim.

"Yes, I do." She stood on the beach in her evening dress, her hands raising the bottom of it to prevent it from getting wet. The sea breeze made her hair dance around her face, and the sight of her made his heart swell. Brightness shone in her eyes as she looked out into the open sea.

"Yeah, me too." He walked back onto the beach and sat down on a rock. Resting his chin on his fist, he tried to imagine what it would feel like to be deep in the ocean again.

"When do you think you'll be ready to go in?" she asked as she settled beside him and dug her feet into the warm sand.

"I'm not sure." He stretched out his legs and glanced at his wet, sand-caked feet.

Narya observed him with her large, curious eyes. "Do you think it's your fault that she drowned?"

Therapists that Louise made him visit had tirelessly asked the same question over and over again. He never really answered them, although he knew what his answer would be. But Narya's question didn't seem rhetorical. She was genuinely asking whether if he blamed himself. Was he ready to let the truth engulf him?

"Yes. Yes, I do."

"Why?" She sat up straight and the sand spilled over her legs. He stared down at them, envisioning what they were underneath.

"I introduced her . . . to this." His finger traced the outline of the diving mask he held. Katie's face appeared in his cluttered mind, and his grip on the mask tightened. Damning evidence of his passion for the sea.

"Diving, the ocean, the whole package. She fell in love with it, and it's what killed her." He grabbed a fistful of sand and felt the tiny grains seeping out of his hand until nothing remained. Everything he tried to protect slipped away from him and got mercilessly thrown into harm's way. Nothing good ever lasted for him.

"But she loved it, right? The ocean?"

The waves rolled in with a thunderous force, as did memories of Katie and their diving adventures. She was always so happy underwater, surrounded by this other realm. It was her passion. It was her life.

"It's not your fault." Narya's tone was decisive and it made him want to pull her near to thank her for whatever it was that made him feel whole again.

"Right." As much as he wanted to believe her, he'd rather be bound by his guilt and not let the memories of Katie fade.

They remained quiet for a while, listening to the sound of the waves crashing onto the shore. The smell of the sea filled his lungs, and he wondered if he would ever be able to breathe easily without it.

He felt Narya shift from where she sat. A small sigh escaped her.

"Want to go for a swim?" She got up and tiptoed toward the water. Her slim silhouette reflected in the water, and her dress glimmered in sunlight that was quickly setting behind them. The sunset cast an orange hue and, as he watched Narya, she glowed like a goddess, standing in the open sea. She turned back with a playful grin and gestured with her hand for him to follow.

He found himself unable to take his eyes off her, her hair swept by the wind in all directions, making her look wild—a side to her he'd only started to see. Her lilac-sequined dress called to mind the violet fish tail he had seen underwater. Everything about her suddenly made sense. This was simply who she was. There was no disguise, no mystery about this girl he initially had thought so confounding. He was falling for her at a speed he felt would suffocate him soon if he did nothing about it. He had lost his remaining willpower and desperately wanted to jump in and join her. *Take me,* he thought, *take me to the deepest blue.*

"Come!"

The spot where she stood took on a soft, light purple hue. He was amazed at the shift of colors as she went deeper into the water.

"Ow."

She was trying not to wince. He didn't have a chance to ask about the physics of her transformation. From the look on her face, he reckoned it hurt each time she turned back into a mermaid.

He walked toward her in hopes of pulling her back out of the water. "Look, I don't think—"

She was completely submerged but then re-emerged with clustered of dark purple, lilac, and silver scales covering her upper body. She threw her wet dress at him, and it landed on the sand near his feet.

"Put on your mask!"

She floated in the water, and he caught a glimpse of her tail that submerged as quickly as it had surfaced.

"It's time that you come back."

She said it like it was an easy task and, for once, he knew she couldn't be more wrong. *But why did it feel so right?*

His hands clutched his diving mask, and he could feel his body tingling uncontrollably with excitement. Earlier, when he had dove into the water to save her, he felt something he hadn't experienced in a long time. A suppressed freedom that he craved for what seemed like an eternity. He tightened his lips and tried hard to justify why he shouldn't just jump in.

"If you come with me, I'll tell you more about . . . *this.*" She swam in a way that exposed the tip of her tail. She was grinning like a child, knowing she was close to winning this battle of enticement.

It was a tempting bargain; she had learned how to maneuver him well. His fingers subconsciously adjusted his diving mask like it was second nature. If he was going in, this swim was going to be well worth his time.

"You can ask me . . . one question. Any question." She changed position, and her tail had disappeared. From the surface, she looked like any normal girl enjoying a carefree sunset swim in the ocean.

"Five." He held up his hand with fingers splayed to give himself a boost of confidence, all the while conscious of his lack of negotiating skills.

"Two." She splashed sea water at him and giggled as she watched him move toward her. Her plan was working. She was, in every way, his kryptonite—his siren of the sea.

"Three. It's my lucky number." He smiled from ear to ear, knowing she would capitulate.

"Fine, you can have three." She smiled in return then dove into the water and began to swim further away from him.

He was knee deep in the water. He tried not to panic, exhaling deeply. This was just a swim. A swim for the advancement of marine biology, he reminded himself. He caught a glimpse of Narya smiling at him, her tail protruding from the waters. It was time. He fastened the mask around his face. Funny how old habits come back so effortlessly. No longer able to control his desire, he dove in after her.

She navigated expertly through the water, swimming much deeper than he was—a few meters further down. The sight of her gliding freely profoundly moved him. He'd never felt as many emotions stir within him—an unexpected epiphany, mixed with an overwhelming gratitude that paved the way for a sense of longing—a longing to live. To stay alive. To have lived until now to be in this very moment.

The glimmer of her tail lit the way, and he could clearly see all the corals and marine life underneath them. They were summoned to life as she swam past them. The bright corals took on a more luscious shade in the evening light, glistening in the water like darkened jewels purposely hidden away only to resurface exclusively to display their grandeur. A mixed group of reef butterflyfish and queen angelfish encircled them as they passed by, their scales reflecting off Narya's tail and creating a bewildering illusion of lights. He had not forgotten the beauty of marine life in the Bahamas, but the love he felt for the ocean flowed back with an intensity so strong he felt an adrenaline rush that made his head spin. A bale of sea turtles swam against the current, one tugging curiously at Narya's tail. She turned back intermittently to check on him, her golden eyes staring into his, inadvertently deciphering his deepest secrets. She swam leisurely at his pace; at times her tail would be almost within his reach, and he was tempted to stretch out his hand to touch it just to make sure she was real.

As they reached the reef area, there was a sudden halt in her movement as though she were waiting for something. He couldn't see much beyond the school of blue tang that stubbornly stuck around. Then he felt a presence before he saw it. He first made out a large, looming silhouette making its entrance among the other fishes that quickly skittered away. Seconds later was he able to see the great white shark making its way directly toward them, its movement slow yet regal.

From where he was, he could see part of its white underside, and its dark blue dorsal area blending with the water. It swam by Narya's side, and it occurred to him that this was the shark they had attempted to tag earlier in the day. Dumbfounded, he watched her reach out to pet it as if it were a tamed beast, and it returned her affection by nuzzling against her arm. With an inviting smile, she gestured to him to come closer, and the shark floated by her, hypnotized by her touch. There were a dozen reasons why he shouldn't get too close to a great white, but nothing had been normal since this morning, and he forcibly pushed logic aside as he made his way toward the mermaid and her unlikely companion.

Narya extended her hand and pulled him closer until he was face to face with the great white shark. Its black, beady eyes stared into his own, and he felt a shudder but tried to bury his fear in the back end of his bemused mind. She took his hand and glided it over the shark's skin. He felt the rough, sandy surface of its placoid scales. From the light that shone from Narya's tail and scales, he saw their shadows cast on the bottom of the ocean floor. He watched, flabbergasted, as he made out the outline of a large shark's silhouette, his own shadow, and that of a mermaid's.

CHAPTER TEN

"So you have a pet shark."

Still panting from the physical exertion and adrenaline of the dive, those were his first words when they surfaced. The beach was still quiet, with no one in sight. He removed his diving mask, and Narya tried to smooth her hair, tangled by the swim. By the time he turned around, she was already in her dress, standing on her two legs. It baffled him to think that, a few minutes before, he had been in the middle of the ocean with the same girl—in her true mermaid form.

"Grey is, more of a . . . friend." She settled on that word like it was an afterthought.

"But—it—you . . . well, I guess you're both . . ." He wanted to say fish, but he wasn't sure if it was an appropriate term.

He found himself unable to form a coherent sentence, and this had become more common since meeting her. He constantly felt under her spell, and now, with this last surprise, he was no longer able to think straight when with her.

"We're what?" She cocked her head sideways, oblivious to what he was trying to say.

"Nothing, let's head back. I think you need to change before you catch something from the cold."

"But I'm never cold." She caught up to him, her wet dress clinging seductively to her body.

"Oh, right. Never mind." He looked elsewhere and directed his focus on something other than the bewitching girl who remained unaware of her intoxicating charms.

After convincing Narya to change into dry clothes—a T-shirt that Louise had left at his place, and an old pair of boxers dotted with yellow submarines—he sat her down with a cup of warm chamomile tea and settled in across from her with a notepad and a pen. He tried to lighten up the mood by putting on John Coltrane as background music. She was curled up on the couch with a blanket over her—at his insistence—and happily sipping her tea.

He cleared his throat, and contemplated on how to best begin his well-earned interview. *How does one go about researching mermaids?*

"You have three questions." She had read his mind.

He dismissed all the trivial questions that went through his head and tried to formulate a proper, worthy question to ask her.

"Yes, I know." He wanted to know everything about her, down to the last detail of her scales. He would finally unlock the mystery that surrounded her like a fog. The same tinge of excitement that had thrilled him during his first year of the program overcame him.

"Make sure you ask the right ones." She looked up from her cup, silently challenging him to try.

He resisted returning her beguiling smile. He needed to maintain authority when conducting research, despite having a research specimen that talked back at him.

He chewed at the other end of his pen as he tried to make

out his own messy writing—random scribblings while he had contemplated how to make the best use of a rare opportunity.

"So . . . is there like a group of you? Of mermaids?"

"I think the right word would be merpeople. There are men, too, you know." She nibbled on a cookie and talked through the crumbs in her mouth.

"Can you give me a number?" He found himself unable to set aside the fact that he was talking to a mermaid who was drinking tea and obviously enjoying a chocolate cookie.

"A number? You mean how many of us are there?" She looked up from her plate, but he couldn't read her expression. Maybe she was about to share an ancient secret. Or maybe she shouldn't but was excited to do so.

"Yes," he said. "An estimate if you can."

"Well, I . . . I actually don't know."

"What do you mean?" He took a sip of his coffee. He could never drink tea. It tasted like weakly-flavored water. Coffee awoke his senses, and he needed to be fully focused while speaking to a mermaid about to confide underwater mysteries.

"I mean. I know how many are in our grid. Our ocean grid—you know, where we live." She grabbed another cookie from the box and took a big bite. "But there are mermaids I've never met in other areas. I guess wherever there is water and marine life, you can find them. *Us*." She tacked on the last word and turned red, embarrassed by having momentarily forgotten where she belonged.

"I see. And how big is your grid?"

"Is that a second question?" A few crumbs fell from her mouth, and he found her all the more captivating, but he had to maintain his composure. He tried not to smile and looked down at his notepad.

"I don't think that's fair," he said. "This is technically the same subject."

"But we agreed on questions and not subjects." She was getting cheeky and flashed him a knowing grin.

"Fine—since you're so good with words, let's scratch that last one. How do you communicate?" This was of special interest to him. Not much of a linguist himself, he was still intrigued by foreign languages, and this one had to be the most foreign of all.

"What do you mean?"

"Do you talk underwater like we're talking now?"

They sat across from each other, separated by a short wooden bookshelf that doubled as a coffee table.

"We don't really . . . talk. I mean, we can speak, obviously, and we all instinctively know the language of the grid we're in. But we . . . read each other underwater."

"Like some kind of telepathy?"

"What is that?"

"It's not real—at least to humans. I guess it's really just science fiction. It's a communication between minds, but without sensory channels or physical interaction." He didn't want to sound crazy. Like Pete. God, what would Pete say if he knew that Narya turned out to be much more than just his prized shark whisperer?

"Like you can read each other's minds," she said, watching him closely. "Like that?"

"Like what?" He scratched the stubble on his chin and moved closer to her. This interrogation was proving more difficult than he had anticipated.

"Did you read my mind?"

He laughed and shook his head.

"I'm not a merman."

"Well, it only works underwater anyway. Keames didn't seem to be able to. He couldn't read any of my thoughts when I tried." She stopped in mid-reach for a third cookie, and guilt began to spread across her face as her cheeks reddened.

"Who's Keames?" Had he met someone who could have been a merman? He searched his mind for someone they might have come across as awkward and uniquely unusual as Narya.

She picked up her mug and sipped her tea, avoiding Nick's eyes.

Who did she interact with besides Louise, Pete, and him? He retraced the past two weeks until a face came into mind.

"Wait . . . Ken Lauer?" The awkward movie star who rose to fame thanks to his boyish good looks and a swimmer's body? Swimmer. *Oh, shit.*

"I don't think he'll ever go back to being one again." She didn't sound sad, but her eyes suggested otherwise.

"So this . . . is flexible?" It had never occurred to him that it might be a conscious choice. Did Narya desire to remain human? Or was she happier in the water? What would she eventually choose, if she had to make a final choice?

"What do you mean?" she asked.

"This change. Or . . . transformation. Can you go back to being a mermaid any time?"

"Well, the theory is . . ."

She had his full attention now. If there was anything he loved more than marine biology, it was theories. She entwined her fingers and struggled to find the right words.

"Every one of us has between seven to nine times to try it out—being human." Her voice grew slightly louder and more confident. "The Elders of each ocean grid—they're like leaders with authority—agreed to allow each of us to experience life as a human. Before we come up, we're given a special kind of seaweed that enables the transitions to take place. *Supposedly.*"

As she explained the process, it began to sound concocted. For all she knew, it could be regular seaweed harvested from her own backyard. Perhaps the transition was something innate, and like Keames had said, there was no limit. Were they all in the dark? She tried to chase away these doubts. Nick's eyes were on her, his hands gripped tightly around the notepad he held. She has never seen him as focused and alert.

"It's to prevent mermaids from venturing out on their own with no support. Most of the time they return and remain a mermaid—usually around the seventh or eighth time. Most of us aren't brave enough to give up life underwater entirely." She pulled the blanket tightly around her.

He knew she wasn't cold; she probably felt apprehensive, or exposed by all the secrets she had divulged. He resisted the urge to wrap his arms around her.

"But it's a *theory*," he said, enunciating the word.

"Yes." This was a secret she wasn't keen on sharing right away. But Nick made her feel safe, and she didn't see the harm of telling him what's been perplexing her. "Apparently there's no limit. According to Keames, who tested it out himself, we get more than nine times."

"I see," he said. Watching her from where he sat, listening to her go on about this, he felt like he could relate to the whole mind-blowing revelation.

"I've changed back . . . *four* times now." She enunciated the number after some pause.

"Theoretically, I have five more, but I can't be sure—unless Keames is an exception." She got up and added more hot water to her tea mug. He liked that she knew her way around his place. They had developed a familiar rhythm of living together, and he never thought he'd grow comfortable with a stranger in such a short amount of time.

"Right," he muttered to himself and thought about the possibilities if she shared Keames's flexibility. Or if she didn't. Could he convince her to remain human and stay here with him? He thought about what she had done earlier, what it meant, and what it must have cost her.

"But you've used one of your transitions for me." He wished he had known this transformation was so limited. He never would have let her utilize it so recklessly.

"Yes, well, that was worth it." She had her back to him so that he couldn't see her face.

His innate fear of the water hadn't evaporated into thin air, but he knew the swim today had changed him. It made him feel less guilty, less trapped. She'd given him a taste of what it would be like to live unencumbered by the past. His thoughts inadvertently drifted back to the day of the shipwreck.

"Why did you save me?"

This was the question he had wanted to ask his anonymous savior for years, if ever he did come across her, and if she actually existed. Now that he had found her, he couldn't help but wonder aloud. More than once he had wished that he'd never survived the incident. That he had remained underwater with Katie and had never surfaced. When he gave voice to this ominous thought to Louise one day, she had chastised him, and he had never brought it up again to her nor to anyone else. When the darkness became too much to bear, he'd curse the person who saved him. Had he not made his choice when he remained by Katie's side? Who was she— this creature—that she should decide he needed her help? But now, as his rescuer's identity was unveiled, and he was face to face with the person to whom he owed his life, he was truly grateful to be alive. To be here—with her.

"You want to know why I didn't leave you there?"

She frowned, a rare expression for her as he had come to realize. He nodded and waited for her to respond. A flash of disappointment came and went in her eyes.

"Do you wish I hadn't made that choice?"

He already knew what his answer would be.

"No."

And it was the truth. She made him feel like it was worth it to be here. That a second chance at a shattered life perhaps wasn't the worst card he was dealt with.

"I'll give you one extra question. Besides, I think you've already asked more than three, anyway." She sat back down and settled beside him with her legs crossed and the tea in her hand. As she shifted, their elbows touched and as cold as she was, he felt an inexplicable surge of warmth.

"Just like that?" He wanted to hug her, but instead rubbed his chin and contemplated what else he could ask his very forward research subject.

"To reward you for your efforts, I suppose." Her eyes sparkled and he wondered if she meant his efforts for the questions or at giving life a second chance since Katie.

"How fast . . . can you swim?"

She nodded to herself as though this were a valid question.

"Well, you know the sailfish?"

Only the fastest fish in the ocean. He nodded stoically.

"I'd say triple its speed."

He ran the numbers in his head. That would be roughly two hundred and ten miles per hour. No wonder she was able to swim her way back to the Bahamas all the way from Vancouver before they arrived by plane. He longed to see this—the image of Narya as a mermaid kept swarming his mind—but he managed to hold back from blurting out such a ridiculous request. It would mean asking her to give up another of her transitions, and he couldn't ask that after all she'd already done for him.

"*Holy shit.*" He tried to contain his reaction. If he were alone, he'd have a lot more colorful comments on the discoveries made tonight.

"This is probably why we're able to stay undiscovered." She spoke fast, excited to share more about her kind. "There are myths out there, right? But whenever we've encountered a human, we've always managed to escape in time so any glimpse of us would be too quick for them to identify anything except maybe an *image* of some kind."

"We and the other species of . . . fish are able to communicate as well. There'd be warnings about divers or submersibles so that we could avoid a surprise encounter. So this . . ." She eyed him with an expression that wavered between hopeful and guilty, and it made him want to reassure her that her secret was safe. She would always be safe with him.

"This would be unheard of. Me, conversing with you— about *us*."

"I understand." He said softly, not knowing what else he could say to assuage her doubts.

She looked down, blowing gently on her tea before taking another sip and suddenly starting to choke.

"Hey, are you all right?" He took the mug out of her hands and patted her on the back.

"Yeah—yeah, I'm fine." She coughed, still struggling to inhale properly.

He blinked fast as he watched her catch her breath. This moment ignited his mind with yet another question. He just hoped that she wasn't keeping track.

"How do you breathe underwater?"

She shifted in her seat and stretched her legs over the coffee table. "Like a fish. You should know this . . . Aren't you a marine biologist or something?"

The sarcasm in her voice reminded him of Louise, and he tried hard to suppressed a smile.

"Yes, but we've never come across any mermaids. You're not exactly featured in our recent textbooks."

"Oh, right. Sorry." She accepted his response as a valid point. "We have gills. Right here." She pointed at her neck and he leaned in to take a closer look.

On the surface of her skin, she had three lines of very faint, faded scars. They were only inches apart, and he could still smell seawater on her, sweet, fruity scented shampoo he bought for her when she first arrived here. He tried not to think about how smooth her skin felt as he glided his fingers over her neck. The scars were bumpy, but almost unnoticeable.

"So when you change back . . . do these open up?" He almost regretted asking the question, but she nodded and reassured him again that he was neither delirious nor crazy.

"It all comes with the transition."

They stayed still, inches from each other, and he resisted planting his lips on hers. *Work has to come first.*

"Do you think we can test it out? I'd like to see how it works."

"I would have to be in the water, though. At least part of my neck does." Narya said breezily.

"Wait, but wouldn't that mean you'd lose another transition?"

She's saved his life once—and technically, revived him for a second time since he had found her on the beach. Asking her to do this—lose another transition—was taking a part of her away for the sake of his own curiosity.

"No, I don't think so. I've spilled seawater on my legs and feet before and it was just for a few seconds. I don't think that counted as a transition."

"Are you sure you'd be okay with this?" Part of him wanted to discard the idea, but to see her in her mermaid form again was too enticing an offer to turn down. He could only blame his selfish human nature.

"It can't be for too long. But I think I can manage to just put my head and neck underwater long enough for the gills to appear."

"Well I got a bathtub." He stood up, unable to tolerate their proximity any longer. Her smell was intoxicating, and he was fighting hard to stay focused, not having his thoughts derailed by other things.

"But it has to be seawater," she added.

He pondered this for a moment, his hand supporting his chin as he crafted a plan to make this research possible.

"It's too dark out there to really see anything." He glanced at his watch. "And I think the surfers will be around at this time."

"We can bring the water back here," she replied.

The version of Narya he was getting to know was bolder than the one he had been getting used to. He wanted to refuse her, but the research itch was too strong for him to ignore it.

"Right. We'll need to find some big containers." He signaled for her to follow him.

This day had turned out to be more than just a regular shark tagging adventure. And this girl—this mermaid—was turning out to be the most precious secret he'd ever kept, and one that he was intent on keeping, no matter the cost.

It took them a few trips back and forth between the

apartment and the beach to fill his bathtub. As Nick carried the last bucket of water up the stairs, he was already huffing and panting. The bathroom was exceptionally bright with all the lights on. He had brought in two desk lights in order to maximize the brightness so that he could get a clear look at her. He kneeled by the bathtub and poured the seawater in while Narya sat on the sink counter, dangling her legs and watching him prepare his makeshift lab.

"Alright, let me just go grab my notebook."

As Nick turned abruptly, he slipped on a small puddle by the door and he tumbled backwards, his arm accidentally pushed Narya as he fell to the ground.

When he heard a splash of water, it was already too late. She lay in the seawater that filled the tub to the rim. Half of her face was hidden by her disheveled hair, and she was on her stomach, her glittering tail protruding out of the water at the other end of the tub.

"Sorry. I don't think this is salvageable." Narya slid the boxer shorts off, already torn at the seams during her quick transition. "And I guess I don't need this anymore." She removed the wet t-shirt as well and passed them to Nick, who remained speechless as he gawked at her.

He took in her every detail: the quietness in her light grey eyes, her toned shoulders and arms damp and shining with water, and the shimmery scales covering her chest that shone like a constellation, dotting the intricate map of her upper body. Their colors were a mixture of dark purple, lilac, and segments of silver and gold. Her stomach was bare, and he saw that the scales began again below her navel, covering the rest of her lower body. Those on her violet tail appeared to be thicker and darker in color, with a mix of light green and gold. He stood by the sink area with his hungry eyes.

"You wanted to see my gills?"

He redirected his gaze to her face and was reminded of his objective.

"Right." He took few cautious steps forward and kneeled down beside the bathtub.

She changed position and sat up straight so that her upper body was fully exposed. The gills were visible, and she breathed deeply in and out. *Like a fish.* Awestruck by it all, he was unable to do much but gawk at her—a mermaid in his bathtub.

"You're not scared of me, are you?"

It occurred to him a second later that she was serious. She appeared to be unsure, and almost sad in a way, and that compelled him to move closer. If only she knew that she was now key to his very own survival—he could never distance himself from her, ever. He stretched out his hand and laid his fingers gently on her gills, feeling their faint, fluttery movements under the palm of his hand. It was a strange sensation, and though he wasn't looking at her, he knew she was watching him. Neither of them spoke; they remained silent as he sat beside her, his hand softly gliding up and down her neck.

A sudden knock on the door shook him from his daze. Narya was equally startled, and he gestured for her to remain quiet as he headed for the door.

"Who is it?" There was no answer, but another knock followed. Cautiously, he opened the door and recognized the hair before seeing a face.

"Oh, hi."

Ken Lauer stood in the doorway in an expensive suit and a head full of blond hair that looked as though it were being blown on cue by the sea breeze.

"Hey, Nick, right? Sorry to intrude, but . . . uh . . ." He craned his neck to get a better look inside, and Nick instinctively stepped out and closed the door behind him.

"I'm sorry, can I help you?" He tried not to sound too defensive. This was the last person he wanted to see at the moment. Merman or not.

"I was guessing—and I hope I'm right—that Narya might be here with you."

"Why are you looking for her?" Irritated by his lingering presence, he could feel himself tensing up. From the corner of his eye, he saw two bodyguards at the bottom of the staircase. He relaxed his fists—using them was probably not the wisest idea.

"Listen, I don't . . ."

Ken looked like he was getting impatient, but he was trying to be diplomatic. Something that a movie star would be good at—acting.

With a small twitch at the corner of his lips, he flashed a polite smile at Nick.

"I just want to make sure that she's okay."

"She's fine. Really, she is." He cleared his throat and had the feeling that Ken was slightly threatened by him. He enjoyed the upper hand and intended to play it well.

"I see," Ken said. He tilted his chin as if cluing into something.

"Why do you have seawater all over you?"

"I went for a swim." Nick furrowed his brow, taken aback by his question.

Ken leapt forward, grabbed the collar of Nick's shirt, and sniffed him like a trained dog.

Before Nick had time to react, Ken threw him to one side and ran past him to open the door to his apartment. Nick tried to chase after him, but he was obviously an athlete, and he already had made his way to the threshold between the hallway and the washroom.

"Oh, fuck, *fuck*! You've got to be kidding me." Ken's distressed voice echoed in his hallway.

When Nick got to the bathroom, Ken was kneeling beside the tub, his head in his hands while the mermaid wore the guiltiest smile he had ever seen.

"Stop freaking out," Narya said as she twirled her hair around her fingers.

"Please tell me that he—" Ken blanched as he pointed toward Nick, his finger trembling uncontrollably.

Nick leaned against the door, unsure whether if he should leave the two alone. A fight was about to erupt, and Nick's first instinct was to stay in case Narya needed protection. Mythical creature or not, she was pretty small in size compared to the towering figure of Ken Lauer.

"Yes, he knows about you, too." Narya said, her eyes tightly shut. She wished that she might dive underwater and disappear. Unluckily for her, she was stuck in a tub.

"What?" Ken threw his hands up in the air and he exhaled a series of muffled grunts.

It all appeared theatrical to Nick, and he tried not to grin at the sight of Ken Lauer in unscripted distress.

"Listen, it's fine," There was very little Narya could do or say to calm the exposed merman down, but she still gave it a shot. "Nick is . . . well, he's a good friend."

"A good friend?" Ken repeated mockingly. "Great, so why don't I just tell all my closest friends in my film circle about how I used to be a merman and harvested seaweed for a living?"

Nick couldn't help discharging a long-suppressed laugh. Narya shot him a warning look, and he dutifully stifled his laughter.

"Look, he won't say or do anything, okay?" Ken still had his head in his hands and refused to acknowledge the fact that his true identity was out in the open.

"It's cool, man," Nick said, approaching the bathtub. He couldn't help wondering about the color of Ken's scales and tried to picture him as a merman.

"Look, I really won't tell anyone. Your secret dies with me." Nick drew a half-hearted cross motion across his chest with his fingers.

Ken made an exasperated sound before he got up and grabbed a towel off the shelf in the bathroom. He used it to wipe away the sweat beads forming on his forehead. This was clearly a stressful conversation for the former merman.

"I came here to . . . get you back." He shook his head as if realizing how wrong he had been.

"I'm not going anywhere," Narya said, gripping the rim of the bathtub, and Nick detected the determination in her voice.

"And stay here? With these *humans*? Are you out of your mind?"

"Look, I made my decision. And neither you, nor anyone can change it." This was a side of her that Nick was only beginning to see.

Ken looked dejected and dipped his fingers into the seawater. He knew this to be true, but was too prideful to admit it. No merman or mermaid can truly be happy on land—that only existed in man-made fairytales. No one should be forced to choose between here and home. He let his arm sink deeper into the tub, feeling the seawater rejuvenating him, triggering a familiar rush throughout his body and sharpening his mind. He felt Narya gently cupping her hands around his and found himself unable to explain his sorrow reflected in her eyes. He had already made his choice to stay. No turning back now.

"You remember what I told you? About the transition?"

"Yes." Narya stared at him with suppressed hopefulness.

"Don't test it out. I'm not sure if it works for everyone."

"Okay." She was beginning to miss him, knowing now that he was finally going to leave her be.

"And if you ever need me, you call this number." He handed her a card.

"Don't worry about me."

"I'm not." He glanced sideways at Nick. "It's the others I'm worried about."

And with that, Keames hurried out the door without looking back. As she sat in the bathtub, she watched her tail sway back and forth in the water, and she felt a pang of nostalgia realizing she had just made her decision to stay—and perhaps to even remain changed for good.

When Nick returned to the bathroom, neither of them spoke while he cleaned the wet floor with towels and a mop. She stayed in the tub, passively soaking up every drop of seawater she could. Nick occasionally turned to steal a glimpse of her. There was no rush for her to get out, and he certainly didn't mind letting her linger.

A loud knock startled them both. Ken couldn't have changed his mind that quickly.

"I'll get it," Nick said, and ran for the front door. He rarely had visitors, and this was the second intrusion tonight.

"Who is it?"

"Damn it, Nick! I tried calling you but you're not fucking reachable!"

Nick recognized Pete's voice instantly and opened the door.

"Hey, what's going on?"

"Well, first, you gotta pack your bags. I got this last minute stint in Pemba, and I'm bringing the whole crew with me. I got a pretty generous per diem package. You're bringing—uh, what's her name, Natalie?"

Pete's words were slightly slurred but he didn't seem that drunk. Nick has seen him in worse states.

"It's Narya." He didn't want to invite him in and remained standing by the threshold, using his body to block most of the entrance.

"Right. Right." Pete began to leave and then turned around as though he had forgotten something. "I gotta use the washroom. Too much beer." He was mumbling to himself as he brushed past Nick and stumbled toward the washroom.

"Wait, Pete!" Nick didn't know if Narya had heard Pete come in, but he also hadn't closed the washroom door.

He heard Pete let out a loud gasp.

He hurried over, his heart racing as he entered the washroom.

"Nothing—I almost slipped on water. Why the hell is your floor so wet?" Pete didn't bother closing the door as he unzipped his pants to relieve himself.

"Sorry." Nick squeezed out an apologetic smile and wondered where Narya had run off to. *Just in time.* He moved away from the door, his eyes following wet spots leading toward his bedroom. Wondering when Pete would be done, he stood guard and waited.

"Alright, my man," Pete's voice said from behind the door. "So the day after tomorrow it is, eh?" He came out of the washroom, one hand zipping up his pants. "Time to start packing!" He slapped Nick forcefully on the back and let himself out.

After ensuring that Pete had made his way down the stairs,

Nick locked the door and headed toward his bedroom. Through the wide-open door, he made out Narya's silhouette on his bed. She lay curled up in the middle of the bed and seemed fast asleep. When he got closer, he saw that she wasn't wearing any clothes, only her long hair shielding parts of her body. She must have gotten out of the bathtub in a hurry and changed in time to escape into the bedroom. He thought back to the previous times she had transformed into a human, and each transition time had become shorter. He tried to ignore the number of transitions she had left. Was it six? Or five now? Would she ultimately choose to live on land or return to the place where she belonged? With Ken Lauer out of the picture, he became her default guardian, and she was his responsibility now. While the feelings that he had for her grew exponentially stronger by the day, he wondered if he would be able to protect her should anything unimaginable happen. *He would just have to try like hell*, he nodded to himself.

The area where she lay was damp, and the window was half-opened; he could feel the sea breeze on his face. As he placed a blanket and over her, his fingers came in contact with her cold, bare shoulders, and he was again reminded that she did not feel the same things he did.

CHAPTER ELEVEN

"Good morning." Dressed in the lilac dress that she finally managed to dry, Narya rubbed her eyes. She favored this dress over all her other clothes, and the thought brought a proud smile to his face.

"Hey." He stood by the kitchen counter sipping his first cup of coffee. He had heard her wake up—the sound of a loud and prolonged yawn that traveled all the way to the kitchen.

"Sorry, I don't even remember how I fell asleep." She pulled a cup from the shelf and poured herself a generous amount of coffee.

There goes his refill.

"That's okay. It was just Pete—well, drunk Pete." He had learned not to take him seriously when he was in an inebriated state.

"What did he want?" She looked around nervously as though he still might be lurking nearby.

She was not the first girl to find him creepy, and Nick didn't blame her.

"He mentioned something about going to Tanzania for research. And wanting to bring us there . . ." Remembering that he was making eggs, he ran back to the oven where she now stood.

"Don't worry, I can do this." She gave him a reassuring smile and took over the pan, flipping the eggs expertly and serving them on a plate.

He was taken aback by her ease around him, and at how much he enjoyed this newfound intimacy between them.

"Tanzania . . . that's in East Africa?" She hopped onto the kitchen counter and grabbed a piece of toast from his plate.

"Yeah. But I don't think Pete was serious. He doesn't mean half the things he says."

"Mmm." She made a face as she bit down on the dry toast.

She jumped down and circled around him to get to the cupboard and searched for the peanut butter jar. Before he could stop her, she was dipping her toast into the jar and enjoying it tremendously as she licked her fingers.

He grabbed a butter knife and handed it to her as his phone rang.

"Hello?"

"Hello, yourself!" Louise said. "How come my visitors schedule is so empty today? You and Narya busy with something I don't know?"

Her voice was edgy, and he could sense her jealousy. He peered at Narya and saw her drinking milk out of the carton. *One of the many habits she will have to change.*

"Sorry, we were up quite late last night." He regretted as soon as the words escaped from his mouth. *Damn it.*

"Oh? Doing what?"

"Just, chatting." He wanted to hang up. He was never good at lying, especially to someone as intuitive as Louise.

"Mmm-hmm." She paused before continuing in a more upbeat tone. "So, did Pete tell you about going to Tanzania? I hope you guys are packing your bags. I'm getting discharged this afternoon, and I've got to get my stuff sorted. I just hope I can find my passport in time . . ."

"Wait, so he was actually serious?" His shoulders tensed. He had traveled extensively but never to Tanzania, and the prospect of studying sharks in a whole new country fascinated him.

"I thought he was just drunk when he came over last night," he said.

"Yeah, well, I'm sure he *was* drunk. Maybe that's why he booked our non-refundable tickets." She snickered and tapped on her keyboard. "I'll forward them to your email in a bit."

"Wait—so all of us are going?"

"Yeah. You, me, Pete—and Narya. She's coming too, right?"

Nick watched Narya licking the border of the peanut butter jar. He made his way over to her, wanting to intervene against any further unhygienic habits she was developing under his roof.

"I'll ask her."

"Okay, cool. I'll see you guys later."

He put his phone down on the counter and reached out for the jar. She was still licking peanut butter off her fingers and making the smacking sound with her lips that he found so endearing.

"Alright, we'll need to set some ground rules here."

When Nick got called away on last-minute duties by Pete, Narya found herself rummaging through his things for her passport. She was convinced she had left it in his bag on their trip to Vancouver, and she'd need it for her trip to Tanzania. She eventually fished it out of the deepest pocket of his backpack, and her job of the day was done. She surveyed the room, unsure of what to do next. All the books in Nick's apartment were ocean related, and she had already flipped through most of them, finding some of the theories absurd or just plain wrong.

As she sat on the ground between Nick's duffel bag and backpack, staring aimlessly at the passport in her hands, it occurred to her that she had someone she could talk to. Someone with useful tips and pointers on how to be human. This would save her from the suffocating boredom of being stuck in Nick's apartment alone on a sunny afternoon.

As soon as she had walked through the sliding doors of the U.S. Embassy, she spotted Alicia working feverishly behind the counter. She was dressed in a buttoned shirt (it was buttoned to the very top, conveniently hiding her neck), her dark brown hair tied in a high ponytail. Her eyes looked tense as she shifted her attention between the papers in front of her and the bright desktop screen.

Narya approached the counter cautiously, keeping an eye out for Jane.

"Hey."

"Hi," Alicia chirped back without looking up from her paperwork.

"It's me." She crouched down so that Alicia could see her face.

"Oh, Narya!" Her fingers continued typing, but her face relaxed into a kind smile.

"Are you hungry?" Narya asked, seeing that the clock read close to one o'clock. She began to feel a gnawing emptiness in her stomach. Ever since she had arrived, she'd developed a keen palate for vegetarian dishes. She had tried California rolls (without the crab meat) several times, and found them to be quite addictive.

"I guess it's about lunchtime," Alicia replied. "I usually eat at my desk, though—"

Narya went around the counter and pulled Alicia by the arm.

"Come on, live a little! Let's go get some real food."

When they sat down at her most frequented sushi bar, Narya ordered a few maki rolls (with no seafood) for herself, while Alicia happily munched on her packed sandwich and ordered a side of fries. She scanned the restaurant before leaning toward Narya.

"How have you been adjusting?" she asked in a low voice. "Has everything been okay? No freak incidents so far?"

Telling the cautious Alicia about swimming in the ocean with Nick didn't seem like a good idea.

"It's been okay." She decided to keep her adventures secret—a harmless white lie.

"I see. I see. But how have you been doing . . . emotionally? Do you miss the water terribly?" Alicia said the word as though it were sacred.

"Yes and no. I'm not sure. I mean, I think I *will* after a while."

Alicia obviously didn't know about the possible limitless transitions. Perhaps she will just keep this to herself for a bit longer until she has the courage to test it out herself.

"Do *you* miss it?"

"All the time!" Alicia carefully folded the brown paper bag she had packed her sandwich in into a meticulously even square. "Sometimes I even dream about being back." Her eyes stared into the distance.

"Have you used up your transitions yet?"

The server brought a cup of espresso for Alicia, and Narya watched her chug it down.

"No, I think I have only one left," Alicia said.

"Oh." Narya wondered what she would end up choosing if it came to this. The more she went over it in her head, the more conflicted she felt. Was Keames truly an exception, or was this number of transitions part of a conspiracy to keep the mermaids from wandering off?

"I'm saving it . . . just in case I can't take it up here anymore." Alicia drummed her fingers on the table.

"I thought you stayed because you liked it here . . . is it Jane?" Narya thought about Jane's stern demeanor, and figured that she, too, would be miserable if she were stuck with her every day of the week.

"What? Oh, no, no!" Alicia laughed and shook her head vigorously. "Jane's great. She actually helped me through a lot."

Narya eyed the last piece of avocado roll. "Through what?"

"Well . . . there was this guy. A *human* guy I met."

She picked up the roll with her fingers and stared at it greedily. Avocado blended with rice was such a heavenly combination.

"And he kind of . . . found out about me. About *us*."

Narya inhaled too quickly and momentarily choked on the rice she was chewing.

"I broke the pact. I had to tell someone, and he was so understanding—and kind . . ." Alicia's hand trembled as she took her napkin and started to fold it into a triangle.

"It all started because he also had a scar on his neck. From a fishing accident. And when I showed him mine, he made comments about how we must have been destined to be together, or something corny like that."

She rolled her eyes, but Narya could see tears welling up and she tried not to stare.

"And then?"

"Then I kind of blurted it out. All of it."

"What happened afterwards?" Narya was fully intrigued now. She thought no one knew. Or at least that no one was ever meant to know.

"At first he didn't believe me. I showed him—in the water. We went to the beach one night when there was no one around. He freaked out at first, but then he turned out to be really supportive . . . and curious. He started to ask all kinds of questions, and . . ."

Narya waited for her to continue.

"Then one day I overheard him talking on the phone." She crumpled the napkin with her hand. "I didn't hear everything, but I think he was going to expose me. To a *research lab* somewhere." She winced, as they were most despicable words she'd ever uttered.

"Oh. I'm so sorry, Alicia."

"That's when Jane came into the picture. I had to tell someone, and she was the one who helped me transition."

"What did she do?"

"Well, I never found out. But I never saw the guy again. Jane and I kept a diligent eye out for the news every day for the next while. We read hundreds of newspapers in print and on the internet every week. But nothing ever came up."

Alicia shifted uncomfortably in her seat, her eyes moist.

Narya put her hand on Alicia's arm. "I'm sorry. You must have been so scared."

"Well, it's over now. Jane saved us all."

Alicia went on about how helpful Jane had been, and Narya's thoughts drifted to Nick. Would he ever betray her? Then there was Louise, who may or may not have seen her scales when she accidentally poured seawater all over her legs. She suddenly felt an inexplicable weight on her chest.

"Sorry, Alicia . . . I just realized I have go. But let's meet again."

Before Alicia could respond, Narya had made her way outside, hoping she would not end up in the same predicament.

She was breathless by the time she got there, but she managed to find Nick after knocking on several lab rooms on the campus. He had brought her here once to drop off his paper to Pete, and she recalled his mentioning he had to stop by the lab to hand over a few things before their trip to Tanzania.

"Are you all right?" he asked, looking concerned. Before turning his full attention to her, he handed a thick folder to a young man wearing a checkered shirt and glasses too large for his face. "What's going on?"

"I . . . I . . ." There were so many thoughts reeling around in her head: the hurt look on Alicia's face when she recounted her story; the man who betrayed her that she imagined would look somewhat like Nick. Handsome, with honest eyes—maybe even studying in the same field. Marine biologists would benefit a great deal from a discovery of a new underwater species. She thought about all the things she had already revealed to Nick. A myth proven real—what a bedazzling discovery it would be for him. Her heart raced as she peered into his worried eyes. After all they had been through together, would he really expose her to the world?

"Do you want to sit down?"

"Yeah, thanks." She needed reassurance that she wouldn't end up like Alicia. Or worse, to have Jane clean up her mess. She closed her eyes, trying to regain her focus.

"Here." Nick handed her a cup of water.

She gulped it down and felt a deep craving to be back in the water, immersing herself in the big blue, safe and guarded, surrounded by her familiar friends. She handed the empty mug back to Nick. "What are you working on?"

He motioned to the young man. "Can you get her more

water?"

Nick obviously ran the lab and that meant he was important—maybe important enough to want to achieve something great.

"Uh . . . nothing major."

Her eyes landed on few papers scattered on a nearby desk. As she squinted to get a clearer look, she saw that one of them showed a drawing of gills. *Her* gills. She inched closer and made out the three thin lines on what was a hastily drawn silhouette of a human face and neck. That was her neck. There were small, illegible notes scribbled around the drawing.

Nick cleared his throat, rose from his seat abruptly, and collected the papers from the desk.

"Look, this is just a stupid sketch."

She wanted to believe him. As silly as it was, she wished she could read his mind, but he'd have to be a merman. A quiet intensity lingered between them, and she waited for him to say something—anything to reassure her of the secrecy he hadn't really sworn to her.

She wanted to give him the benefit of the doubt, probably trusting him more than anyone up here. "Do you remember what we talked about?"

"Yeah, I do." His tone was apologetic. She hoped she hadn't place her bet on the wrong person.

"You have to promise me that—"

"Yeah, I know." He met her gaze with an unwavering confidence.

They stayed silent, looking at each other as though making a silent pact.

The young man walked between them and handed Narya a mug of water.

"Okay then." Narya snatched the papers from Nick's hands

and crumbled them into a ball. She threw them into the wastebasket behind him.

"I'll see you at home?"

"Sure." He got up from the chair and walked her to the door, his eyes lingering on her back as she exited.

CHAPTER TWELVE

E-20. Louise glanced at the cabin seat number. She threw her backpack onto the seat and picked up her carry-on to place it in the luggage compartment. A man who sat across from her got up and motioned to see if she needed help. She shook her head with a half-smile and mouthed 'I got this.' Despite her petite size, she was physically fit, and probably stronger than most men she knew. Aside from being sarcastic and bold, she was known to be self-sufficient and fiercely independent. She'd never felt she needed anyone, nor wanted to be committed to anyone—until Nick came long. While they did put an indefinite pause on their relationship, she never thought she'd see the end of it, but this was becoming more evident ever since Narya appeared.

As she settled comfortably into her seat with the airplane blanket tucked around her, she put on her headphones and closed her eyes. She had drifted off under the hypnotic spell of Daniel Caesar's voice when an unwelcome tap on her shoulder woke her up.

"Pete! How humbling of you to come into economy class where us peasants sit."

She and Pete had parted ways during boarding; she knew he had upgraded his own seat, abandoning her in the economy section.

"Is anyone sitting here?"

"Nick will be, and I think he's almost here. He just texted me." She winced as he sat on her blanket and wanted to pull it out from under him before it picked up his scent.

"Good—I want to talk to you before he gets here." He held a champagne glass—one of the business-class perks.

"Oh, please. We went over this three times already. What kind of idiot do you take me for?" She rolled her eyes and started to put her headphones back on.

"All right, all right. So where's the girl? She's still coming, right?" He suddenly felt alarmed at Narya's absence.

"Yeah, yeah. Nick said she had to delay her flight by a day to attend to some personal stuff." Pete's eyes darkened with concern. "And no, he didn't explain what. But I'm sure everything is still going according to your genius plan."

"Uh-huh." He rubbed his chin, his glasses sliding down as he nodded.

"Look. She'll be there. Nick was pretty affirmative."

Pete took a big gulp of his champagne. "Does he—did you tell him about our plan?"

"No, I don't think that would be a good idea."

"Right. No, probably for the best. He's pretty taken by her, isn't he?"

"Well, I wouldn't know." Louise grabbed his glass and drank the rest of his business-class perk.

"Do I detect some jealousy?" Pete jokingly nudged her with his elbow, and she grew more annoyed. Another touch and she knew she'd punch him in the chest. Hard.

"I think it's time for you to get back to your fancy cabin, Pete." She forcibly pulled her blanket from under him, almost causing him to lose balance.

"Just let me know when Nick gets here." He frowned at her bluntness but smiled agreeably. She was a much-needed ally in this situation.

The water was calm as she swam at a leisurely pace with migrating whale sharks. The gentle giants encircled her at first, curious to spot a lone mermaid so far from her original grid. One young male brushed against her with his pectoral fin before swimming away to join the stately procession. She was in no rush, as she was already ahead of her schedule, and took in all the underwater sights she had missed during the past few days. She had few transitions left, and although the reality unnerved her, a rebellious part of her craved to test Keames's theory.

The ocean floor was delicately lit by the full moon. A perfectly orchestrated school of angelfish danced around her before scurrying off toward their destination. A lone tiger shark moved in the distance, its shadow mirrored over the open ocean floor. As she made her way into the Indian Ocean, she felt a change in temperature, and more foreign fishes came into sight. A Southern right whale, which she'd only ever read about in Nick's books, swam toward her. From its body language, the whale was as nervous as she, and she was so transfixed by its presence, they almost collided before it swerved out of her way.

She spotted a seagrass meadow from a distance and knew she was close to another grid. This was her cue to stop and ask for directions. Though she knew the Caribbean Sea like the back of her hand, she had not the slightest idea of how to get to this particular island from the Indian Ocean. She slowed down and looked around carefully to see if she could spot a group of merpeople. Rumor had it that those who reside on this side of the ocean were of a shyer, more skittish breed. As she made her way into the narrow opening of a deep trench, she found herself surrounded by a few dozen black swallowers, eyeing her unwelcomed presence. There, in the midst of the darkness, she spotted the bright reflection of a mermaid's tail. She approached carefully so as not to scare her away. It was obvious her tail was still not of mature formation. Some of her scales were still shedding in preparation for the new, brighter ones that would eventually replace them. Her skin was darker than most mermaids she'd come across.

Narya smiled at her and tried to appear calm and unobtrusive. She wondered if her thoughts were being transmitted as she watched the girl's blank expression and hollow eyes. She swam a bit closer, and her sudden change of pace inadvertently spooked the mermaid, who bolted away. The cavernous area was dark, and vampire octopuses lurked nearby, making Narya think twice about chasing after her.

As she turned away, ready to search for a friendlier grid, she felt a gentle tap on her arm. A mermaid about her age, who bore a striking resemblance to the young mermaid, had somehow materialized. Her hair was dark, unruly, and long, reaching below her waist. Narya was able to obtain the information she needed from her, but there seemed to be something else the mermaid wanted. Her eyes were large and emitted a strange sadness, and as Narya stared into them, she sensed a warning from her about the place she was heading to.

An unexpected, powerful current sliced through the water, and her vision, along with all of her other senses, became clouded. In the blink of an eye, she found herself alone again, staring into the darkened cave that held a lifetime of mystery.

The water was dark and murky as she navigated the foreign

territory. There were no signs of other mermaids, but she sensed them nearby or occasionally spotted a familiar glimmer from a tail. She focused on looking straight ahead, trying hard to keep the mental map communicated to her by the mermaid, but her mind was preoccupied with invisible threats lurking in every corner.

She felt it before she saw it: the shadow of a large fish hovering over her. An innate sense of relief swarmed over her. *Grey.* She quickly swam ahead and felt his snout poking her belly, a familiar gesture that showed his affection. With the large shark swimming beside her, she felt as though she were invincible in this foreign part of the sea.

"What time is Narya arriving?"

"Huh?"

Nick snapped out of his daze and found Louise glowering back at him. He had been thinking about Narya's journey underwater the whole time he was on the plane. When she had agreed to go, she explained at length the hassle it was for her to fly, along with many excuses, all pointing to the fact that she was terrified to be on a plane again. When she had proposed swimming to Tanzania and meeting them there, he could only shake his head in disbelief. This was his parallel reality—having a debate on whether to swim or fly to their destination with a mermaid, and a stubborn one at that.

When they had agreed to meet in Stonetown, the city on the coast of the Unguja island in Zanzibar, the first stop of their journey in Tanzania, they had to figure out the exact spot where he would wait for her. It took a few hours to figure out the many different beaches on the island, but they finally settled on one that had no hotels or tourist traffic nearby. Narya reassured him she would simply ask for directions, and as much as he wanted her to elaborate on the subject, he dismissed the thought. Ever since she had stopped by the lab with that distressing look on her face, she feared for her safety. He tried to avoid asking her mermaid-related questions in case he scared her again. They had ended the evening with a movie of her choice—one not starring Ken Lauer.

The next morning, they took Pete's speedboat and drove it far from shore until the island was a small dot. Though he knew Narya was returning to her natural habitat, he couldn't help feeling he was sending her into the unknown, somewhere far beyond his reach or protection. Not that he had really offered her any—if anything, she was more than capable in taking care of herself and others, and all he could really do was to stand by back and watch in awe. Letting her go was a difficult thing to do. He wanted to turn the boat around and convince her otherwise, but her excited anticipation of being back in the water set his mind at ease. He knew she was glad to be returning to the deep blue where everything was familiar—not a bad place to be.

"You ready?" He turned off the boat engine and admired her from where he sat. Her hair was ruffled by the wind, and her eyes were wild with excitement as she stared at the open sea, a hypnotic oasis for the both of them.

"Yes."

Before she dove into the water, she turned back and gave him a playful wink. He watched her dive—the girl he found himself undeniably attracted to, transformed into a siren of the sea. This time, she did not resurface, and he wondered whether any of it had been real. Had she really just turn into a mermaid? He looked at where she had sat, and her absence made his heart sting. He cursed himself for having become so weak.

Tonight, he was on the shore of Unguja island, the spot he and Narya decided on—their meeting point. This morning, since arriving in Zanzibar, he had been distracted by thoughts of Narya. Would she make it?

Louise pinched his arm a few times to make sure he was listening to her. Obviously, he wasn't and didn't pay the least attention to anything she said. Pete laughed off his absentmindedness and blamed jetlag, but Nick sensed she knew something was up. She said nothing; instead, she fumed silently and glared at him whenever she caught him in a daze.

When he excused himself after dinner, he told them he wanted to explore the city on foot. He took the number of a cab driver from the hotel then made for the door. Narya and he had agreed on her surfacing in the evening, but they hadn't specified a time. It all depended on how fast she would get here, if she didn't get lost on the way. He made his way to the beach, settled down on the sand, and dug a hole for his feet. Feeling the warm sand under his soles was one of the best sensations he'd become accustomed to since he moved to the Bahamas. That and the starry skies that knew no limits. He stared into the darkened African sky and counted the stars as he waited for his mermaid to make her long-awaited appearance.

He barely noticed the two hours or more that passed. The evening breeze was a welcoming contrast to the humid temperature that lingered in the air. He sat on the sand, watching the dark waves roll in and out, a natural certainty he'd always enjoyed observing. As a new wave swept in, he thought he spotted a distinctive movement— the flutter of a fish tail that emerged from the water. He jumped up and ran to the edge of the water.

Narya's face was abovewater, her features glowing and her eyes shining as she signaled to him. He wanted to reach his out hand to her, but he had forgotten something.

"Oh, shit."

"What?" She waited in the water, her mermaid body safely submerged, hidden from the outside world.

"I forgot your clothes." He couldn't believe that he had forgotten such an important detail. They had been left it by the door as he rushed to meet her.

"Well, then, give me your clothes," she said, motioning impatiently.

"What?"

"I can't walk around here naked."

"What am I supposed to wear?"

"Well, don't you have underwear? Just give me your clothes, Nick."

He opened his mouth, trying to formulate an alternative to stripping down to his boxers, then shortly realizing this was the only quick and logical solution. He took off his shirt and brought it to Narya, opening it wide and turning around so that she could undergo her transition. She no longer groaned in pain, nor did he hear her breathing quicken as he had before. He heard her stand, her feet splashing the water as she stabilized.

"Wait!"

He felt her hand tug at his pants.

"I'll need these, too."

He shook his head in defeat and unbuckled his pants and handed them to her over his shoulder.

"Thanks."

She came up behind him, and he turned to her. She stood before him in a shirt too large and his pants folded several times around her waist to keep them from falling. He couldn't help but smile at how ridiculous she looked, and she shrugged at his reaction.

"I wouldn't look so funny if you had brought my clothes."

She was displeased with her appearance, and it seemed to him the first time she actually cared about what she wore.

"Well, I think you look just fine."

They walked away from the beach toward the lights in the city that sparkled in the night.

"This reminds me of the first day we met," he said.

She giggled softly as she recalled how he first found her on the shore.

"Alright, let's get going. I think Pete and Lou will be wondering where I am."

Pete sat upright in his chair, listening intently to the person on the other line. Their conversation sounded very top secret, and though Louise tried to eavesdrop, Pete wasn't speaking much and seemed to be taking instructions. They were in the empty hotel lounge by themselves. Tourists preferred being out of the hotel, which worked out even better, since Pete insisted they go over the details of the plan for the next few days. He didn't divulge much to her except that she was to distract Nick tomorrow afternoon while he took Narya to a lab.

When he finally hung up, he scribbled more notes in his book. She craned her neck to see if she could make out any interesting information but couldn't get a clear view.

"All right. My colleague, Mike-something, is coming over tomorrow for breakfast, and he'll take me and Narya to the lab while you—"

"Yes, I know, distract Nick." Louise had her doubts about this plan. What would Nick do when he found out what they were up to? This seemed like a pretty low move, even for her. But Pete had promised over and over again to include her in the research that would revolutionize marine biology, and all the accolades and possible grants that awaited her were too tempting to turn down. She had shoved her uncertainties aside along with any goodwill she had felt toward Narya.

"Your colleague's name is Mike-something?" Pete was horrible at organizing anything, and now she was having another round of doubts about this risky project.

"Hey, I don't know anyone's last name. What's yours, Smith?"

She rolled her eyes at him. "Pratt."

"See? I don't care much for formalities." Already tipsy, he staggered over to the bar and ordered another drink for himself. "Anything for you, Miss Pratt?"

"I'm good. I'd rather be sober for the big plan tomorrow." She was tired, her mind constantly busy with thoughts of Nick's inevitable disappointment in her. But then, this could all be a big misunderstanding. *Mermaids*, she thought to herself, and scoffed aloud. If Pete was wrong, they would all have a big laugh and go home. But if he were right . . . She pursed her lips. Then it would change everything.

Stonetown was as vibrantly alive at night as it was that afternoon when they arrived. The old town was filled with imposing, ancient-looking architecture of Arabic influence, and the lack of adequate lighting left it looking mythical at night. The busy streets were filled with people, excited to be out and about, chatting loudly or selling food and goods from the stands that crowded every corner. Local vendors called out to them as they passed by, others eagerly greeted them in English. Nick wanted to get Narya back to the hotel, but her curiosity slowed her usual pace. To make matters worse, he wore nothing but his boxers and tried to ignore some very disapproving glares, some people yelling at him in a language he didn't understand. He stopped by a stand to buy a touristy T-shirt and what he could only assume were second-hand swimming trunks.

"These can't seriously cost this much." He handed a fifty-dollar bill to the smiling vendor who had sold him the mismatched items.

"Can we go this way?" Narya was already walking away from him as he put on the swimming trunks. Trying to catch up with her, he cursed while tripping over his own legs.

"Hey—the hotel is not this way!"

Narya was transfixed by the exoticness of the setting and continued on ahead of him. As they walked, she paused at every food stand to inhale the pungent smell of local herbs and spices, shying away from the ones that proudly showcased freshly grilled seafood skewers.

Small children trailed behind them, laughing and pointing at their foreignness, and Narya reciprocated with her bell-like laughter. Soon, they were surrounded by large crowds of children, some braiding Narya's waist-long hair, which she didn't seem to mind. Nick watched her, enchanted by her charms. She was a stranger to this place, but in less than an hour, she had become immersed in the local culture so effortlessly. He found himself wishing transitions could be endless, as Ken had guessed. That she could belong in both worlds without being forced to choose. He would be lost if she chose to leave.

When he was finally able to pull her away from the children, they entered a narrow alleyway dimly lit by small candles and kerosene lanterns.

"Wewe! Wewe!" A frail-looking elderly woman reached

out to Narya, her sunken eyes open wide in shock. Her dark skin glowed under the candlelight, and she spoke in the local language, frantically sputtering out words they couldn't understand.

Narya stood still as the woman pulled her close, their foreheads almost touching. She whispered to Narya, her lips moving fast, as though chanting an unknown spell.

"Hatari. Hatari . . ." The woman kept repeating the same words, and her grip on Narya tightened.

Other vendors began to murmur, and approached them looking concerned. They had attracted unwanted attention, and Nick stepped in and gently pulled Narya away.

"Let's go." He had his arm around her, and as they made their way out the alleyway, the woman rushed toward them and tried to block their way.

Nick let Narya go ahead of him while the woman grabbed unto his arm. A glimpse of her profile showed a familiar scarring on her neck. The scars blended in with the wrinkles on her skin, but the memory of Narya's gills was still fresh in his mind. He managed to detach himself from the seemingly distressed woman. As he turned, he searched for Narya frantically with his eyes, before finding her standing near a food stand ahead, safe and out of the alleyway. He looked back to where they came but could no longer see the woman.

"Well, that was weird." Narya rubbed her arm, recalling the woman's tight grip.

"Yeah." Nick was lost in his thoughts. He wanted to tell Narya what he had seen, but he was afraid the information would set her off again. In retrospect, perhaps they were just scars. It could mean nothing at all.

"This way," he said, ushering her through the crowds in the alleyway until they had made their way back to the hotel entrance.

The hotel was nestled in an old building in the heart of Stonetown. A sultan's ancient residence had been converted, and it still retained its palatial charm. As they walked through the open courtyard, a stray cat skittered by and hissed at them before being shooed away by a hotel staff member.

"Hello, Jambo." He was dressed in a white tunic with an intricately sewn decorative pattern on the neckline and wore a matching kufi hat. "My name is Baraka. Welcome to Stonetown Palace Hotel." He presented a reassuring smile and gestured for them to follow him.

"This place is beautiful," Narya said, her eyes taking in the details of the splendid building. The tall, white stone walls were more than a dozen feet high, and the white, marble floors were impeccably maintained and sparkled under the moonlight.

Baraka led them to Narya's room, between Nick's and Louise's, and he offered a quick tour of the room.

"I think we're good." Nick smiled politely at him, wanting some time alone with Narya before the crammed day that Pete has planned for them.

She busily explored the room, awed by the fabric of the beaded bed runner.

"Of course," Baraka said, turning to leave.

"A quick question," Nick lowered his voice as he watched Narya on the other side of the room, seemingly distracted by the view from her window. "What is the meaning of the word *Ha-ta-ri?*"

"*Hatari,* sir?" Baraka seemed puzzled by the question. "It means *'danger'.*"

"I see." Nick glanced at Narya. It could have been a warning. He tried to remember what he saw. Were they gills? Or just scars?

"Is everything okay?" Baraka's voice sounded concerned.

"No, no. It's fine. I saw the word on a sign somewhere, and

I wondered what it meant." He felt a strong urge to stay by Narya's side.

"Thank you, Baraka. Goodnight."

"Good night, sir."

The door closed and Nick turned to find Narya already in bed, her hair in disarray as she buried her face in the pillows. He quietly approached her and covered her with the thin, cotton blanket. The temperature was still high outside, but the fan on the ceiling helped cool the room. He made sure all the windows were locked, settled into an armchair, and put his feet up on the ottoman. He still felt deeply unsettled by Narya's encounter in the alleyway, but after spending considerable time trying to connect the dots between the woman at the shop and Narya, he gave up fighting the will to sleep.

CHAPTER THIRTEEN

"Good morning."

Nick was shaken from his deep sleep in the armchair. Narya knelt beside him, her hands cupping a mug of coffee, their faces inches apart. He smelled a mixture of saltwater and caffeine—two of his favorite scents.

"Hey." He rubbed his face distractedly then smoothed his hair with his fingers. He looked at his watch. It read nine-thirty.

"Oh, shit."

He shot up from the armchair and quickly headed toward the door. He was supposed to meet with Pete an hour ago. He pulled out his cellphone from his pocket and saw three missed calls from Pete, and five from Louise.

He gestured for Narya to hurry up as he started returning calls. Knowing her appetite in the morning, she was undoubtedly starving.

"Hello, Pete! Sorry, I overslept. Yeah, she's here, too. We're on our way down."

"How do I look?" Narya asked. He glanced up and saw that Narya had changed into a new outfit. A simple, white T-shirt with a pair of denim shorts. Louise's shopping advice seemed to have worked on her. She was looking more normal—more human—by the day. He nodded approvingly and tried not to let his eyes linger on her curves and her long legs that became more tanned every day.

"You look good." He searched through his bag and dug out his black-and-white checked bandana. Without a word, he tied it around her neck, covering her scars. She didn't question his action, as she quickly understood as to why he did it.

He slung his bag across his shoulder. "Alright, let's go. Pete is going to kill me if I don't get down there now." He rushed her out the door, his eyes following her as she skipped down the stairs. *Keep her safe.*

"Well, hello! Look what the cat dragged in!"

Louise and Pete sat at the breakfast table, their bowls and plates already emptied save for a half-eaten croissant on Louise's side plate. She was in a foul mood, partly due to the effect of the humidity on her short hair, and she complained incessantly about forgetting her straightener. Nick thought her messy curls were one of her best traits—her *sexiest* trait, as he had once said.

He smiled apologetically and tried to form a logical explanation of why he was late, but Narya interrupted him with a loud squeal.

"Is this breakfast?" She pointed to the long table filled with three different types of muesli, a large bowl filled to the rim with fresh fruits, and several baskets full of freshly baked pastries.

"Yes, yes, go crazy!" Pete laughed as he picked his teeth with a toothpick and then spit out a piece of food.

Louise made a disgusted face at him.

"Sorry I'm late. Did I miss anything important?" Nick pulled a chair back and a voice called out from behind him.

"Ah, welcome to Zanzibar!" A tall, tanned man in his mid-forties walked in with his arms wide open. His physique was robust except for a slightly protruding stomach. Nick couldn't help but notice the can of beer he was holding at nine o'clock in the morning.

"Pete! How long has it been, mate?" He spoke with a thick, Australian accent and smiled as he greeted everyone at the table. His gaze lingered on Narya in a way that made Nick uncomfortable and involuntarily defensive. The warning from yesterday was still fresh on his mind.

"Mike! You haven't changed one bit!" Pete gave the man an affectionate hug, something oddly out of character for him. Louise raised an eyebrow and looked at Nick. *Weird*, she mouthed silently.

The two men exchanged pleasantries, although they sounded a bit more forced on Pete's part.

"I should probably introduce my assistant, Craig," Mike said, pointing to a clean-shaven man who looked to be in his early thirties loitering in the doorway.

He wore a baseball cap, a light blue fitted Polo shirt and khaki shorts and stood awkwardly in a highly polished pair of beige loafers. He was tall, good looking and appeared too meticulously put together for a research assistant. Most of the assistants Nick had known were uniformly scruffy in appearance, with long beards that had been ignored or forgotten for months.

Craig approached the group with a feigned smile and unsure whether or not to join them at the table. "Hi, I'm Craig."

Pete rubbed his hands together and exhaled dramatically. "Great. Well . . . I guess I should be making introductions. To our left here, is Nick; he's one of my most trusted assistants, and one of the best shark taggers one could hope for in the Bahamas."

Louise cleared her throat.

"Yeah, getting to you next, sweetheart. And right here is our lovely Louise Pratt. Other than being a major pain in the ass, she's one of the most organized researchers I've ever met in the field. She takes all my notes, ha-ha!" He nudged Mike with his elbow and they both let out a hearty laugh.

"And who's this?" Mike directed his gaze at Narya, already standing at the buffet table filling her breakfast tray with fresh fruits.

"Oh, well, she's a friend of Nick and Louise. And . . . a part-time shark whisperer." Pete pulled out a chair for Mike and motioned for him and Craig to take their seats. His usual authoritative manner crept back into place. "*Na-ree-yah*! Come here, sweetheart. You can go back for more food as many times as you want."

"Organized? I get organized?" Louise muttered under her breath as Nick took a seat next to her. She was fuming, and he didn't blame her. He gave her a sympathetic smile before reaching for the french press.

"I already got one for you. Black, no sugar." Narya placed a cup of coffee in front of him before sitting down.

Pete laughed. "Well, isn't that *nice?*"

"So, Narya. How do you like Zanzibar?" Mike asked.

He had one of those smiles that irked Louise—somewhere between half-sincere and overly enthusiastic, and in under thirty minutes of observing this man, she had classified him as '*fake as fake can be.*'

"So far I like it. But I just got here," Narya replied, picking a seed out of a small cube of watermelon.

Lousie watched her indulge in her plate of fruits. *For someone so slim, she sure can eat.*

"I see. Well, we'd love to show you around Stonetown, but I believe we're all headed to Pemba shortly." Mike nodded at Pete, who, in turn, agreed with a low grunt while concentrating on his phone.

"Anyway, I think you should all go pack now—we'll meet back here in about forty minutes and head to the airport." Mike stood up, and Craig followed suit.

Louise noticed that he hadn't spoken since he sat down. Granted, the conversation was pretty much hijacked by Pete and Mike, both smugly boastful about their own achievements. They continued vying for possession of the greatest number of accolades in the past decade. Craig had a quiet demeanor, but there was something about him. Every so often, she saw his eyes move nervously around him, as though looking for someone who might be listening to their conversation. She wanted to ask what kind of work he did for Mike, but every time she opened her mouth, the conversation would inevitably be steered toward Pete or Mike, and they'd much rather talk about themselves.

As they went upstairs to pack, Louise trailed behind Narya and Nick, who went ahead to their rooms. As she watched them, a sense of jealousy was anchored deeply in her mind, and she felt unwillingly obsessed by it. The secret glances, the subtle smiles that passed between them at the breakfast table. Jealousy had indeed reared its ugly head, and she despised herself most when she felt vulnerable. The only way to rid of it—well, was to be rid of *her*. She tried to chase the shadow of her conscience away, but it stubbornly followed her through every decision she made. Should she go to Nick's room and confess the details of Pete's sinister plan to him? Should she confront Narya and question her about whatever it was that Pete suspected her of being? Or should she just return to her room and pack her things and carry on with the plan?

She heard the sound of Nick and Narya laughing behind closed doors and she let the rising rage within her decide for her.

Once they arrived at the airport, they boarded a bus that took them to a small plane, the kind that would make an infrequent flyer's teeth chatter. Nick watched Narya, anticipating her reaction. She smiled nervously at him, her eyes distressed at the idea of getting on a plane for the second time in her life.

He purposely let Craig and Mike go ahead of him so that he could linger behind with Narya for a bit longer.

"You alright?" They were the last ones to board, and the airport staff impatiently waved at them from the plane.

"Sure. Yeah, I think so."

"It's a really short flight." He tried to make the best of the situation, and signaled for her to go ahead of him.

Narya took a big step forward toward the plane. As she entered, she caught a glimpse of the wings and tried not to think about the plane debris she'd seen underwater. While whole ships usually sank to the ocean floor, plane wrecks were never in one piece.

Nick watched her settle into her seat before taking the one beside her by the window.

Louise sat up front with the pilot, asking technical questions about the engine. Nick could hear the annoyance in the pilot's voice as he responded monotonously to her endless probing.

He pulled out his headphones and handed them to Narya. "Hey, do you want to put these on?" The last flight they took, the music had calmed her down.

Narya gladly took the headphones and her smiling eyes showed her appreciation.

"Let's play this one." His finger scrolled down on his phone, searching for a song most suitable to calm a mermaid during a plane ride.

When the music started, he saw her eyes lit up in recognition.

"I heard this one before," she said, proud that she had

remembered the melody.

"Yes, you did." It was the same song he had played for her when they took off to Vancouver only a week ago. Much had changed since then, he thought while watching the infinite blue horizon ahead.

"All right, everyone," the pilot said. "We're ready for take-off." He turned on the engine, and as Narya's eyes filled with fear, Nick turned up the volume, hoping music would drown the noise out and distract her for the shaky ride ahead.

The island was surrounded by clear blue, pristine waters that sparkled under the blazing sun. Their resort—generously paid for by Pete, as he had claimed—was set in the far south end of the island, surrounded by lush green forest. Its main lounge area was elevated, and as they looked out to the open sea, they were encircled by exotic birds that Nick had never seen or heard of before. After dropping off their bags in their rooms, they all met for a late lunch in the main restaurant. Within minutes of settling down at the table, Mike began to speak of the wondrous, exotic marine life that surrounded Pemba Island.

"Did you know that we get the yearly whale sharks' migration right around here?" He made a broad circle with his hand. His demeanor was more genuine than Pete, but they shared the same kind of arrogance that shone in their eyes whenever they spoke of what they knew best.

"That's nice," Louise said, unimpressed with this piece of information. She already knew this, never having gone anywhere without putting in hours of research.

Nick grinned knowingly. She probably knew just as much as Mike, if not more, about this island.

Mike shrugged his shoulders and chuckled at her indifference. He raised his beer glass to Pete and they made another round of cheers—their third since the beginning of the meal.

Louise gulped down most of her martini. "So tell me, Craig, what do *you* do exactly?"

Craig was caught off-guard and he stammered his answer before Mike rescued him.

"He helps me out with research here and there. Paperwork, mostly. Boring stuff, huh, Craig?" Mike nudged him with his elbow and released another outburst of overly buoyant laughter.

"Yeah," Craig said, shifting uncomfortably in his seat.

Nick saw that Louise was dissatisfied with his answer. She was not that easily fooled nor did she ever give up when she was on a mission.

"Yeah, but, what do you specialize in?"

"Endangered species . . . mostly."

"Mm-hmm," Louise held her chin with her hand. "Name one."

"Whale . . . sharks." Craig's voice slightly faltered at the second word.

Louise smiled triumphantly as she gave Nick a knowing look.

"Right," Mike said, clapping his hands enthusiastically. "Who's ready for some fresh grilled seafood?"

Craig remained silent through the rest of the meal, and even Nick started to seriously doubt his identity. He clearly didn't have a clue about the subject of Mike and Pete's conversation. Even Narya offered some opinions of her own regarding marine conservation, the heated debate at the table; Craig, however, was noticeably obtuse in his search for words to answer Louise's questions. What exactly did he do, and why was he given a seat at a table made up exclusively of marine experts?

Nick saw Craig's gaze drift across to Narya from time to time. Maybe it was the encounter with the old woman in Stonetown that made him feel more paranoid. Narya was unusual, but he felt that this was more than just a curious glance.

"Are you even eating your food?" Louise frowned at him disapprovingly as she eyed Nick's plate—a fancy lobster dish with a tangy mango salad—still untouched. This was fresh seafood, and he was wasting it. Pete and Mike were already done with their lunch and were smoking at another table, their loud bouts of laughter echoing throughout the dining hall.

"Yeah, I'm not too hungry." Nick stared down at his plate, looking apologetic. The lobster lay on his plate, its shell still fully intact.

"Well, don't mind if I help you with that." Louise grabbed the lobster from his plate, and as she did so, she saw Narya's face distorted in disgust.

"I'm sorry, I think I need to use the washroom," Narya said. She pushed her chair back seat and hurried down the hall.

"Well, I know she's not a fan of seafood, but that shouldn't stop anyone from enjoying the fun, right?" Louise shrugged and began to tear the lobster apart with her fingers.

Craig excused himself from the table, and Nick followed him with his eyes. He sprang up and rushed after him.

"Hey—hey!" He caught up with Craig and saw that his forehead was dripping with sweat. "Are you all right?"

"Yeah. It was a bumpy flight over here." Craig laughed nervously, and he tried to wipe away the sweat with the sleeve of his shirt.

"I guess," Nick replied, not completely convinced.

Narya emerged from the women's washroom, and he let his guard down.

"Sorry, you go ahead." He stepped aside and Craig entered briskly into the men's room.

After the waiter brought the coffee and dessert over, Craig excused himself to go to his room early, and Louise saw the moment as an opportune time to corner him with her questions.

She caught up with him at the stairwell and blocked his way down. Smiling beguilingly, she eyed him as if he were a vulnerable prey out in the open with nowhere safe to run.

"You don't really look like a marine biologist assistant."

"Well, neither do you." Craig tried to appear calm, but his body language suggested otherwise as he awkwardly stuffed his hands into his pockets. She was dressed in a tight, sleeveless maroon dress, her hair in a stylish up-do. She enjoyed dressing up when she traveled and felt the need this time since Narya posed such constant competition.

"Yeah, but at least I talk like one." She stood close to him with her arms crossed.

"Who brought you here? Pete? Did he tell you about the big plan?"

"Pete? No—no, I just met him. I'm with Mike."

"Mm-hmm. As his *assistant*?"

Craig lowered his voice and looked around to make sure no one was nearby. "Look, Mike is my uncle. I'm just tagging along because I was curious."

"Curious about fish? Or about a specific kind of fish?" She couldn't be sure whether he was competition or the imposter he had just admitted to being.

"You know what kind." His voice was small, but she heard every word.

He backed away skittishly, and his footsteps echoed in the empty hallway.

When they finished lunch, Mike proposed that they take the kayak out, while he, Pete, and Craig would stay behind for the preparation of the tight schedule tomorrow. Nick didn't feel particularly excited about the activity, but Louise jumped in and nagged until he agreed.

"How about you, Narya?" Louise gave her a nudge. "Come on, you can't say no to kayaking in tropical paradise!"

"I'm not sure . . ." She was hesitant to join, but at the same time did not wish to stay behind where Pete inevitably would be.

"Look, I know you can swim for a fact, so don't tell me that that's the reason," Louise said. She pursed her lips into a thin line. "Besides, you don't want to stay here with Pete and Mike." She grimaced as she mentioned their names.

"Yeah . . . okay, you're right. I'll join you guys on the kayak." Narya was still reluctant, but at least she didn't have to deal with Pete's incessant stares. Whenever he was near her, she felt a kind of premonition—like when she could sense a fangtooth nearby, its presence obscure, but the threat deceptively evident.

"I'll take you," Nick said.

Louise knew she was green with envy, but Nick was too preoccupied with Narya to notice. He had volunteered gladly—a little too gladly.

"All right, we're off! See you at dinner!" She make a small courtesy wave to Pete and Mike before scurrying down the stairs, taking Narya by the arm.

Nick waited for them at the dock while Louise and Narya went back to their rooms to change. He fiddled with the oar in his hands while watching a small crab poke its head out of the sand, reluctant to leave its hiding place. The sun was strong, and he felt his back already burning. He slowly approached the edge of the water and soaked his feet. He closed his eyes and imagined what he would see underwater if he and Narya went for a swim right now. All he really thought about these days evolved around her: venturing out in the water with Narya; pestering her with mermaid-related questions; sketching her and outlining her gills on scraps of papers when he was bored at work; protecting her from harm. The face of the old woman Stonetown resurfaced in his mind, and the thought of danger awaiting Narya gnawed at him. The longer it took her to arrive with Louise, the more unsettled he became.

When they went back to their rooms to change, Louise lent her tank top to Narya, who was unsurprisingly short of outfits, and told her she would meet her at the dock as she would likely take longer to get ready.

"You should go first. Nick will be waiting for us." She left Narya alone in her room.

Returning to her own room, she texted Pete, "Ready." Then she locked her door and waited, as instructed.

Sitting quietly on her bed, a multitude of thoughts swarmed her mind, blasting her conscience to a degree so great she had trouble remembering where she was.

Five minutes passed, and she heard Narya's door creak open.

She cautiously pulled the curtains open and saw her step out of her room. Her hair was down, as usual, and she wore the pale yellow tank top she had borrowed with a pair of denim shorts. Her long, straight legs had become more tanned, compared to her snow-white complexion on the first day they had met. The scales she thought she had seen at the hospital were nowhere to be seen now. No matter how many times she went over that afternoon in her head, she knew she wasn't imagining the scales emerging and multiplying when she spilled the seawater on her legs. They had been a mesmerizing mix of dark and light purple, with specks of gold and silver that had dotted across her legs. They had glittered underneath the sunlight that crept through her open blinds in the hospital room.

She waited a bit longer, her hands nervously twirling her shoelace as she sat with her arms wrapped around her legs. With no texts from Pete, she assumed all was going according to plan. *His plan.* And what was that exactly? She couldn't remember if he had given her relevant details. All he had said was that he would do some research on her to prove his theory right. Pete's face came to mind. That smug look annoyed her to no end—that malicious grin he had flashed when she agreed to be part of his plan. And his accomplice, the equally arrogant asshole, Mike. And what about Craig? She couldn't figure out what his role was in all of this. And where would they take her, or do to her? She buried her face in her hands as she tried to focus on what really mattered. Nick. It was for him. To protect him . . . but from what . . . from Narya?

She felt sick to her stomach. What had she done? Her heart beat violently against her chest, shutting out all other noise. Who could help her now? Nick would know what to do. Seconds later, she found herself on the beach, running toward him, shielding the sun with one hand and clutching her sunscreen with the other. She knew that Nick would forget to bring any, and she also knew how easily he burned. She remembered how she used to poke fun at how pale he was before they started their diving adventures together. They had so much history together; surely this interlude with Narya wouldn't destroy the bond that they had. *Honesty*, she nodded, *honesty would get them through this.*

"Hey." He stared directly at her with a puzzled look, clueless as to where Narya was.

"Where's Narya?"

"She's not here," Louise replied. She was flustered and covered in sweat from the run.

As with most things, she had a love-hate relationship with the sun. She loved its warmth but hated the effect it had on her hair and skin. She realized now more than ever that she was filled with paradox. Her very existence itself was a paradox. Her mother had wanted to abort her after learning she was pregnant with a fourth child. She had found this out one day when she came home to a house filled with tipsy adults at a family gathering. She was fourteen years old at the time—a moody teenager on the verge of pimple breakouts and overwhelmed by all the uncertainties of life. That was the fateful moment her mother had announced that she had been an 'accident.' Perhaps it all had stemmed from that: her overly sarcastic personality, her rebellious stage that had never really ended, and her snappy comebacks to almost everything anyone had to say. Except when she was with Nick. He made her feel better—like her life finally had some meaning, and that she was more than just an accident. That she had been brought serendipitously into the world to cross paths with him. He made her better somehow. Looking at him now, she knew this to be true. Maybe her being here now was to save the life of another.

"I can see that. Where did she go?" Nick's voice had an edge to it.

She closed her eyes briefly, imagining his enraged face, his disappointment in her when he found out what she was up to. She had no choice now—she had to tell him.

"She's with Pete," she replied, feeling instantly relieved. That stone pressing relentlessly on her chest was finally dropped.

"Pete? Why?" Nick was frowning, and she could see this wasn't going to get any easier. Best to come clean with it.

"Listen . . . and try not to freak out and kill me." She felt tears welling up in her eyes. "He has this plan."

CHAPTER FOURTEEN

"Hello there."

She recognized his voice before she saw him. There was something chilling about his voice. It always sounded a bit hoarse, like he was getting over a bad cold.

"Oh, hi, Pete." She detected something in his eyes— something malevolent and secretive. It made her wish she was not alone.

"What do you say we go for a little walk?" He held out his hand to her, and she shrank back a little, unsure of what to do next.

"I'm supposed to meet with Nick and Louise." She looked around but couldn't see anyone nearby. She was about ten minutes away from the dock. If she ran, she could probably make it in less than five. She had gotten used to her legs. Not the fastest runner, but she was getting the hang of it compared to when she first surfaced.

Pete seemed to have read her mind, and he grabbed her forcibly by the arm. Trapping her like this seemed to give him satisfaction. He winked at her as though his action was normal and harmless.

"It won't be long, trust me. Nick is coming in a bit, so you don't have to worry, sweetheart." He held her close, one of his arms draped over her shoulder, while the other locked her arms in his. His scent was musky with a tinge of alcohol, and she shuddered at his touch.

Her body went limp and the will to escape she had felt a moment before was gone.

They walked for a few miles before reaching a door that seemed purposely hidden by bougainvillea and local shrubs cleverly masking the entrance. Pete knocked five times with a distinctive rhythm, indicating a signal code. The door opened and Mike stood at the threshold, holding a small needle in his hand.

"Hello, again." His smile was wide, but his eyes were serious and suggested that something insidious was about to unravel. Narya's stomach churned, and she felt a sourness rise in her throat.

She felt a sting on her arm; her vision slowly blurred and the surrounding sounds became increasingly muffled until she lost consciousness.

She was underwater now. It was dark all around her, but the capepods that floated nearby sparkled faintly, offering a glowing spectacle on the ocean platform that made her feel less alone. She knew others were nearby, too. Grey never strayed too far from her, and she sensed that her family roamed somewhere behind the rocky outcrops. Rows of sea lilies swayed gently back and forth, and the motion relaxed her as she began to fall back into a deep sleep. The twinkling lights from the capepods began to fade, and she could hear her own panicked breathing, followed by a sound of metal clanging, echoing through an empty room.

She was not underwater.

When she opened her eyes, she saw her reflection staring back at her. Sitting upright in a chair, she had been stripped down to her underwear—a mismatched top and bottom that Louise made her hurriedly buy before packing for this trip. Her hands were tied with ropes, and her feet were shackled with metal cuffs. In the mirror, she could spot one blurred figure behind her, filling up a bathtub-sized glass tank with a bucket of water. The room had grey concrete walls with high ceilings, and although it wasn't very big, there were large and intricate looking machines that blew steam and made a distracting buzzing sound. She has never seen the inside of an operating room before, but she suspected that it would very much resemble the one she found herself in now.

Cameras were set up in all four corners of the room, aimed directly at her from different angles. Her eyes frantically searched for Pete, but he was nowhere to be seen.

Someone approached her, but she couldn't sense where he was coming from. The long, slow footsteps made her heart race, and she tried not to whimper. Someone's face came into view, and small gasp escaped her.

Craig.

He had removed his cap, and she could see he bore a faint resemblance to Nick with his dark brown hair. His eyes were glazed, and he stared at her in silence. She felt his fingers on her neck, softly touching the scars of her gills. He opened his mouth to say something, but the sound of the door squeaking open stopped him.

"Are we ready for this?" Mike appeared from behind him, and while his friendly demeanor hadn't changed, his tone was jollier, as though he anticipated something grand about to take place.

But of course. She was at the center of it all. A sudden nausea hit her, making her head spin, and her vision started to blur again. It all had been planned—from the very beginning. Where was Louise? And Nick? Were they in on this, too? She shook her head and tried to focus on keeping her mind clear. Her vision slowly came into focus.

Pete appeared by Mike's side and motioned for him to follow to the other side of the room.

"Craig, we'll be right with you," Mike said before he joined Pete to discuss something in hushed tones.

"Would you . . . like some water?" Craig asked. His expression was apologetic, and his voice was almost gentle.

How he could be part of something as monstrous as this? Her lips were sealed with tape, and she nodded.

He poured a cup of water then paused when he was about to hand it to her.

"Sorry. Let me . . . take this off for you." He smoothly removed the tape from her lips.

She winced at the pull but thankful for the chance to speak.

"Listen, I'm really sorry about this," he said. His hands shook slightly.

"Do you know what I am?" she asked in a hushed voice. She had nothing else to lose at this point; she was about to be exposed, and she had no way out.

Her eyes fixated on his kind face, and she wondered if she could convince him to let her go. Then her gaze lowered and paused at his neck. He had a visibly long scar like hers. A human with gills? It triggered the memory of her conversation with Alicia before she left. He must be the guy. The one that threatened to expose her.

Perhaps he could help her. If he was as kind as Alicia had said, there might still be hope.

He appeared surprised but not entirely thrown off by her question.

"You do?"

Pete and Mike still had their backs to them and were engaged in debate. About what to do with her? Whether to keep her alive for experiments? She shut her eyes before she gathered her strength to speak again.

"Do you know?"

Craig kept his eyes lowered.

"Alicia?" She pressed on urgently. "Was it Alicia?"

He looked uncertain about what he should say next.

"Is she okay?"

"Yes. Or at least I think she is. I met her about a week ago." She saw Pete turn to them and knew she had very little time left. She wished she knew what Craig was thinking. Did he truly care for Alicia? Would his kindness extend to her own grave predicament?

Before Craig could say anything more, the sound of footsteps started them both. Craig shrank into the background, leaving her defenseless with her captors.

Mike was suddenly beside her, holding a large bottle of water. He knelt down beside her, whistling as he stared at her bare legs.

"It'd be a shame if these aren't your real legs, now, wouldn't it, darling?"

He twisted the cap open and spilled a small amount of water on her left leg. Within seconds, dozens of her scales surfaced, the glitters dotting random places on her leg where the water had been spilled. She could barely feel the sting and wondered if her transitions had come to an end. Or was it her body adapting to the transformation? A small glimmer of joy sparked inside her. Perhaps she could have both worlds after all, and she could stay human and mermaid for as long as she wanted. But as her eyes met Mike's intense stare, she knew she couldn't be more wrong—*everything* was about to change.

"*Fuck me.*" Pete kept blinking, making sure that what he was seeing was what he had thought all along. "I was right," he whispered to himself.

"This is. . . beyond fascinating." Mike bent down, cautiously touching the few scales that dotted along both her legs. She squirmed at his touch and tried not to make a sound.

"Was this what you saw, Craig? On that other mermaid friend of yours?" Mike spoke without taking his eyes off of Narya's legs.

"Yes." Craig's voice was small and passive.

"Incredible," Mike muttered, his eyes still fixed on her mutant limbs. His shoulders shook as he began to laugh aloud, his eyes gleaming with anticipation. Without warning, he poured out enough seawater to drench both her legs. As he watched her transition, he stepped back and nearly stumbled into a metal shelf. He remained speechless as he saw the girl in front of him slowly morph into a mermaid's likeness with shimmering, scaly legs. The only thing missing were her fins.

Narya knew her feet would have to be immersed in seawater for them to complete the transition. The reflection of her scales from the mirror created a radiance around her, and they all shielded their eyes from the brightness.

"So you weren't crazy after all, eh?" Pete said, nodding at Craig, as he distractedly scratched his chin. "The US Embassy back in the Bahamas is going to be thrilled to know that their very own tried to cover up one of the biggest discoveries of the twenty-first century. Hah!" He tried to make sense of it all. "What was her name again?"

"I don't remember. Jane—maybe Jane something?" Craig's voice shook, and he saw the recognition in Narya's eyes.

Mike was inches from her face, and she could smell the musky aftershave from his chin.

"Now you really have to wonder what this Jane was up to, covering up a huge scientific advancement! Is she a friend of yours? A fellow mermaid, perhaps?"

Her eyes turned cold as she stared back at him fearlessly. All those talks and endless teachings about preserving their kind; all the tedious preaching surfaced all at once, and her ears buzzed with words she had always taken so lightly. Up until now, she never had felt as strongly about protecting those she loved. Her indignant scowl trigged something in Mike. They both knew they were really of one kind because of their capability to understand and empathize with each other—much like what they were doing now. Still spellbound, he stood transfixed by a creature he'd only ever heard of and dreamed about, and something like a conscience tugged at his heartstrings. But his eyes hardened and the momentary warmth vanished. His ambitions undermined most other things, and this may be one of his biggest triumphs yet.

He took a step back, needing to distance himself from this creature lest he be distracted again.

"This calls for a toast! A celebration for a scientific breakthrough!" He had snapped out of his daze and shouted, addressing no one in particular.

He and Pete exchanged glances and started to laugh uncontrollably while slapping each other hard on their arms.

"Craig! Get the tub ready! We got a live mermaid show coming right up! We're going to get the champagne!" Mike led Pete away. They were both ecstatic, drunk on uncontainable excitement and the inevitable fame that this specimen of a groundbreaking marine species would surely bring them.

Narya began to panic. This would be the end of her—of

them.

"Listen, Craig. I can't be exposed. It'll change everything." She had little time before Mike and Pete come back, and she tried not to think of what laid ahead. Her eyes pleaded for him to help her.

"Alicia . . ." She saw Pete turn and start to walk back in their direction, and she bit her lips to stop them from trembling. "She said that you were . . . *kind.*"

His eyes widened in horror. Memories came flooding back and along with it, a pang of guilt.

"I—I shouldn't have made that call," he whispered. "I was just stupid, and scared shitless—you know?"

Narya was quiet. She knew all about being scared.

"I came because I wanted to see you. And to see if you can get a message to Alicia for me. That I'm sorry—I never meant to hurt her. But I'm such a coward, and I let this happen. I had no idea it would get this far." He made a fist and remorse and dread fill his eyes.

"It's okay—we still have time . . . right?" Narya couldn't see Pete anymore, and she could only hope he was still savoring that champagne with Mike.

Craig took a deep breath and tried to steady himself.

"Listen, they're going to take your blood sample in a minute, and then they should be distracted for a while."

He gave her a reassuring look when she began to panic at the word 'blood'.

"It's just a small prick. And then I'll try to get you out. It's the least I can do." He stared solemnly into her eyes. "I'm going to get the keys for those, all right?" He pointed to her shackled feet.

"Okay—okay." She nodded nervously. She had no other options; he was her best bet. Whatever Mike and Pete were going to do with her blood wasn't something for her to worry for now.

"*Na-ree-yah!*"

She flinched at the sound of Pete shouting her mispronounced name. She needed to stay calm and give Craig the benefit of the doubt. She met his gaze and he gave her a quick nod before hurrying off. He'd better be back. Alicia better be right about him.

"Here we are," Pete said as he came closer. He made a hissing sound as he exhaled.

He reminded her of a malicious sea snake that released its venom on anything blocking its path. When he got beside her, he stooped and ran his finger from her ankle to her inner thigh, lightly tracing her fading scales like he was playing a game. Her legs slowly took on their human form again as the seawater dried off. She needed to stay human to escape, and she breathed a sigh of relief when she saw that there was no water bottle nearby. His finger paused as he reached her lower waist, and she felt her skin crawl. She felt a small prick as Pete peeled a scale off her skin.

It lay on his index finger. Anger filled her chest as she saw that he had forcibly took something that rightfully belonged to her. He inspected it keenly, trying to get a clearer glimpse of it under the florescent light.

"Amazing, truly *fucking* amazing," he mumbled, still watching her purple scale with a gold undertone reflecting off the ceiling light.

Its removal didn't hurt much, but having a part of her taken so carelessly infuriated her.

"You know, you might just be the prettiest fish I've ever seen." His hungry eyes took in her long limbs covered in scale glimmer, exhibiting a half-human, half-mermaid appearance. He took out a small plastic container and carefully placed her scale inside.

From another pocket, he pulled out a small needle attached to a tube.

"This will hurt, but only a little bit." He wet his lips as if anticipating a delicious meal.

Narya shuddered when he neared her, and she turned away when he injected the needle into her thigh.

"All done." His voice was masked with kindness as he pulled the needle away and waved the tube of blood in her face. "This will revolutionize marine biology like nothing before. Hell, maybe even a step forward in stem cell research!"

He walked away as Craig approached. She saw him discreetly take out a small key from his pocket, and her eyes lit up with gratitude.

"Do you see that door?" Craig pointed to her right, and she nodded in anticipation of her release.

"You have three seconds."

She felt the shackles on her ankle loosened.

"Run!"

And she bolted.

She heard the shackles fall to the ground, and the noise alerted Pete and Mike. She heard them shout angrily at Craig.

"Hey!"

She heard someone calling out and running behind her but she knew she was going to make it. The door was so close, right within her reach.

Her hands still bound, she approached the door sideways and attempted to turn the doorknob. She felt a hand on her shoulder; the grasp was firm and it tried to pull her back. Unwilling to succumb to whatever they had planned for her, her willpower to escape was strong and she turned abruptly, and bit down hard. She heard Pete yelp and curse something incomprehensible. Clutching the doorknob, she twisted until the door swung open and her legs sprint forward as though they were not her own.

CHAPTER FIFTEEN

"Nick!"

The run left Louise panting. They had searched for Narya all over the resort with no luck, and he hadn't spoken to her since they left the dock. "They can't be far. Pete said the lab was right around here."

To her left, she heard a rustling of footsteps, and a figure emerged from the bush a few meters from where they stood. It was Narya, frantically running towards the open sea.

Nick shouted her name. She had her back to them, her long, wavy hair dancing in the wind as her legs raced forward. Without turning back, she dove into the water and vanished among the rolling waves.

As they chased after her, they saw Pete running in the same direction, with Mike lagging behind, struggling to catch up.

Before Louise could stop him, Nick dashed up to Pete and swung a punch at his face that landed him on his hands and knees.

"Damn it, Nick!" Blood streamed from his nose, and he tried to wipe it clean with his hands.

Nick wasn't done.

"What the fuck did you do to her?"

All the fear he had bottled up, all the angst felt about protecting Narya, all of it was unleashed. His eyes were red-rimmed and blinded by fury. He pulled Pete up by his bloodied collar and punched him again. Still cocky, even in defeat, Pete let out a dry laugh.

"You have no idea . . . what we could achieve, Nick . . ." Pete labored to breathe in between his gasping words. His lips curled into a half-smile as he stared back at his pupil, believing he could be tempted with the prospect.

Nick eyed his teacher with an unreadable expression. His grip tightened and he heard Pete gasp for air. As he watched him squirm, Nick saw the greed that endorsed anything in the interest of fame and money.

"You're sick," Nick said. He loosened his grip on Pete's collar and threw him back on the sand, disgusted by his ambition and reckless drive to succeed.

Mike ran up to them and appeared unsure of what to do, his hesitancy propelled by his innate cowardice. Only when he saw Nick back away from Pete, he ran to his friend and helped him up.

"Don't tell me . . . that you haven't thought about it," Pete said. He wheezed audibly but managed to squeeze out his words.

He shrugged Mike's hand away and stood by himself, undefeated, his eyes wild and confident. Narya's bloodwork was still in his possession. *Oh, the things he could do.* His hands shook as he gesticulated dramatically. "Imagine the discovery of a brand new *species.*"

Nick didn't answer right away. He silently held Pete's gaze before he flinched.

"I admit that I thought about it." There was guilt in his voice; he knew he wasn't exempt from the battle between his conscience and their shared ambition.

"But I'd never do it, Pete." With that, he stepped away from him, sickened by the future that Pete envisioned for them.

Pete scoffed loudly and kicked the sand under his feet, inadvertently getting some into Mike's eyes. "Sorry."

And as if remembering her only now, he turned to Louise and winked. "How about you, sweetheart?"

"Fuck off, Pete." She scowled at Pete, wishing that Nick had thrown a third punch on that arrogant face.

Nick and Louise spent the afternoon in silence, and he acted as though she were invisible. She might have deserved the silent treatment but she hated being ignored; still, she swallowed her pride and tagged behind him. After leaving Pete and Mike, they sat quietly in the lounge. She sipped on a mojito while Nick buried his head in his hands. It frightened her to see him like this, eerily reminiscent of the week Katie died. He didn't speak, nor did he eat anything, but he drowned himself in anger and unresolved frustrations.

He followed Louise's gaze to Craig standing nearby at the bar. His left eye was bruised, and there was a small cut near the corner of his bottom lip.

"What happened to *you*?" Louise asked.

"I'm really sorry about what happened," Craig said.

He didn't look the part of the culprit, but Nick felt that he also deserved a punch. He closed his fist and tried to resist the urge to take a swing.

"So what happened?" Louise asked again.

Craig kept his head down as he told them without skimping on any details.

When they got back to their rooms, Nick rested on the couch. Louise sat on his bed, watching his chest rise and fall until he fell into a deep sleep. Listening to Craig's recounting what happened in the underground lab had taken a toll on him. It only confirmed what they both already knew: Pete was both an asshole and a creep, and it brought to light Narya's identity as a mermaid and that Pete had her blood sample in his possession. No one knew what Pete and Mike had in mind. Louise could only guess they'd be sending it to a top-secret lab wherever there was advanced enough equipment to analyze the specimen extracted from a live mermaid. *Holy shit.* Louise envisioned Narya in her mermaid form and shook her head in disbelief..

When she opened her eyes and realized that she too had fallen asleep, she was alone in his room. She jumped out of bed and started for the door.

Outside, the air was cooler, and she felt the ocean breeze on her bare shoulders and legs. The skies darkened, harmoniously blending the vividness of purple and orange to create the perfect sunset. From a distance, she spotted a lone figure walking toward the beach. She ran as fast as she could until she was able to make out his silhouette, the contour of his diving suit, and the oxygen tank that he slung across his shoulders.

"Nick!" She shouted from where she stood.

Unsure if he heard her, she sprinted ahead, but before she could reach him, she heard a loud splash, and he was nowhere to be seen. She felt an urge to run back to her room to gear up and follow him into the water. There was something that made her resist—a sharp reminder that this was how Nick dealt with his demons. He needed to do this alone.

She didn't know how long she stayed where she was, but by the time he came out, the stars dotted the clear evening sky. She sighed in relief as she watched him walk sluggishly toward her.

"Did you find her?" she asked, knowing it was a stupid question by the sullen look on his face. But she had to say something—anything to alleviate the deafening silence.

They traipsed silently back to their rooms.

The next morning when they went down for breakfast, the dining area was eerily quiet, except for the sound of glasses clinking as the waiters poured freshly mixed juices at the tables. Craig was nowhere to be seen, his absence in no way missed. Mike and Pete sat at a table in the corner of the restaurant, conversing in hushed tones.

When the two men saw them enter the room, they acted as though nothing had happened and greeted them with a smile. Nick took a piece of bread from the breakfast table then walked outside.

Seeing the lavish breakfast bowls that were displayed on the table, Louise realized she had skipped dinner and was, in fact, famished. She lingered behind, devouring two big plates of breakfast food.

"Anything planned for today?" Pete sat crossed-legged, his eyes smiling as he waited for a snappy comeback from Louise.

Sometimes, she wondered if this actually excited him. *Sick sadistic bastard.*

"Yeah." She grabbed a piece of watermelon and took a large bite before shooting him a warning glare to back off. "Your funeral."

Louise stared at the fins Nick carried under his arms. His

gaze was fixed on the open sea. He hadn't said a word to her since that morning, and she had grown tired of the silent treatment.

"Are you going back in?"

"Yeah. I'll see you later." Nick tried to smile with a tremendous amount of effort.

She nodded and tried to be as supportive as she could be by staying out of his way.

"Sure, I'll see you in a bit." She stood behind him and watched him put on his diving mask, adjusting it tightly around his head.

He did a quick check of his equipment and tightened the diving cylinder on his back. As she'd seen him do hundreds of times before, he stretched his shoulders in a circular motion and tilted his neck slightly. As depressing as the circumstances were, she actually enjoyed seeing him returning to his old, diving self.

She had three transitions left and was visibly shaken when she got back underwater. At first, the surrounding fishes skittered away, obviously affected by her darkened mood. Her energy seemed to have set off alarms wherever she swam, and she felt like an outcast as she swam deeper and deeper, anxious to find another mermaid, anyone who could soothe her with the familiarity she craved. She was so close to being exposed, although she couldn't know for sure what Pete had planned for her. She tried not to think about the details, and focused on where she was going. She needed reassurance.

As she anticipated being reunited with the community underwater, she found her thoughts constantly drifting back to Nick. But how could she resurface now, after what she had been through? But she didn't want to be exiled from the world up there—not just yet. And she couldn't possibly go home. Her community would know something horrible had happened and they'd collectively force it out of her, and she would never see land again. She decided to remain exactly where she was until she figured out what to do, but she also needed rest. She gingerly scanned the area around her and decided to venture into an unexplored cavernous area, where only lone fishes roamed.

He was unfamiliar with the area and didn't want to risk getting lost, so he chose to stay close to the shore. For once, he cherished the thought of being alive.

He couldn't really justify what he was doing. He only knew that he needed to see her again. She couldn't have gone far either. What did he expect out of this? Maybe seeing her underwater in her true form would be a wake-up call. They were from different worlds, and surely a relationship so complicated as theirs could never really flourish.

He swam until he was low on oxygen and turned back. Passing a cavernous area, the water became murkier, and he felt disoriented. He'd have to resurface to see how far he was from shore.

As he began to make his way up, he sensed a large being looming above him. A great white shark made its way toward him, its presence non-menacing and triggering no sense of alarm. The shark paused midway and they stared at each other as they as they floated in the deep blue. The shark turned, and Nick saw the distinctive scar on its pectoral fin. *Grey.*

Elated to have recognized the shark, he was convinced now that Narya couldn't be too far away. He swam beside Grey then reached out and latched on to his fin, instinctively knowing the shark would bring him back to shore.

As they neared the coral reefs, he let go of Grey's fin. He swam faster now, anxious to refill his oxygen tank and to devise a plan to find Narya.

Louise sat on the sand wearing a wide-brimmed hat that shielded half her face. He was still angry with her, but he knew he'd need her for his plan. He took off his fins and mask and settled down beside her.

"I need your help," he said, keeping his eyes on the horizon.

"Of course," she said. "Anything." Her guilt ate away at her.

She had never been so agreeable, and this new side of Louise made him chuckle softly. Still smiling, he turned to face her. His reaction had obviously spooked her, and she stared at him, unsure of what was so funny.

"Did you bring your Bluetooth speaker?" he asked.

CHAPTER SIXTEEN

"How long do you plan to be down there?"

They sat in a kayak, floating aimlessly. A night dive made navigating more difficult in an area unfamiliar to them. But they had come equipped with a compass, a satellite phone that Louise had managed to steal from Pete's bag earlier in the afternoon, and some snacks and bottles of water taken from the mini-bar. She smiled at the thought of Pete paying the hefty hotel bill at the end of the trip.

She had also geared up in case she was needed. Part of her wanted desperately to be in on the dive, if only this act were enough to redeem herself—but Nick insisted that she remain in the kayak.

"And what am I supposed to do with this?" She held an oar that had her Bluetooth speaker stuck to it with masking tape. Nick hadn't said much when he took it from her room, and now she wondered if he wasn't high on adrenaline. What exactly was he planning to do—lure the siren with music?

"Here, take this." He handed his phone to her. The screen showed a playlist of his songs.

"You want me to play all of these?"

"No, just this one." His finger glided over one particular song. "On repeat."

She made a scoffing sound.

"You think she's going to hear it all the way down there?"

Nick cocked his head. "Just do it, please."

She rolled her eyes at him as she turned on her Bluetooth speaker. She held the oar so that the speaker was facing over the water.

"This is beyond crazy."

"Yeah, I know."

With a loud splash, he was gone, just like that. Gone searching for his siren of the sea.

As he dove deeper, the music became more muffled, but he was confident his plan would work. *It had to.* He held on to his hope in the midst of all the uncertainties that encroached on him. As he neared the cavernous area, he paused and remained still in the water. Something told him that she would come. If he'd wait long enough, she would come to him.

At first, Narya thought she had imagined it, but the melody kept ringing in her ears. She sat up from where she lay and poked her head out. The fishes around her scattered nervously. Something was unsettling them. She heard it again, more distinctively this time. She swam out of her hiding place, willingly lured by the familiar melodious song that echoed in the ocean.

Nick counted twenty-six minutes. The song had been repeated seven times; he was keeping track. A sense of despair crawled over him. She was either too far from shore or she was not willing to see him. A scene from the day before went through his mind. The way she ran—he'd never seen her panic like this. As much as he wanted to stay put, he began to realize his mistake by coming up with this foolish plan. It was time to leave.

A small flicker of light caught his eye. Thinking it was the scales from a school of angelfish, he swam toward them, and they skittishly dispersed, paving the way for what awaited him.

He recognized the unmistakable flaxen hair that flowed in front of her and, like that day at the shipwreck, her enchanting face emerged from the murky water. The mermaid he had been aching to see magically materialized before him. Her tail sparkled with its colorful scales as it swayed back and forth. She stared back at him with eyes that took on a golden shade underwater. His outstretched his arms pulled her in and embraced her tightly—the only reassurance he would ever need to feel alive again.

"No fucking way!" Louise cursed under her breath at the sight of a fishing boat approaching.

Pete leaned forward, his arms looped around the railing. As they neared, she could make out the wide smile on his face—smug and triumphant.

"You didn't think I'd give up this easily, did ya?" he shouted as he gave her a sarcastic half bow.

"I wouldn't jump in there if I were you," he said when seeing her prepare to dive in.

With a wave of his hand, she saw a large fishing net being lowered into the water.

A sudden thud made Nick release her involuntarily. A sense of panic overtook him when he saw that a metal fishnet had been cast over them. Narya looked at him in horror, and regret flooded through him. His hands fumbled for the pocket knife he kept with him. He opened it swiftly and tried to cut through the metal wires. As hopeless as it seemed, he had to try.

The metal net was old and rusty, and Nick couldn't cut through the wires. They were trapped and appeared to have no way out. His hand clutched his pocket knife, and he stared at it intently, wondering what else he could do. Turning to Narya, the look on her face sent a chilling sensation down his spine. Her eyes were a fiery golden and they appeared to be burning. She must surely have thought he was involved in this ruse. He felt his heart sink. As his grip around the pocket knife tightened, he felt a sharp pain and realized he had accidentally cut himself. Without a second thought, he took the knife and pressed down as he cut deeply across his palm. He watched the red liquid gush out of his hand. If Pete thought that he was the perfect bait, he couldn't be more right.

As the net was pulled up, they saw a familiar shadow coming toward them. *Grey.* Nick could feel Narya's body tense. The shark approached the net and Nick saw that he was infuriated. Grey circled around them until Narya reached her hand out of the net and calmed him with her touch. Grey sank back then suddenly lunged forward with a violent force, charging full speed at the fishing boat.

Louise sat in her kayak, torn between staying still or diving in and taking a look for herself. She heard a loud thud coming from underwater. The fishing boat shook violently as though being attacked. The crew began shouting in Swahili, and she could see

Pete's uncertainty and fear in his body language.

"Pull it up! Now! *Sasa hivi!*" Mike commanded the ship crew, all of whom were panicking and shouting. When the shaking stopped and the water became still again, Pete moved forward to get a closer look. The boat swerved again, causing him to lose his balance and fall overboard.

"Screw this." Louise decided to let her curiosity get the better of her. She'd feel safer underwater than on this tiny kayak anyway. Whatever was causing trouble was worth a look. She put on her diving mask and gear and jumped in.

A great white shark, astonishing in size—one of the largest great whites she had ever seen—had its jaws clamped on the fishing net. Its magnificent rows of teeth were visible as it pulled at the net with a mighty force. Narya and Nick were trapped inside the net, and from what she could see, the shark was trying to free them. And she had a *tail*. Narya stared back at her, stunned to see Louise underwater.

The scales that Louise had caught a glimpse of at the hospital were now intricately dotted over Narya's upper body, and they formed a colorful tail where her legs had been. Dumbfounded, Louise remained motionless in the water, trying to take it all in.

As the shark tugged violently at the net, it began to loosen. Soon, the upper right corner broke free, and Narya escaped, followed by Nick, through the small gap.

She was about to swim toward them when she saw a shift in the shark's movement. It headed speedily toward the boat then paused as though searching for something, or someone. She saw Pete's legs kicking in the water, trying to make his way back to the boat. But the shark advanced menacingly and began to charge again. This time, Louise wasn't sure if she was brave enough to look. She quickly surfaced; her hands frantically searched for the rim of the kayak and she latched on.

When Louise emerged from the water, her eyes looked for any sign of Pete. As much as she detested him, she was not prepared to see him torn to pieces by an angry shark. She was astounded to see him again, terrified, as he floated in the water. The shark was less than one meter away from him. Its snout was out of the water, its jaws wide open, but it appeared hypnotized by something as it lay immovable in the water.

Then she saw her—the girl she had doubted to be a true shark whisperer, who now had her hand atop of the shark's snout. She pulled it close and put her forehead gently against it, her lips moving as though murmuring a secret language only they shared. The shark seemed to have understood whatever was being communicated, and it slowly sank down, its fin disappearing into the deep blue.

Louise saw Pete let out a deep breath and watched his teeth chatter, not from the cold, but from the fear of being devoured by his favorite research sea specimen.

She made her way toward them, and as she swam by Narya, her hands accidentally brushed against her tail, feeling the uneven surface of her scales.

"Nice tail," she whispered to her mermaid friend.

"Thanks." Narya smiled faintly and made her way to Pete, her tail hidden below water. An audience had formed aboard the ship, heads poking about to see the daring heroine that saved Pete from what could have been a gruesome death.

Pete wheezed as he scrambled to hold on to the ring buoy one of the crew had thrown down. He didn't see Narya until he heard her speak.

"I'll need those back." She held out her hand to him, confident that he knew exactly what she demanded from him.

"What?" Pete was either playing dumb or had been disconcerted by his narrow escape from the shark.

Narya made a quick circular motion with her hand, and a large fin emerged from the water. She laid one hand on the fin and held out the other to Pete. He was in her territory now, and he may be the ocean expert, but she was its guardian, and both she and he knew she was in control of his fate.

Pete stammered for a few seconds before his hand fumbled in his vest pocket, and he hurriedly retrieved the blood sample and the plastic container that held her scale. Staring at them in the palm of his hand, he was reluctant to let them go. These were his most prized possessions; he would revolutionize marine history. Only moments ago, he had the road to success within his grasp.

Detecting his hesitance, Narya nodded, and he saw the great white shark emerge from the water. This time, his jaw was fully visible and slightly parted, just enough for Pete to see the fearsome rows of teeth that would be his fate should he fail to hand over the specimens. He was greedy, to be sure, but he was no fool. He threw the tube and the container to Narya, and she caught it in mid-air. He shut his eyes, and when he opened them again, the shark, along with the mermaid, were nowhere in sight.

"So, Pete, how'd you enjoy your midnight swim?" Louise swam past him, her tone suggesting how much she had relished the show put on by Narya and the shark.

The boat crew threw down a rope ladder and yelled for Pete to grab on, but he didn't react. His eyes stared straight ahead, and he was obviously still in shock, unable to move from where he was. His fingers stayed fastened onto the ring buoy, unwilling to let go.

"I told you we were planning your funeral. You'd better

leave before she changes her mind again."

Her words woke him from his daze, and he wholeheartedly heeded her advice as he speedily climbed up the ladder.

As soon as he reached the boat, he was seething in anger as he approached Mike, who was still in shock from what he just witnessed.

"Get me the fuck out of here—now.

"The boat's engine rumbled and soon Louise felt the vibration in the water. Within minutes, the boat moved steadily further away. She waited until it was a small dot before she swam out in search of Narya and Nick.

Neither of them spoke for what felt like an eternity. Nick hung on the edge of the kayak, floating with Narya in the water. If he could, he'd choose to remain by her side. She was here, within his arm's reach, but now seemed to be drifting further away from his world, his reality. Her tail occasionally popping out of the water, a hauntingly beautiful, glistening accessory—reminding him what was at stake here. Under the moonlight, he made out the contour of her gills, opening and closing as she breathed. Had it been only a few days since he first saw them, touched them? There was so much more he wanted to know about her, not just the mystifying underwater realm she came from, but specifically her. Unasked questions multiplied in his head, forcing out all logic and ultimately leaving him no room to think straight. He inched closer to her and, in the darkness, he felt her hands clasping the sides of his face. He couldn't tell who leaned in first, but it didn't matter. The moment was sublime and electrifying—exactly what he wanted at this moment. His mermaid was kissing him back.

CHAPTER SEVENTEEN

She was the one to pull away first. Being in Nick's embrace like this made her feel as though she had betrayed her own kind. There were no specific rules forbidding Changed Ones from situations like these, but she hadn't yet made up her mind. Her heart throbbed at the thought of leaving him indefinitely; still, she needed time to rethink all of this.

"I have to go back." She ran her fingers through Nick's damp hair, his soft curls now straight and wet. If only she could bring him underwater with her. She ached for them to co-exist in a world without her having to give up anything—an ideal world, to be sure.

"Yeah."

His eyes had lost the luster so tangible only seconds before. He must be disappointed at her decision. She wanted to say something—anything—to reassure him. But there was not much she could think of that would do, so she kissed him again— briefly this time.

"I'm not sure how long before I can come back," she said, the last few words are almost inaudible. Nick was not a merman, but she felt he could read her mind better than anyone she knew underwater.

"That's fine. I'll be here." He nodded at her and smiled, his voice confident.

Seeing him like this made her heart swell. Right now, at this very moment, Nick was so different from when they had met when she first surfaced. Or the lifeless Nick she had rescued from the shipwreck. He was so full of spark, and it made her feel like he was a strong current propelling her toward where she needed to go.

When Narya returned to her ocean grid, she remained as discreet as possible. She avoided the merpeople she knew and, when asked about her transitions, gave only short, curt answers that painted an uneventful life above water.

There were also a few brief encounters with the Elders from her grid.

"How sure are you that we only have nine transitions?" she questioned more than once.

Most shrugged off her question, while some took on curious and defensive looks. She grew bolder each time she asked the question, her voice firmer, and her stare a confident one. After ten days underwater, a young merman, not much older than she was, approached her. He projected an unspoken authority, eyeing her with an air of superiority. He must surely have been sent by the Elders.

"You should stop asking questions here.".

"But I—"

The merman dismissed her with a wave of his hand.

"You should ask elsewhere." His cold gaze lingered before it flickered upwards. Was he hinting at something? Up, as in on land? Who would she seek for help? And then Jane's face—that icy look and her authoritative air—came to mind.

The merman remained motionless, his thoughts quiet. But a

small grin escaped him when he read her mind. He swam away after successfully having relayed his message.

Tossing on her seagrass bed, she barely got any sleep. As exhausted as she was, her mind kept replaying the recurring scenes of the narrow escape from Pete's lab, and the last words she had exchanged with Nick. But it was time to go now—she pushed herself up with her arms, swishing her tail as she prepared to surface for what may or may not be the last time.

Earlier today, she had been able to sneak into a meeting of a group of merpeople anxiously preparing for their transitions, and she found out about several landing points. She needed to go back but couldn't do so without any clothes. She reckoned that the possibility of her running into any more benevolent strangers were slim.

And now, as she swam behind the two mermaids that were going to surface on the beach where Nick first found her, she had to keep a safe distance until they were close to shore. Knowing what lies ahead for them, she wished them well—all the luck that they would need to get through the first days. Unfortunately for them, however, they were not off to a good start, mainly due to what she was about to do. As they neared the shore, she quickened her pace, and sped past them, as she hurried to their destination.

She emerged from the water first and marveled at how the air rejuvenated her insides as she breathed. Near the landing-point rocks, she saw a pile of neatly folded clothes along with a large beach towel. Her transition took less than five seconds, and she barely felt the pain on her legs other than a faint tingling sensation. Now familiar with the use of her human legs, she hurried toward the clothes, fearing the other mermaids were not far behind her. She finished changing and spotted a woman with her back to her.

She had almost run past her when the woman turned around.

"Narya!"

Alicia was dressed in a black jumper, her face shielded by a large-brimmed, black sun hat. She was obviously trying to appear discreet, but her odd outfit succeeding only in doing the opposite.

"Oh, hi! I . . . have to borrow this." Smiling guiltily, Narya pointed to the clothes she now wore. "You should go and get more clothes. There are two more transitions behind me somewhere. I'll see you later!"

She quickened her pace before Alicia could say anything else, kicking the sand as she ran.

"This is it. The end of our careers as marine biologists as we know it," Louise said. "Oh, shit. We didn't even start yet, did we?" She grinned at Nick, who looked equally exhausted.

For the past two weeks, they had rushed through their final thesis paper—a sudden deadline that Pete had decided to surprise them with upon their return to the Bahamas. Despite his notorious reputation, he was considered a fair grader, and she sincerely hoped he would not let their personal clashes affect his assessment of their hard work.

"Yep, here it goes." Nick knelt and took the two envelops representing their sweat and blood for the past two years on the island and slid them through the crack under Pete's door.

Louise patted him sympathetically on the shoulder. "Well, it wasn't all for nothing," she said. If Pete failed them, she had plenty of alternatives planned anyway. One of them involved trashing his boat and vandalizing his beloved Mercedes Benz.

"Let's get out of here," Nick replied, signaling for her to follow him.

It was strange not having Narya around, and whenever her name did come up, an awkward silence would swiftly follow. Louise wanted to talk about it—she excelled at confrontation—but Nick had made it clear he wasn't up for it. Every time, without fail, he would respond to her probing with silent, deadly glares. So they left it at that. The Narya Problem remained untouched and unresolved. The fact that she was a mermaid she was a mermaid was simply ignored, shelved into the deepest drawer they could find in their awestruck minds.

They walked to the nearest bar, and Louise hopped onto a stool at the counter, while Nick settled into the seat next to her. This would be her first drink of the day, and definitely not the last.

"I'll take a mojito. And make that double shot," she said breezily.

"It's three o'clock in the afternoon, Lou."

"Exactly, the night . . . well, the afternoon—is young, my friend."

"Well, Lou, I don't know what I'd do without you."

"Me neither."

Nick was her anchor. It unsettled her to see him so lost, and it made her sick to know that she had been instrumental in Narya's disappearance.

As if on cue, the big screen above the bar lit up, and a perfume commercial featuring Ken Lauer began.

Louise was almost salivating before Nick stood up, his face

unreadable.

"I just remembered that I had something . . . I'll see you around."

She knew exactly what she was going to do as she entered the familiar building. She walked past Alicia's desk before she could be stopped and entered the office without knocking. Her visit was likely already expected.

Jane sat in her chair, facing the ocean view from her office window. Her face was hidden, but her stiff body language indicated she sensed Narya's presence.

"Ah, Narya."

"I have three transitions left," Narya said.

Jane swiveled around in her chair. She sat upright with her legs crossed tightly against each other. Her hair was pulled back in a tight bun, and she was dressed in a somber grey suit, exactly as how Narya remembered her when they first met.

"Is that so?" She began to shuffle papers around on her meticulously clean desk, appearing to look distracted and busy.

"But I think that I have more," Narya spoke slowly, her mind anchored unto a conspiracy theory brought to light by Keames. "In fact, I don't think there's actually a limit."

Jane's hand paused as she reached for her pen.

"No limit?"

Narya tilted her chin and leveled her gaze with the former Elder of her grid, something she wouldn't have dared do underwater a few weeks ago. But they were both in foreign territory with a different set of rules.

"Yes, I think it's all made up."

"I see. And, who do you suppose—made this up?" Jane

leaned on her elbows, her fingers interlocked like she was preparing to pray.

"I can only suppose the ones who want to keep us away from here."

Jane shook her head slightly and her eyes rested on Narya. A look of resolution crossed her face.

"Everyone has a choice, you know that."

"Yes, but most make that choice based on fear. Fear of not being able to go back." Narya's thoughts drifted to Alicia and all the others who had returned underwater having been convinced they had neared their final transition. Few merpeople had the courage to remain changed permanently.

"Then it's up to everyone to take that risk—that leap of faith." Jane got up from her seat and she paced leisurely around the room.

"Not everyone has the courage to test it out." She picked up a framed photograph and dusted it with the corner of her sleeve. "The limit . . . well, to be frank, I don't think any one knows for sure how many make up the limit. Perhaps there isn't one."

Narya inhaled deeply. Was she finally on the right track? Was Jane admitting to the fact that the transitions are in place to keep the merpeople away from land? From exploring the half humanness that they all possessed and instinctively craved?

"If there's no limit, then why did the Elders come up with a number?"

"That was the case in the past. But now, as you've evidently found out—that number has changed. We have changed—evolved . . . somehow." She let out a small sigh, as though this were a trivial subject she had spent too much time explaining.

"Possibly because everything around us is changing. The climate, the reefs, the ocean itself—you know this. The limit is there simply to . . . simplify things." She narrowed her eyes and nodded, as if to convince herself.

"That's all? There's no better explanation other than *things are changing*?"

It was not the answer she had hoped for. She wanted to hear that the transitions would be unlimited. That she wouldn't have to choose. That, somehow, she would have an easy way out. She didn't expect vagueness from Jane, who usually aimed to be meticulously certain about everything.

"I'm afraid not. So it remains a mystery. As with most precious things, don't you think?" Jane's shoulders relaxed. She returned to her chair and laid her head back.

"Tell me, what would you choose?" She folded her hands and looked at Narya, anticipating an answer, appearing genuinely interested in what she would say.

"I haven't decided," Narya replied. "But I will, soon." She ached to see Nick again, but to stay here, so close to her home grid and unable to return underwater for fear of her transitions ending— that would be torment. And she may not be able to bear it.

"And after all this time, you've decided to stay here? For good?" she asked the former Elder.

"Well . . ." Jane looked at her as though this was the silliest question she had ever heard. "Who else would ensure the smooth transitions of the Explorers up here? Alicia?"

She cleared her throat and Narya knew this was as much as Jane would divulge.

"I see," she muttered softly. Everything remained uncertain. She was still swimming in murky waters; there was no clarity for her, nor for anyone else.

"I will give you one piece of advice, though," Jane said without raising her eyes from the document she was reading. "Steer clear of marine biologists."

Narya couldn't help but smile and leave Jane's counsel unanswered. This was one recommendation she was unwilling to heed.

CHAPTER EIGHTTEEN

Since returning from Pemba, Nick found himself more drawn to the sea than ever before. He felt most alive when he was underwater. The air he breathed on land was shallow, and it often felt suffocating on boring, stale ground. He began to do three dives a day. Promptly at sunrise, he went for a two-hour dive. The morning ritual awoke his senses, rejuvenated his tired body, fed him the fuel he needed to get through the day. He took a midday dive to savor all there was to see underwater, discovering new colors as well as fishes he'd seen before but never observed closely. They prickled his skin as they passed, and he tried to stay unobtrusive, blending into one with the marine life in this other realm he called home. The ocean had adopted him ever since he lost his parents, and he had vowed never to return after losing Katie. He felt like the prodigal son returning to his roots.

When he had seen Keames appear on the television screen, he immediately thought of Narya—the girl who blurred the line between dream and fantasy. He knew, somehow, that she was calling out to him. Perhaps she was part of a plan to bring him back to where he belonged. So he came to the beach, sat on the sand; and simply waited.

At dawn, when the setting sun ignited the sky into a blazing montage of gold and orange, he knew that it was cue for the last dive of the day—to return to the place his heart no longer repelled but fully and deeply embraced. The thought of Katie still hurt, but he had become more and more able to cope. Healing was manifested through his diving obsession, which Narya had reinstated into his life. There was an atmosphere of peace in the deep blue like nothing else anywhere, or that anyone could offer him.

She swam back to her home grid with two transitions left. As she navigated through her home area, she managed to avoid meeting anyone and discreetly made her way into her cavern. All her favorite collections, from unique seashells to anything interesting she pulled from shipwrecks, were stored there. She dug through her chest of jewelry until she found what she was looking for. Dangling the chain in front of her, she watched the tiny pearl sway from side to side, bringing back memories that both soothed her heart and made it ache. She had it all figured out just moments ago.

Why was she wavering now?

It wasn't until he glanced at the calendar hanging above his desk that he realized what day it was. It didn't unnerve him as much as it used to. On this particular day, he would run for miles without stopping, pausing only when he felt dehydrated to a point where he'd be at risk of passing out on the street. For the past few years, he had dutifully followed a stringent ritual. When he woke, he'd go to the gym and transfer all the blame and bottled-up guilt he had put on himself to the punching bag. He worked out for hours until his knuckles turned black and purple. A brisk stop at the bar would also be required. He'd pour a drink for Katie and one for himself— the lucky bastard who had stayed alive. Katie's cup would remain untouched while he downed an impressive amount of beer and spirits until his head clouded and his vision blurred. This alleviated the pain that poked at him incessantly on this day.

After drinking, the next thing on his list would be a game of darts with the regulars at his favorite bar. They were familiar with his story by now, and he was convinced they felt nothing but pity for him. Once back home, a bottomless supply of alcohol was inevitably the last sacred ritual of the day. He would drink himself to sleep and wake up the next day sore, bruised, and hungover.

But today, when he read the dates aloud, he made no attempt to chase away the memories that had haunted him for the past three years. Nor did he immerse himself in the morbid ritual. Instead, a sense of relief crept into his mind, shot deep into his veins and straight to his heart until he felt a jolt that sent him running to the beach.

It was time for a visit.

As he dove into the water feeling the waves crashing over his body, he lost himself in the quietly heartening sensation of descending deeper and deeper into the serenity of the ocean. An indescribable peace filled his whole being, empowering him with the courage needed to follow his plan.

When he neared the shipwreck, its silhouette sent shudders through his limbs. But he soldiered on and swam straight toward the familiar wreckage. It was only when he was close enough to count the railings that he noticed something that shone in the short distance away. He quickened his pace, curious, though he knew he had already guessed what it was. The seashell necklace he had given Katie on her birthday hung on one of the protruding metal poles. It floated in the water with a purpose.

It struck him who might have been the benefactor of this long lost gift. Feeling a shudder that crawled the length of his spine, he turned back, only to find a pod of curious dolphins swimming around about the boat. He blinked at the sight of the necklace he now held tightly in his hand. It was a sign that gave him purpose. All this time, he had been searching for a glimmer of hope in the murky waters.

He left his door unlocked on most days, wishing and hoping that she would show up. She never said so, but he was sure she would return eventually. Every night, as if on cue, he dreamed about being underwater, zigzagging in and out of caverns, led by his mermaid.

Tonight would be another one of those dreams. He sighed and laid his head on the pillow, trying to muffle the sound of the waves rolling in and out. The sea breeze taunted him with the tempting smell of seawater, luring him back. Tonight, he would dream about her again.

As he fell into a deep sleep, he saw her ever so clearly. Her long hair flowing in the water, her slender arms wide open, inviting him to come closer. He caught a whiff of her signature scent, a hint of seawater, as though she were right there in front of him. It filled the air, and when he opened his eyes, he found himself staring into the same grey-gold eyes he's been dreaming of. He raised his hand and let his fingers glide across her cold cheek. The familiar chill pulled him out from his daze at once. She was no longer a dream.

Her eyes crinkled as she smiled. He knew that look well, and it comforted him to see she was just as he remembered. She inched closer to him, and as the coolness of her skin brushed against his arm, it ignited every sense in his body.

"You're back." He resisted the urge to rub his eyes in case

he was still dreaming.

"Yes, I am."

"Let's go for a midnight swim." She took his hand and pulled him out of bed and into the dream that was now reality.

The night sky was intricately dotted with stars, and though Nick was unable to recognize all the constellations, tonight, the stars were especially bright, putting on a light spectacle exclusively for them to marvel at.

They stood at the edge of the beach, hand in hand, staring into the darkened horizon of the sea, making it seem more infinite than it was.

Narya had on a simple white T-shirt and a pair of khaki shorts—an ordinary outfit cloaking a girl with the most extraordinary secret.

"Wait—how many transitions do you have left?" Nick asked.

"Well, theoretically, just two. So after this swim, I'll just have one left." Her tone was surprisingly calm.

"And then? What's your plan after this?"

Was this goodbye? Nick couldn't tell. He had every reason to ask her to stay—selfish reasons that he'd conjured up in his mind since discovering her time on land was limited. But he restrained himself from spilling his heart. In the end, it was ultimately up to her and her alone.

"I don't know."

She shook her head and he knew this was precisely how she felt. All her doubts were written clearly across her face, with nothing held back.

"I just wanted to see you again . . . so I came back. I haven't made up my mind yet about what to do after."

He had not anticipated this answer. Her honesty was like a bridge that linked them together, unexpectedly filling the gap that once divided them. They stood before a dilemma, and she was entrusting all her uncertainty to him. He was as lost as she was, but this emboldened him to follow her wherever she desired to go.

"Well, I guess we'll find out later. No rush." His fingers closed in on her hand, and he took the first step forward. If this was to be their last swim together, then it would be damn well worth it.

Stunned by his reaction, she tried to validate what he had told her. Her eyes shone brightly, and she saw his steadfast support for whatever she would decide.

"Let's go for that swim," he said.

Under the moonlight, two silhouettes dove simultaneously into the ocean. They moved side by side, gliding freely toward the boundless horizon, unburdened by the past and unencumbered by what the future held.

It was a swim like any other swim for a man and his mermaid.

My soul is full of longing / For the secret of the sea,
And the heart of the great ocean / Sends a thrilling pulse through me.

~ Henry Wadsworth Longfellow